D0093211

HEARTBROKE

ALSO BY CHELSEA BIEKER

Godshot

HEART BROKE

Stories

CHELSEA
BIEKER

Catapult
New York

This is a work of fiction. All of the characters, organizations, and events portrayed in this novel are either products of the author's imagination or are used fictitiously.

Copyright © 2022 by Chelsea Bieker

All rights reserved

ISBN: 978-1-646221-27-1

Jacket design by Nicole Caputo
Book design by Wah-Ming Chang

Library of Congress Control Number: 2021940566

Catapult
New York, NY
books.catapult.co

Printed in the United States of America
1 3 5 7 9 10 8 6 4 2

For my father,
across oceans

It wasn't my life she was after.
It was more. She wanted to eat my heart and
be lost in the desert with what she'd done, she
wanted to fall on her knees and give birth from
it, she wanted to hurt me as only a child can be
hurt by its mother.

—DENIS JOHNSON, "Dirty Wedding"

Contents

HEARTBROKE

Mamas, Don't Let Your Babies Grow Up to Be Miners

Dedicated to Mary Glim,
whose writing inspired this story

Now I didn't know a thing about mining when I got into it with Spider Dick one night working at the Barge. I was the only lady bartender on, so you can imagine all the miners, off from their dirty shifts, covered in the soot of the earth, flocking right to me like I was handing out the Lord's blessing. And who was I attracted to then, my eyes wide as the deer I'd nearly smashed into on my way up from the valley to the mountains where I was employed that summer, but Spider Dick, of course, who introduced himself that way, and I said well, what's your Christian name? And he laughed and said that was it. Then he really leaned over the bar close to me and I smelled all that whiskey on his breath and thought, I haven't been giving him whiskey tonight, I've been giving him beer, and he said, "Want to come powder your nose?"

I burned with shame, thinking my nose was shiny, thinking this man, with dirt in his eyebrows, was noticing my shine. I ran to the bathroom first chance I got, and there he was in the women's stall waiting for me, lines of white drawn across the back of the toilet seat. He was ready to give me an education, which is to say my nose wasn't shiny at all.

"Now why they call you Spider Dick?" I asked after I snorted up that white like I'd done it before.

He leaned against the stall door. He smiled this weird way like he could see through my shirt, through to my bra with the safety-pinned strap, through to my heart and right out past me into some long future life where there was a strong likelihood that I would one day be able to describe why he was called Spider Dick with more detail and confidence than even his own self. I would know him and he would know me, so why rush tonight, his look seemed to say. My heart sped up. Colors of the bathroom got brighter. I got brighter.

"What's your deal?" he said.

I cracked my knuckles like my mam used to hate. "I'm nineteen and enrolled in two courses at the city college," I said. "Stage Makeup and English Composition 101. Figure I'll get me a job doing up ladies' faces at the mall."

Spider Dick looked at me and nodded. "But I'm gonna need you all the days of the week."

I could let Stage Makeup go easy enough, I considered. All we did was spread pancake foundation on one another, which then made my face break out in mounds of pimples, and watch silent films of women in modest swimwear while the professor ate potato chips and worked on what he called a screenplay. But the English class. Well. I liked it. After the first day, I'd left feeling different. I'd done something called freewriting and it seemed to unchain the fighting dogs in my chest. But it faded from view there in that bathroom. Looking into Spider Dick's eyes I could actually see the want in them aimed straight at me. It was like I didn't have no choice in the matter. If you've ever been stared at in that fashion, it's a powerful drug.

"Well, I'm not that sort," I said, thinking of how my mother spent her life under a man's thumb, how it had shoved her right into an early grave. I liked to imagine I could have both a life of my own and the love of a man but I had never seen such a combination turn out. It was one or the other and I wanted my own sports car, a job where I wore a leather miniskirt and read the newspaper some mornings. But goddamn I saw he wasn't gonna give up on my love and, despite all I knew, a thrill ran through me. There I was in that bathroom imagining myself an old lady telling passersby that I was one of those people who knew right away. Spider Dick would be frail next to me, having endured several strokes but living on still because of my devotion, all the wonderful years we'd spent bringing oxygen to our hearts side by side.

"I'll turn you," he said simple.

I kissed him then, just like I knew not to. My mam, had she been alive, would have told me I'd fallen under a fool's spell.

✦

Spider Dick worked all the time. He was a hydroelectric miner in the mountains near Shaver Lake. A dangerous job. He talked about his work every evening, laying his head across my lap and describing each shift like he had survived a war while I played with his long greasy hair. He'd do all that sad talk and then he'd need me. The first time we was intimate I learned the reason for his nickname. There was a black widow spider tattooed on his thinger and it isn't special science that the spider got bigger when he saw me. I said, "Why on earth you get something like that?" And he looked hurt and his face darkened in a way I hadn't seen on him yet, and I thought goddammit, Alma, you've gone and ruined your intimacy with this love of your life, but he shrugged it off fast.

"I just woke up with it one day," he said. "Don't remember."

Then I started laughing hysterically and he tackled me and tickled me until I couldn't breathe. A thought came to me, how my mam once said you never could trust a tickler, but I pushed her aside. What right did she have anyhow, intruding on me at a time like this, a time when finally I was happy. If she wanted to give me advice she should have kept two feet on living soil.

I was in love in love in love. Later that summer I moved in with him and I only went home for Sunday lunch with my daddy and his live-in cousin Rina, who was saving her pennies for a facelift while actively letting the rest of herself fall right apart, bird bone frail drinking from bags of wine she kept in the bathroom cabinets. Why she thought this was a secret from everyone I'll never know. I would sit across the table from her while she cut her pork chop into baby bites, moving them all around the plate in a huff before sending the whole mess of it into the garbage, and I would seethe. I had taken up a hatred for her because she seemed to think she was my mam based on nothing but her proximity to my daddy. But my mam hadn't been alive since I was sixteen years old and she wasn't going to be replaced by this mumbling half-wit. Rina didn't notice the awful way I'd stare at her because most the time she was goo-goo eyed looking at my daddy. After we'd eat she'd situate her bones on the couch, right in the middle so he would be forced to sit next to her no matter which cushion he chose, their thighs a press.

"What is this?" I finally asked them. I'd wanted to ask for so long and now I was thinking that if I was special enough for Spider Dick's love then I could ask my own father a question like this, one that should have been asked when Rina had first shown up like a middle-aged orphan last year.

"What's what?" my daddy said to me, eyes on the television playing one of Rina's Lifetimes.

"This," I said. I stood and thrust my plate so hard into the sink it broke. My daddy didn't wince but Rina shriveled like a shy princess flower. It was my daddy who liked to throw dishes, right over my mam's head after he'd had too many beers, and so we had taken to eating off paper plates, but then he started shredding her clothes instead, ripping them from her closet and turning them into a strange confetti that littered their bedroom floor, and so we went back to using real plates so he could get his aggressions out on something she didn't have to wear. I thought I'd forgiven him for that but seeing him sit there with his dingbat cousin like they were lovers made me realize there was no forgiveness to be found in my heart.

"It ain't right," I said. I picked up my purse. I waved my hand at them. "Sick," I said. "Sick sick. My mam is turning over in her grave." I looked to Rina. "Before she died my mam always said that you fell from the ugly tree and got beat by every branch on the way down." My mam had never said that exactly, but instead had thinned her lips when Rina was around and made a point of calling her other names on fake accident: Lina, Mina, Whatser. Oops, she'd say, stone faced, and then flub it again.

Rina put three fingers in her mouth and began chewing. "Everyone thinks I'm your dad's wife," she said, eyes on the TV. "Kind of funny, ain't it?"

"Well, I, on the other hand," I said to them. "Am in rightful love with someone who ain't my relation."

Rina perked up. Leaned forward to me. "Who's it?" she asked, excited, like she had no memory of the ten seconds prior. "Gonna have a baby? I'd like to give a baby some vanilla icy cream. See how it likes it."

"Don't put it in your calendar. You won't be seeing me much anymore. I got a new life. My beau's a miner."

"La ti da," my daddy said. "A miner."

Rina shivered into a silent laughter. Slapped my daddy's knee.

"A miner," my daddy repeated like it was the single stupidest thing he'd ever heard.

I stopped going to see them after that and I didn't hear anything until an envelope from my daddy arrived at the Barge weeks later and it was the notice from the city college that if I didn't show up soon I'd fail my classes and still have to pay tuition. My daddy had opened the envelope himself and read it, no respect for my privacy, and then re-taped it. *Don't ask me for money, cuz I ain't got it!* he'd written on the paper. My face burned because of course I'd been spending my money on Spider Dick's rent and a number of delicacies he liked to eat—pickled pig nose, mock lobster, canned scorpions, chicken livers—and on several full lingerie suits that were far more expensive than a handful of lace ever should be. I shoved the paper in my purse. I'd been meaning to talk to Spider Dick about my dreams and school. I'd just been waiting for the right time.

But the right time was hard to find. Spider Dick liked to talk about discipline instead when he was on all that white powder, and he'd make up adult games for me. He would leave me notes before he left for work, instructions for my day.

No eating fruit.

Stretch to learn the splits.

Dye your hair blonde like Marilyn Monroe.

My heart flew when I'd read his notes. They were like nothing I'd ever experienced. My whole body trembled. I wanted to check off the lists each day to please him; I wanted to know what would be on the list the next day. Some nights I couldn't sleep thinking of it, and I'd try to pry the answers from him, but as he said, the ideas came to him in dreams and I'd just have to wait.

I'd wait. I liked that he wanted me a certain, specific way. Lying next to Spider Dick in bed, I knew I'd never be bored again.

Only frozen green beans today.

I tried to tell Dani at the Barge about it. She was as close to a real friend as I had and I was burning to brag.

She looked me up and down, wiped down the counter, and clucked her tongue. "Aren't you Miss College Girl? What happened to that? Weren't you on about transferring your credits to a real school? Get a real degree? Believe you said, 'Dani, I'm gonna get out of this place. I'm gonna go to a school with a two-story library.' Blah blah blah. Now here you are, with the very one who's gonna do you the worst."

"What do you know about it?"

"Please tell me you don't think you're the first woman around here to get caught up with a miner. Just you wait. Clock's ticking on that time bomb."

That night she flirted hard with Spider Dick to try and prove something to me but she failed. He kept looking over at me, winking, making her all exasperated. She was no match for the greatest love in the universe.

After I completed my tasks Spider Dick would place a happy face sticker in the color of my choosing on a repurposed child's potty chart that he had named *Alma's Chart of Eternal Happiness*. I would clap my hands when he'd place the sticker and feel a real sense of accomplishment.

One day he asked if I had a mother. The question caught me off guard as we didn't discuss me much, mainly him and his worries and ghosts. His own mother with her nervousness and his father with his COPD. But he asked and when I fell silent he held me to him and said go on, let it out.

It was hard to explain to him but I tried. My mam died a strange way. I didn't like to think about it too much because I couldn't make no sense of it. Either something had been quietly the matter in her body for a long time and she chose not to tell me, or nothing was ever the matter and she was taken fast as lightning by no logic of man. Each possibility was a puzzle of its own horrors. A friend I had at the time suggested my daddy had something to do with it. She had seen on *Matlock* that glass shards in food was quick and quiet, and that maybe he had done her in, right under my nose. The weird thing was, when she said it, it didn't seem improbable to me.

I didn't tell Spider Dick about that though. I said she died unexpected and left me without explaining all the things I needed to know about life, and then I mentioned Rina and got started on all that. I was breathing hard about it and Spider Dick looked at me, amused.

"Don't you ever just want to mess with her?"

"I don't want none to do with that Rina," I said. "I don't want to think about her at all."

"It's fun to mess with people," he said. "It's fun to make people think you're one way and then boo! You're another."

His pupils were all small when he said that and there was Mam again, right next to me now. I could practically see her, the downturn of her tired eyes, the little hairs escaping her ponytail, saying *Honey, don't you see? Don't you see?*

But I was covered in love and all I could say was *See what?*

So things were good until the fall. I'd fully shit the bed on my summer classes, and now my transcript had Fs on it. I was surprised at how low this made me feel, like a badness had locked into me. I wanted to erase the Fs. I wanted someone to look at me and at least see Cs. Before my shift at the Barge I went to the small library a few minutes down the road to look at the computer. I could register for new classes. I could start those and talk to a counselor about how to fix my first bad semester. I found the English class I'd have to retake and I entered in a credit card number I had never used before, one I hadn't shown Spider Dick for a reason I wasn't sure of, and I paid. I thought of how dumb this would seem to my daddy, paying so much just to take the same class I'd already failed. I thought of Spider Dick at home waiting for me with a new list, how chipped off he'd be if he knew I'd signed up for a class without at least talking to him about it. That's how we were now. He said we were basically the same person, we were tied together in every way. The thought of him finding out sent a sharp shooting fear into my stomach. I didn't like the feeling, but it wasn't new to me, was it? I raced home to him.

But when I got home he wasn't there. I paced around the cabin until it was time for my shift and when I arrived all the girls were huddled around a phone, hysterical. A tunnel had collapsed at the mine. One of them pulled me aside and told me all about it, how it had crushed Spider Dick's ribs and cut off his middle finger, killed his best buddy Jimbo instantly. He had been airlifted to the hospital in town. I wondered if the class I had signed up for had caused the accident, cosmically. Oh, I felt guilty. So I went back to focusing on my one true love, whose finger was gone and replaced by a thick bandage. He said they had tried to save Jimbo, but that everything happened fast, a quick black of space and time, the thick air suffocating, and then nothing. He said his last thoughts had been of me, and of the angel version of our child, a blonde little girl. Me and the angel child were calling to him to come back and so he did. Now all he had to live for was me and that child, whoever she was, waiting inside of him to be shot into life.

I threw my body over him and wailed when he said that. I

really cried. I felt so much for him. I loved him, so damaged and frail and talking about me like I was a piece of his destiny. What more could I have ever wanted? We were above everything else.

Back at the cabin I fed him creamed corn and washed his hair over the sink. I stayed by his side, but he stopped with the lists. I figured they would return but instead he became angry with me if his soup wasn't the right feel in his mouth, if I came home a few minutes later than he imagined I should, and he didn't want me going for drinks or lunches with the girls at the Barge no more. He said all that was energy I was putting elsewhere, into other things, and energy was finite. My energy was for him and for our little girl, whereabouts unknown. The unknown part was my fault, he said, because he put his seed in me every day, carefully of course, because of the ribs, but my body was not doing what it was supposed to do with it. He told me long stories about his ex-girlfriend that made my ears burn, the way he described her as being *so beautiful and full of goodness, sooooooooo laid back*—and how his main regret in life was getting her pregnant and making her get rid of it, how he should not have done that. I sat there listening and petting him but the stories made me feel real weird and even worse when I got up to pee and the toilet water was tinged red.

"I'm on the rag," I told him when I sat back down. I reached to rub his shoulders but he brushed me off, stood up, and slammed his good fist into the wall behind me and howled.

He looked at the hole and then at me. "Call your daddy to fix that," he spat.

"My daddy don't fix nothing."

"Yeah, don't think I don't know you go there all the time, whining to him, poor me poor me, telling him how poor we are. I got your number, little girl."

He was another person, it was plain to see. He was talking total nonsense.

"What's wrong with you?" I asked.

Then he dropped to his knees before me, put his face in my lap. "Jimbo is dead," he said, exasperated suddenly as if he'd just found out.

I bled for a full week and then some, like my body was really putting on a show of it. Spider Dick was eager to get going again with his seeds. But I knew it wouldn't work. It had something to do with energy, our two opposing forces.

One day when he was napping, I went snooping into his wallet and found a picture of a bucktoothed blonde and on the back it said *all yours baby*, and I thought so here she is, the famous ex-girlfriend. I hated her for a moment until I imagined her getting rid of her baby. He had *made* her, which told me she had wanted it and then I felt bad for the both of us for having been with Spider Dick at all. I wondered where she was. I wondered what it would be like to call her.

I put the picture back. I didn't want me a baby. When I

tried to think of myself with one, for some reason I could only picture myself alone, writing a paper on my own computer. The little click of the keys under my hands. I would know how to spell and how to turn all the thoughts I had into sentences that could be read and read again. In high school they told me I was dyslexic, and I accepted it as I did everything else, but I had begun to dream of the sound of those keys. I had begun to see my name at the tops of the papers, a little "A" written in the corner. *Nice job!* I supposed perhaps my mam was channeling her desires for me from behind the veil of death. She had always secretly worshiped women with an education. *She's educated,* she would say when she bitched about some other mom at the school meeting, or a loan officer who'd turn her down when she'd try to buy things like a car of her own. She'd roll her eyes, but I could tell that behind the eye roll was a big jealousy. In any case, things weren't fun with Spider Dick most of the time now and my mother's warning voice, much as it annoyed me, had begun to make sense. Had begun to feel like a comfort.

Late September I decided I'd try out that English class I'd registered for. I waited to tell Spider Dick until after he had eaten all the funfetti pancakes I had made him just like he loved, with his strawberry milk in a little cup on the side. The class was that afternoon. I had time to warm him up to it. He sat slack-jawed, eyes dull, staring at the wall as I made my case.

"So that's what I'm doing later," I said. I slipped to the back of the cabin where I raced to get ready, shirtless, upside down spraying my hair, and when I stood back up he was there leaning on one crutch, his bandages dirty in the light of the window, his eyes darting.

"Not gonna invite me?" he said.

"It's a two-hour class," I said. "Besides, you ain't a student."

"You think you're so smart, trying to trick me. Saying you're going to English when you're really going to see some other guy." He gripped my wrist and I dropped the hairbrush. I locked eyes with him.

"That's gonna bruise," I said. "Someone might see."

He looked at his hand holding my wrist and nodded. He knew I was right. But then I saw my mistake take form in his eyes, the idea I had just given him.

He gripped my hair and slammed the back of my head into the wall. Little silver lights appeared in my vision. I sat down. It hadn't hurt the way I would have thought. It was dull and not sharp. I touched the back of my head. No blood. I looked up at him.

"Better?" he said.

"You think I have time for another guy after taking care of you all day?"

"Don't make me do that again," he said. "Alma, I don't take pleasure in it."

I was quiet. I'd wait for him to reach a resolve of his own. If I'd learned anything from growing up with my daddy it was that it never helped to reason. You just had to be quiet or agree.

He picked up my hairspray and sprayed some in his hair and ran his fingers through it. He really was good looking. I thought of the blonde girlfriend. I wondered how she'd gotten herself out of this mess.

"Get in the car, school girl," he said. He smelled bad, and there was chili on his shirt. It struck me that I was embarrassed at the thought of being seen with him, his limping body and wild eyes.

I got up and he looped his arm through mine, and chuckled. I could see he was happy with himself, that he thought we'd be driving to nowhere, to my lie.

My mam used to brush my hair and talk to me about her life as if I were not a part of it. She would tell me about my daddy and how I should never take up with a man like him. That was the last thing she wanted for me. I asked her a few times why she had chosen it for herself and she would just shake her head. She seemed to think she had no choice in the matters of her life. I didn't understand that. "Okay, Mam," I'd tell her, "we'll escape in the night." She would just nod and nod but nothing would ever change. I worried after Mam died that my daddy would take to picking on me instead but he didn't. He sort of regarded me as a lump that lived in the same house, something to sidestep in the hallway. Sometimes he'd come out of himself and into another, nicer, livelier form and he would do something wild like buy a bag of frozen shrimp at the Pac 'n Save and we would sit on the porch and he'd light the little barbecue and we'd eat burning hot shrimp with our hands and I would think in those moments I could see why Mam fell for him, or I could imagine him a real good daddy, and I'd start thinking I'd made up all the cruelties of the past. But then there he'd go again, that shrimp father retreating back into himself, sometimes offering a symbol of the shift, a tousle of my hair on the way to crack open the fridge for the first beer of the night.

Spider Dick became sullen as we parked at the campus. We were hours early and the car was hot. The air conditioning didn't work and I was sweating all my makeup off. I could tell he felt bad for the way he'd treated me. He put a hand on my knee, soft as a butterfly landing. "Kiss me, Alma," he said.

"You're ruining my first day," I said quietly. Then I did what I was told, and kissed him.

I pulled out and we drove through McDonald's where I bought us McFlurries and fries and we cruised in silence until it was time. Before I got out, he leaned and pulled my head into him. He put his lips real close to my ear and whispered, *You ever lie to me, I'll kill you.* I got out of the car slowly. I straightened my skirt.

"Have a good class," he said.

In the classroom I tried to remain calm. I tried not to picture Spider Dick outside. I imagined for one horrifying moment a new friend asking for my boyfriend's name and the only answer I'd be able to give was . . . Spider Dick. Truth seemed to be rushing to me now. I tried out a few smiles at different classmates. I did what everyone else did and sat quietly with my notebook. One of the students stood and walked to the front and started writing on the board. I felt sort of embarrassed for her, thinking, what is she doing up there? Then I was the embarrassed one when it was clear that she was our teacher. Now that I really looked at her, she might've been in her thirties, with a frizz of bleached hair and orange lipstick. She seemed like someone I wouldn't normally come across, not in the mountains and not in the valley. She seemed smart with herself, nervous in the body, flitting around, hands trembling, but her voice rang out clear and true with everything she said. I wondered how she saw me. Young but rough maybe, in my tight skirt and my three spaghetti-strapped tank tops, and my cowboy boots and my dark eyeliner. I had thought I looked real pretty but the teacher had this weird effect on me. I wiped my fuchsia lipstick off on my arm. Wondered why I'd caked over my delicate freckles with foundation thick enough to paint a house.

"Freewrite," she said. I had done this in the other English class, but I still felt stumped so I just signed my name over and over, until more words finally came from the pen, ones I hadn't even intended. It seemed a sort of magic. I looked down at my page. *My name is Alma, My name is Alma, My name is Alma,* I wrote. *I don't like lovers' quarrels, no I don't.*

I crossed it out. My hands started tingling. This was all

wrong. I needed to get back to Spider Dick before he got any madder. I remembered how my mother would take me school shopping and everything would be fine until suddenly it wasn't, and then she'd be rushing me, worrying over my daddy being left alone for so long.

I put my notebook back in my bag. I got up and walked out of the classroom. I stood against the wall outside, unable to breathe. I sensed the teacher there behind me.

"I'm not good at writing," I told her. I wanted to tell her other things, maybe ask if there was a room she could lock me in at the school where they could tend to me like an experiment child, raise me up again, the way I should have been raised in the first place, so I'd never be in a situation like this with a Spider Dick ever again.

"I don't expect perfection, only that you try," she said.

I saw my mother next to her. *No one will believe you, Alma, and even if they do, no one cares.*

"Can you agree to just do your best?" the teacher went on. "That's all I really care about. If I could hand out dolphins for grades, I would."

"This is college," I reminded her.

"Exactly," she said. She smiled. A small diamond ring gleamed on her marriage finger. I had some sense that she had made good decisions for herself and some sense that I wasn't going to have the same lot in life no matter what I did.

"Everything will be fine," she said.

She walked back in the classroom and I followed.

◆

The homework was to begin writing an essay about something you are the expert on. Something you know better than anyone else. I looked around at my life. I thought of the Barge. Surely I knew all there was to know about serving drinks as an underage girl. I knew how to make the miners smile after a long day. I knew miners better than anyone else because I lived with one, like an expert would, I supposed. Yes, miners I knew best.

The next week I got ready for class and hoped Spider Dick would calm down, would just sink into our new routine. I told him about the expert assignment and he froze up, got real cold.

"You ain't the expert on nothing," he said, eyes on the television while it played a show about men fishing in perilous conditions.

"That looks dangerous," I commented. I sat close to him on the couch. I thought he might put an arm around me. I decided right then if he got romantic I'd forget school and stay with him. He just needed to be nice to me again.

I almost thought to tell him that my topic was mining, that my focus was still on him, but instead I got up and finished getting ready. In the mirror was a cute girl, I thought. Could I be a smart girl? I felt the back of my head under my ratted hair. I couldn't feel my sore spot anymore. My body had eaten it.

"I don't think you should go," he said. "Clear to me you're getting dolled up for them boys in the class. Bet them boys never worked an honest day in their lives. They're probably still cuddling their mommies, trying to work their way up to manage the Arby's. Bet you like that idea, a man in charge of scheduling, buttons all the way down his shirt."

I couldn't even remember if there had been boys in the class. I could only picture the students who had sat around me, women of all ages and sizes, and then of course the teacher, where my eyes had stayed most the time.

I sat back down and leaned in to comfort him. The difference between him and my daddy, why I wasn't like my mother at all, was that Spider Dick was romantic. All the girls at the Barge called him the sweetest thing. They were so jealous. Oh, were they. My daddy never put on a sweet front for no one, never wrote my mam lists. I knew deep down Spider Dick was good, knew it was my job to pull that part of him out again. He had been the victim of a horrible accident, but he could be healed. I put my lips on the broad side of his neck, felt the blood pumping beneath skin. We stayed like that and then I felt pain. The pain seemed to come from somewhere outside us, a third party surely, I thought. I yanked my arm back. He'd pinched me so hard the skin was deep purple. I had never seen something turn dark so fast.

I sprang up. "What the hell?"

"I don't mess around with floozies."

Now, please forgive me. I'll beg for your forgiveness like

my mother begged for mine every time she didn't run. Because standing there, my mind couldn't put together how this man I loved had just hurt me or said the thing he said. Everything in me said it couldn't be true.

"You talk to the blonde girlfriend like this?" I said.

His eyes rolled around the room, looking for her maybe. "What'd she tell you? She been calling here?"

"You do this to her, too? This your thing? Tell me now so I know. Just tell me."

He looked at me sort of pleading. Hunched his shoulders. His ribs seemed fine now. The cast was off his finger. "I'm awful," he said. "I don't know what to do about it."

A message like a cloud in the sky rose up before me and said, YOU'RE IN TROUBLE. I saw my mam shaking her head at me, saying *well how'd you go and do it this way, Alma, after everything I taught you?*

Forgive me, Mam.

And she said, *I will not.*

During the freewriting in class I wrote what I knew nice and slow, thesaurus on one side, dictionary on the other.

> The following list of nicknames are authentic. The miners' actual names I will not supply. However, I will assure you they are somewhere, alive and well. All except Jimbo, rest

his soul. Muckerman, Loadin' Pole, Jarhead, Suitcase, Two Belly, Hard Rock, Half a Bubble, Quarter Bubble, Two Story, Crown Bar, Sparky, Mumbles, Hardway, Pig Pen, Cupcake, Nuts and Bolts, Animal, Weasel, Spider Dick, Nasty, Boots, and Pretty. To illustrate multiple generations of miners within one family, which is not uncommon, their names are the following: High Ball (father), Low Ball (oldest son), and Eight Ball (youngest son). Low Ball and his wife had a little girl and her nickname is No Balls.

I didn't know if this was what the teacher meant by expert writing but once I got going I found myself enjoying it. I found myself looking forward to the next time I'd be able to write, maybe back at the cabin, on the toilet, my knees crunched up, listening for stirrings from the living room, Spider Dick coming in and out of consciousness while the TV blared.

Don't you ever just want to mess with somebody? he'd said to me about Rina. I didn't know. Or perhaps I did. My mother had visited me in the kitchen that morning, told me what to do: add a little something, an extra pill, to his cocktail of painkillers. Set out a nice morning beer next to the spread to wash it all down, for he wouldn't say no to a morning beer. This became how I was able to get my writing done for class without him breathing down my neck. And in that brief period of quiet, it hit me: There wasn't no blonde baby girl inside me and there wasn't never going to be one. When was I going to tell him, became the new question of my life.

> Miners also have unusual slang phrases. The following will have their interpretations: Hay-Bag: woman, Hump Up: hurry up, Tar Hills: miners from the south, Dumping Shift: not showing up for work, Hoosier: mother and father, Hang a Rigging: mistake, Show Me: a person who acts like he knows it all, Gimmer Miner: want, Block Down: go to the station, Muck: shovel, Saddle Up: rock and roll, and Coast to Coast on a Piece of Toast: traveling across country with very little money to the next job.

Weeks passed and Spider Dick got well with all that rest. He was fast moving again and had started rejecting the pills altogether. He wanted me at all hours like a scrambling pup. No more hits. My head felt clear. I kept writing in my notebooks and he accepted it mostly but wanted to know what I was writing about. Finally I told him I was writing about miners and he seemed to like that.

"You really are here for me, baby, aren't you?"

He seemed sorry for it all, all the strange behavior that we now blamed on the painkillers and the accident. It was bliss. He even toned down the talk about the blonde little girl. But then one day I threw up. My body went dim and I slept through my English class completely. I woke not knowing what day it was. I woke to him holding a preggo test over my face. "Take it," he said. "Take it now."

I peed on the stick already knowing. Here was that blonde little girl come to ruin my life. "I'm late for work," I said, and I scrambled out of the house, drove like a madwoman to my daddy's. For what reason I didn't know.

Once there, Rina was skittish and my daddy was nowhere I could see. "What's going on?" I asked her. But she was wringing her hands and moaning at me, something about him not feeling well. I went up the stairs and there was Daddy in the bed with the doily sheet pulled up around his neck and his eyes were closed. He snored. I stood and looked at him and waited for feelings to come. I had always feared something happening to him because then I'd be truly parentless and there would be no more chances for redemption. I saw a little movie in my mind of all the things I wished he'd been. I saw our hands holding shrimp bodies. I wanted joy for him, and it was the strangest thing. I wanted joy for him despite all he'd done to my mam, despite him not wanting joy for me. I felt a sadness come over me, the heaviest feeling I'd ever known. The love I had for him had nowhere to go, but yet it wouldn't evaporate.

There he was, still life yet in him, and I knew none of it would be for me.

Rina tapped her toes behind me. "I haven't been able to leave the house for days, him laid up like this. He wants fried chicken. Then he wants oysters from a can. Then he wants chicken again and all I know how to do is the Shake 'n Bake."

She was holding two small gold chains in her hand. She saw me looking and dangled them in front of my face. "I been meaning to get to the jewelry place to repair these. I wear them all the time. Snapped."

"How'd they break like that?" I said.

She shrugged. Drew her eyes down at her feet. Oh, I saw it then. Why I hadn't before I didn't know.

"He pushing you around?" I said to her. I put my hands on her shoulders. Thought back to the times she'd been in the hospital with a broken hip, a broken wrist, a broken ankle. Frail, I thought of her. Weak.

"He don't feel well," she said. "Can't you see he's ill?"

"Well," I said. "If he wakes up, tell him he's gonna be a granddaddy. And tell him he ain't never gonna see me again."

"I knew you was gonna have a baby soon enough, I did," Rina said, bouncing on her toes. "I been saying it all along."

I got real close to her face. "He isn't ever gonna stop pushing you around," I said to her. I saw something flash in her eyes then. She backed up closer to my daddy and put her hand on his bed. She had already decided on her life. But I hadn't decided on mine. A laugh fell from my lips. I hadn't.

The English teacher had said we could stop by her office anytime. I carried my journal full of all my writing. My mam rode in the car with me, somber and translucent like always. *Perk up,* I told her. *You're depressing me.*

You're a mother now, she said. *Get used to depression.*

I went in and knocked on the door. The teacher was looking at her phone and making different faces, posing. She startled when she saw me. "Alma!"

"Here's my writing." I handed her the thick notebook. She thumbed through it and smiled.

"This is great stuff," she said.

But how did she know it was great? She wasn't really reading it, she was just looking at the evidence of my pen on paper.

"I've got a man and now a baby inside." I decided to just tell her.

"Congratulations!" She smiled. "That's wonderful."

"You think I can be a writer?" I asked. I wanted to know. What I was really asking was should I give this all up and focus on my writing? Just keep going to school and taking her classes and then try to work somewhere, should I do it?

She looked back at my pages. "Well," she said. "I think we're all writers in different ways."

"All of us, huh?"

"Sure," she said. "Yeah."

"Okay," I said.

I felt real tired. The little blonde girl was taking it all out of me. I already didn't like her. Mam was still in the car when I got back and we sped up windy roads back to the Barge. I looked at Mam and I wanted to cry. I thought she might advise me what to do now. *Keep driving,* she'd say. *It will all work out.* But her mouth quivered for a moment, concealing a little smile. It was the same smile she'd worn when I got the stomachache she predicted after I ate a whole bag of gummy bears.

> It might be noted that miners are in a high risk job. Casualties happen at a high percentage. This may explain why miners have a different attitude toward their fellow workers. The main difference is the bonding that occurs. These men depend on each other for their lives. Each and every day might be their last. Usually families don't understand the risk they endure. Their wives and girlfriends least of all. They especially should be understanding of their miner's sacrifice.

I told my mam to get out of the car. I didn't need to see her no more. She gave me a solemn nod and didn't fight it. She was tired too. I resolved to never see my daddy and Rina again. Spider Dick would also be dead to me. I'd work this night and get my tips and then I'd hit the road. I was no writer, fine. I was no Alma at all. And I was certainly no mother, but yet, I was.

After my shift I went to the cabin of our love and Spider

Dick wasn't there. He was healed now, partying with the miners again. But there it was: he'd left me a list.

Write me a letter, tell me what you want to do to me.

Steal a bag of pork rinds from the Quick Stop.

Marry me so you and me and that little baby girl can be happy ever after.

My mam was back then, shaking her head. *How will you support yourself alone?* she said. *He's a hard worker. You think you can raise a baby alone? I never could.*

I do, actually, I told her. *I do.*

All in all, I would like to add a word to the wise: Mamas, don't let your babies grow up to be miners.

Say Where She Is

Selena's father bags groceries at the Pac 'n Save. His nametag reads Marcus but she calls him Daddy Marc. Selena is good at making names for people. She started calling me Colt in second grade when we compared underpants beneath a desk. Now she says it was because I reminded her of a little sad horse crouched under there, legs folded in, face long and still. She does the impression. She likes to pull it out when I annoy her, or when she wants to feel prettier than me, superior, but joke's on her because it was never up for debate: she is prettier. I try to remind her that the name came about because my underpants had tiny horses all over, not because I have the homely face of a horse. But Selena denies this. She says my underpants had little broken hearts on them and that I do look like a horse. Sometimes she'll add that I should be proud, that horses are majestic and beautiful. Everyone loves horses. Mother, who calls me by my Christian name, Briley, said no woman wants to be compared to a horse. In any case, the name stuck in our tiny town, teachers even sing it out on the roll call, and I try to remember that a nickname from Selena, no matter what it is, is much better than nothing at all.

Daddy Marc scans the cereal, buttermilk, candied nuts, and bags of semisweet chocolate chips I buy for Mother. I won't eat any of it. I'm on a hunger strike for Selena, on account of her being missing for three whole weeks now. I've lost twenty pounds I didn't have in the first place, and my thinning has received many compliments. But Daddy Marc keeps his eyes on the cashier's screen.

"Hello," I say.

He blinks. He's ignoring me. Acting like I'm not Selena's best friend, practically her sister.

"When she comes back I'm gonna eat a whole pizza to myself. And a bag of Nabisco Oreos. Not generic. You be sure to keep some in stock for me. Send in an order now maybe. I think she's on her way home. I can feel it."

He hands me a special-order pad and gestures for the next customer to come on forward. Fine.

The morning she disappeared, I had gone to pick her up for school like usual in what we called the Vulva, which was a beatdown Volvo someone had abandoned on the side of the road in town. Mother had it towed to the repair shop. She said, "Imagine having a Swedish car in our driveway." Selena said, "Imagine being so low-down you give your daughter a car you found on the side of the road." The lettering had mostly fallen off the back, and I had to admit Selena was right: it did look like it said Vulva. So I was a horse in a Vulva, wearing a light crinkled dress that had once belonged to Selena as I idled in her driveway. First period with sexy Mr. Fairfield and we didn't want to be late. But she wasn't home. No one was, not that I could see. I called and called her cell phone. I got out of the car and peeked in her little bedroom window. The blinds were drawn. I rang the doorbell. I walked around back and stood near the fig tree. I broke off a tiny branch and chewed it to rocky bits and spit it out in the dirt. She would never ditch Fairfield's class, I thought. We had waited all of high school to finally take senior lit with him.

I tried a door. Locked. I needed to get inside. I depended on using Selena's makeup, which her mother spent all her waitressing tips on each month, driving us out to Sephora in Fresno. Selena would make videos of herself unboxing the haul, holding the tubes and compacts up, turning them to show each angle, doing *swatches* of the colors and textures on her wrist. Then came the detailed tutorials on eyeliner winging and brow filling. "What I just did here," she'd said to me, gesturing to my face after she'd manufactured my cheekbones from thin air, "this is art." Our report cards had come back and she'd gotten a D in art class. "I should get extra credit for this."

When she'd finish a recording she'd say "Upload" to me and flop on her bed eating Red Vines and I would begin writing captions and listing the products she used. *Publish.* It was true her followers were growing. She liked to say she was weeks away from free shit coming in the mail. That was when you'd really made it.

I squatted on the side of the house and peed and my ankles caught a mist of backsplash. A breakfast noise came from inside, dishes shifting in the sink, and I jumped, afraid Daddy Marc had seen me with my panties around my ankles. I ran to the car and slammed it out the driveway. I went to school alone, pimples uncovered and gleaming. I was mostly concerned then that Selena had spent the night at Farley's house, had finally ditched me for the popular girls like she sometimes threatened, the ones who had tattooed a swirl of all their initials put together on their lower backs. Selena would look at them from across the quad and say to me, "I could be so much cooler. But I love you. Don't feel bad you're holding me back, Colt." I lived in fear that she'd finally decide to join them, but just when she'd get me scared enough of losing her, she'd come back stronger than before, holding my hand, hanging all over me in the hallways as if for dear life. I was the only one who understood her. Who knew everything.

A few days later her picture was up on every pole, in every shop window, and those who were skilled at prayer communicated with God through microphones in the field outside the one church. *Bring us our Selena, Lord, let her walk back into the arms of the community.* The tattooed popular girls stood misty-eyed with linked arms and signs that read SAVE SELENA. WE LOVE YOU, GIRL. They were interviewed and photographed for the paper, answering questions in shrill voices, saying, "O-M-G, this could have happened to one of us!" But no one cared like me. As I reminded Selena often, they would have never added an S to their design.

I stood in the shadows, watching it all. Selena would have loved the uproar over her, and I couldn't wait to tell her about it. People care so much more about you when something bad happens.

But it's true that the hunger of those first few weeks is beginning to die down, and I miss all the concerned faces and how people even brought nice things to our house, like bundles of wildflowers and homemade cakes. Mother ate cake every night for dinner, giddy over what kind would arrive the next night, calling them Selenacakes like they were a new brand. "Try some," she'd say to me, and I would refuse. I am a good friend if nothing else, and besides, when Selena finally returns I will be so much skinnier than her.

They send out fewer search teams lately. Some folks were certain her body would turn up in the canal, where bodies are not an uncommon find—but there was no Selena, and now it's just the same group of Jesus freaks who don their SAVE SELENA shirts and wear their dollar-store capes and go into the fields over and over, angrier each time they return without her. They also know that if you wear your shirt and you look field-weary, Ned's Family Valley Dining will give you a complimentary ten-piece buffalo chicken wings platter. I have seen some of them in the parking lot change into their shirts before walking in, mothers forcing stiff cotton over toddlers' heads, spanking them hard when they cry. Selena's posters are fading in the sun so I printed some fresh ones. I have about a million pictures of her. The Jesus freaks keep offering to pray with me, but I prefer to pray alone. I request dreams from God, to be gifted with a vision. My best friend Selena, nowhere at all, but everywhere to me.

I never had a daddy, so Daddy Marc was it, I guess, because we were always hanging around Selena's house instead of mine. Selena said my mother depressed the shit out of her. She's not wrong. Mother sucks the air from the room. I often feel out of breath around her. She lies in bed and polishes the tiny glass cats she orders by the dozen off the Home Shopping Network. She laments my father, a man she barely knew, but thought she would be with forever. *He looked like Merle Haggard, Briley, like James Dean.* I tell her those men look nothing alike and she says *mmmhhhmm*, not able to agree or disagree. Without Selena to report to, there seems to be no humor in it. What's funny about a woman who zips herself up in her old prom dress, seams straining down the back, and stays that way for days without taking a bath? Nothing, if you really think about it.

Selena's mother was always working and sighing, too tired to make dinner, complaining of extreme bunions, saving for surgery one day. She looked the other way when her Virginia Slims went missing, but once she called Selena a whore when she caught her making out topless with a gas station worker in my Vulva, dumbly parked right in their driveway. I'd been sprawled out on their front lawn, keeping watch to make sure Daddy Marc didn't wake up from his drunken slumber and come out in a rage, or to alert her when her mother's car turned up the street. I fell asleep, though, and woke to her mother dragging Selena out of the car, screaming about teenage pregnancy.

In the doldrum of long afternoons, Daddy Marc made it his business to supervise us. When we got ready for makeup videos, it made him happy. He'd watch us and sort of shake his head from Selena's doorway like we were miraculous and unknown creatures. Coors in a koozie, he'd mutter stuff we'd pretend not to hear, like how if he didn't know any better and saw us out someplace, he'd think we were at least eighteen and then . . . and then.

Sometimes we'd play along, ask him what he thought of our eyeshadow, or a new lip gloss. But one afternoon a few months ago Selena slammed the door in his face. She waited until he flipped on the TV and blasted the NASCAR race before turning to me. "He ain't my daddy," she said.

"What do you mean?"

She positioned the computer just right to capture her face in the natural light coming in through the window. I stood behind her and locked eyes with her on-screen face.

"Look at him. I'm Mexican. He has red hair and a burnt neck."

"What does your mom say?"

"She says I took after her heritage," Selena said. "But she was running around."

"Does Daddy Marc know?"

"Come on."

"Don't it make him mad?"

"Turns out, he likes that I ain't his," she said.

Selena didn't look like either of them, I thought. She looked like she came from somewhere beyond us all.

"The problem is, he likes it." She got all weird then, closed the computer and shut herself in the bathroom.

I haven't been sleeping much and when I do it's sweaty and part of me is still awake. The ceiling fan whirs always above, too cold with it, too hot without. Last night I got down on my knees and I prayed to feel her presence. I know this can happen. I have been researching other missing girls, and many times someone comes forth with an image from beyond, like a street sign, or someone's face, and then they find the person right away. I can't accept that police suspect Selena is dead. Something about how after two days the odds of a missing person surviving goes down to almost nothing. But they don't know her at all. It will be me who leads them to her and Selena will always remember it. Those search dogs are useless. I'm the only one who can pull her scent from a crowd, the deep vanilla that makes something in the pit of me ten degrees warmer.

The first week they suspected Daddy Marc because of his criminal history. After Selena went missing, people started reminding each other how years ago he'd been arrested for taking his dick out in broad daylight near the elementary school. He had said in the report that he was urinating when the kids happened to come out for recess. I mean, he *was* telling the truth. As a day drinker his judgment wasn't always too sharp and he did have to pee a lot. We all accepted it as unfortunate timing, but now with Selena gone, people feel like it's a clue. So until she is found, police are tracking Daddy Marc with a GPS system they slapped on the bottom of his clunker truck. They document his trips from the Pac 'n Save to home, home to the Pac 'n Save. A policeman named Officer Geary asked me if I ever had reason to fear Daddy Marc. I felt confused about the question and told him no, he was all right. But later, an hour into biology, I ran to the bathroom and vomited, then pressed my face to the cold tile floor.

That night, I sat by the phone, picking it up and setting it back down. I should have called the police and told them more, told them something different. Maybe told them about the time Daddy Marc had barbecued all day, in the heat of the valley sun. Sweating over the grill, searing thick burgers and dogs, hunks of chicken breast. How Selena's mother got a migraine and went inside. How the three of us ate on the lawn of their small backyard as the sun set behind rooftops, and Daddy Marc drank his beers and got sentimental over his high school days, and all the pretty girls he used to love. He told us about each one. He told us about the first time he ever tasted a girl, and I watched as Selena sucked an orange pop, tapped her foot to the country music playing on the radio. He drank beer after beer and when he started saying that one of his sweethearts looked a damn sight like me, like she and I could be sisters, when he invited me onto his lap and Selena lit up one of her mother's cigarettes, when all that happened I felt the elastic of Selena's bikini that I was wearing cut into my thighs, felt her top too snug and felt myself too big, and I got up, said I had to go to the bathroom, figuring Selena would be close behind. I went to her room and waited. But when she didn't come right away I started to worry this was the kind of night she had told me about. The kind where Daddy Marc got ahead of himself. But she had said that wasn't really happening anymore and I had believed her. I took off the bikini and put on some of her soft cotton shorts. I got up to go get her, stopped before the sliding glass door, and stared. I could see the glow of their cigarettes. I could hear the low push of their voices.

"What are you doing?" Selena's mother said from the couch. I jumped. I hadn't seen her there in dark.

"About to see if Selena is coming inside."

"She's happy out there," her mother said. She sounded slow and heavy, weighed down by her migraine medication. "She needs a daddy around. Girls without daddies end up all ass backwards. They end up slutty is what I'm saying. I ain't gonna let that happen to my girl."

At the Pac I ask Daddy Marc if there's been any word as he scans Mother's requested multi-pack sandwich cookies and powdered raspberry water flavoring.

"You'd know it if there was," he says, eyes on the groceries. "Everybody would."

"I'm sure she's fine," I say. "I just feel it. She's going to come back."

Daddy Marc turns the register screen so I can see the total. He didn't apply my usual discount. "Go on, Colt, this ain't a good time."

"I need to talk to you," I say. "When are you off?"

"I don't think so," he says.

No one is behind me in line. "I got more to say to the cops," I whisper. "Afraid I may have to go back and tell them right."

Daddy Marc closes the register. "Say whatever you please."

"You're in love with her," I say. "Aren't you?" I feel tears behind my eyes.

"Anyone's in love with her, it's you."

Well, so what if I am? is my first thought. *So what if I am.*

I walk off leaving the groceries. I go behind the market, fall to my hands and knees, and scream.

I count the days. I wait for a message. I write notes to the Lord on notebook paper that I fold into tiny ships and release in the canal. I ask Him questions but nothing comes. I tell myself at night that what I did is separate from all this, has nothing to do with it. I tend to think if anyone should be blamed, it's Daddy Marc. After all, he was the first bad thing to happen to her. And if no one finds out that she didn't go missing that morning, that she didn't get kidnapped on the way to school, but that she streamed out into a new life the night before as we all laid deep in sleep, then they are much more stupid than I thought.

I join Bible study with the Jesus freaks, something Selena would make fun of, but there was no other option. The usual girls had come by the house to save our souls like always and this time I held out my hands and let them. They told me how the Lord anoints some people with the ability for prophecy, and I told them about Mother's favorite show about mediums where they say you have to first acknowledge that you have this power within you. You have to invite it. "Can you all help me with that?" I asked. They said they could. They told me about many kinds of miracles taking place within their church, feathers floating from heaven, glitter too. I said, "But have you handled something like this before?" And they smiled so bright, they said, "God has seen it all." So maybe I can take care of my own forgiveness while I'm there, too. But it's tricky, what needs forgiving.

Last spring Selena and I wanted the same boy. We became obsessed. We shared a journal where we would write notes about him, things we had observed about his looks and habits, like his three crooked teeth and his left pigeon toe. Things we noticed when we would follow him around town, always allowing a few cars between his truck and the Vulva. It felt like a shared thing, sealed in the protection that neither of us would ever have him but we would always have each other. He was only to look at, only to fantasize about as we lay cocooned together on her bed, as we braided our legs and popped each other's zits. But then he asked Selena to the junior fucking prom.

"I manifested it," Selena had said as we walked laps around the track in matching gray gym shorts. "I was sending him vibes."

"That's not fair. I could have been sending him vibes too, but I wasn't 'cause I knew you liked him."

"Last night he rang my doorbell," she said. "I had just showered so my hair was all wet."

"Does he *like* like you?"

She did a high kick, her knee almost reaching her nose. "He said he has liked me all year."

"You and I were going to drive to the beach and say whatever to prom."

"I never agreed to that, Colt. That's what you want to do. Look, I'm not a loner type. I actually like socializing."

"I'm not a loner," I said.

"That's right. You're a 'one on one' type. Isn't that what you call it?"

"I do better one on one because you can really get to know someone that way. You can know everything about them. Like I do you."

"What is that, a threat?"

"Never."

She laced her fingers with mine. "If you were my real friend you'd be so happy I'm going in a limo with Farley and the girls. I can maybe get you in. They're gonna have so much alcohol and someone's gonna get E from Fresno."

I wanted to shake her. These were the people we'd always made fun of, we'd always thought they were such losers because they would peak in high school while she and I had our whole futures together. "Fine," I said instead.

The night of prom I stayed in and watched movies with Mother and got sick drunk on red wine. She twisted my hair into hundreds of tiny braids and strung each one with beads. They were plastic and glittery, depositing tiny flecks of shine across my collarbones.

"Heartbreak is horrible, Briley," Mother said. "I bet you're imagining them together, ain't you? Having so much fun, holding hands and kissing."

"She always gets whatever she wants," I said, standing up in front of the entryway mirror. The braids were too many. "This makes me look even more like a horse, Mother."

"Sit back down," she said. "Let's add some Sprite to that wine."

Selena and the boy hung out for a few weeks and I made up reasons why I was busy. Then he moved to Fresno and stopped coming around. We went back to normal, and I stowed the journal in the box under my bed with my other Selena stuff. My pictures of her and a few of her hair ribbons, a small bottle of her vanilla lotion.

After the boy left, Selena changed. "He should have taken me with him to Fresno," she said a lot. "He said he was going to, and then he just ghosted." She darkened and shifted. Became obsessed with finding an older man, a real man, she said, that could get her out of here. "I thought I was about to leave all this," she said. "I thought I'd never have to spend one more night in my shitty house."

I had just uploaded one of her videos, a mermaid waves tutorial, and was busy looking over her comments section. Usually I deleted the comments that came in by the dozens from her super fan, Kevin$$843. They were desperate lines, always asking her to message him privately, boasting about new cars and boats and vacations he wanted to take her on, a place I had never heard of that was somehow one place but seemed like two: Turks and Caicos. He very much wanted her address so he could mail her outfits. I played a game with myself then: if he left a comment in the next five minutes, it was meant to be. I'd finally write back to him. Maybe he was a nice guy. He could be very romantic. I clicked his profile page and saw he was actually super-hot. There he was jet skiing without a shirt. There he was throwing a peace sign drinking something frosty from a glass as big as his head. I clicked back to Selena's page, to her new video. I looked up at her, her sadness. I knew it would be easier on me if she left town with the likes of him versus drifting away to become popular. It would be an abandonment I could get behind. And maybe he'd have a friend for me. "We just aren't meant to be in a small town like this," I said to her. I refreshed the page.

Please email me! I can't stop thinking about youuuuuuuuuuuu.

That night I stayed up late pretending to be Selena, typing back and forth with this Kevin from a fake email account. He said he lived in San Francisco. He had a condo where you could see the Golden Gate Bridge from the living room window. Everything was perfect about him. He would make her so happy. He mentioned how women often just wanted his money and he needed to make sure she wasn't like that. *Was she drama?* No. *Do you love me too?* He asked a few times and each time I ignored it but finally, before I fell asleep, I said, *Yes. I do.*

The police want to know everything about Selena and me. Old Officer Geary has come by several times since she disappeared. He putters around our kitchen, acting right at home. He wears a white horsetail braid down his back and his denim looks ink blue, like it could rub off on fingers.

Mother raises her eyebrows from her place sunken down into the couch, says, "Need something?"

And he says, "No, ma'am, please don't get up."

"You come here to tell me you all found her?" I say, sitting at our small kitchen table in my nightshirt.

"No, see, that's the problem, we can't seem to find your girl anywhere," Geary says, taking a seat across from me. "Her daddy called me up and said you might be holding back."

"Daddy Marc has himself confused," I say. "With him being a sex offender and all."

"What would you say you and Selena's biggest best friend secret was?" he asks.

"You mean, what our secret *is*," I say.

"Of course. Is."

"We once hid scissors in our purses and cut the security tags out of the nice jeans at Macy's in Fresno," I say. "Will that help you find her?"

Geary smiled. "You never know what could help."

"She's probably off with some man," I say. "Did you think of that? Maybe she has a brand new life."

"Any man in particular?"

Well, Kevin, of course. Things had really escalated with him and he had started sending pictures. His penis had been hard in the photos and he gripped it and pulled it sideways a bit. Not big, but I guess not small. I had no frame of reference. I had looked at the pictures until my eyes were dry. He wanted her address so he could bring her roses. She would love that, I had thought. It would be a story she would tell me and then finally, finally, I'd tell her I'd known all along. That I'd helped get them to her. Then we could start planning her new life in San Francisco. I'd help her pack. Maybe I'd come too.

"All men loved Selena," I say again. "She could have had anyone."

Officer Geary stands up. "Do the boys ask you out?"

"Not really," I say. "I'm shy."

"You don't strike me as shy," he says. "You strike me as coy."

"What's coy?"

"Ain't the same thing as shy," he says. "Look it up."

"Need something?" Mother croaks from the couch. "Briley's stocked the cupboards near full of them Ore-Os. Briley, get the man one of them Ore-Os and a glass a milk. She's gonna binge them all when Selena comes back, that's what she says."

"Don't open those," I say to her sternly. She shrugs.

Geary paces before the hall like he is going to step in my room and my heart falls from my chest to the floor. But he walks out the front door, tipping his felt hat to Mother as he goes.

"What's about it?" Mother says without looking at me.

"More Selena stuff," I say.

"Why don't you tell them what you all were up to?"

From the window I watch Geary pull away from the curb. Our neighbor Trish walks by, bends down, and picks up a cigarette butt off the street and pops it between her lips.

"He's gonna keep coming around," Mother says. "If you just tell him, he ain't gonna think nothing of it. Just two little girls having some fun."

Mother knew about the emails. She had used my computer one day to research how much her Beanie Babies were worth and found them. She was angry with me at first, saying we were too young for something like that, and grounded me for a day.

"Selena hated you," I said.

"I feel like I don't know you much these days, Briley," Mother says. "If you ain't careful, I'll show that old man into your room. Let him figure all that out."

"There's nothing to see," I say.

"Let's hope for it."

Anyone would tell you that friendship boxes are something a lot of girls have. I've been the collector since we were little. I've protected the important things. I saved up for a camera a few summers back and bought black and white film at the Pac 'n Save. I took pictures of Selena lying out by the school pool. She struck silly model poses in some of the photos, pouty with a serious face, but my favorites of her are the ones when she didn't realize I was shooting. There's one with her arm up shielding her eyes. She had untied her suit strings and you can see a crest of boob.

"Colt, let me take one of you," she had said.

"Okay, but tell me how to pose. I want it to be good."

"Take off your top and, like, hold your tits together," she said.

"Like this?"

"Wait, take your hands away." She appraised me. Shrugged.

"What?"

"Don't worry, there's a man for every type of tit."

I put my top back on.

"No, girl, I was messing with you." She laughed. "I want to take the picture. Hold still."

The picture is weird to look at now. It's a body I don't recognize. It's the only one of me from that day, and my hand is moving over my breasts and my face is sad. I don't know why I've never thrown it away.

I saved the hair-ties she threw to the floor, a pair of panties she let me borrow, a container of wax she used to carry when she had braces. I sent the bikini pics to Kevin when he requested nudes. Told him, *One step at a time.*

I take the box and drive to Tent City, a dump turned homeless encampment on the county's edge, and bury it there. There are used needles on the ground and I am glad I wore close-toed shoes.

I didn't do anything wrong, but I can see how someone might wonder about the box. How could they understand our bond? She told me everything. Told me Daddy Marc sleepwalked into her room some nights, curled his body around her in her twin bed and slept, a heavy and unmovable sleep, and on those nights Selena never slept at all. Remember, please remember, I just wanted to save her from all that.

✦

Bible study happens at a girl named Denay's house. Denay is a top believer in the church and says when the Holy Spirit goes into you, He comes out your tongue on fire. So she squawks and hums and speaks in tongues while she lays hands on each of us. I have yet to speak like this, but I think I will soon. Denay says the Holy Spirit is reawakening inside me and when He comes out I will be changed. I will have answers.

"Prayer requests?" Denay asks us girls, four of us sitting in a circle.

"Me," I say. "I need a vision of Selena."

Denay looks at the two other girls, Taffy and Lacey May, and raises her eyebrows. "You think the Lord is too busy to handle Miss Selena on His own?"

"I'm worried," I say slowly. "That something went wrong. At first I thought she was just busy in her new life someplace but she should have called me by now. She would have called me if she were okay." In truth by now I had pictured myself also living in San Francisco in Kevin's spare room that he had said was open for Selena's best friend.

Lacey puts a hand on my shoulder. "Maybe Jesus has her out there to teach her something. Think of that?"

"And if He already took her home," says Taffy, "then it ain't no business of ours."

"I feel called to know what's happening," I say. "Please."

"I have a prophecy." Denay stretches her arms upward and closes her eyes. "The Lord says to look within yourself, Briley."

"What else?" I say, eyes closed.

Denay lets her hands drop. "And that she's dead already."

Lacey gasps. "Oh, fuck."

"Lay hands," Denay commands. She walks over to me and forms a chokehold around my neck and the other girls entwine themselves around me, around each other. Taffy kneels before me and hugs my shins.

"Lord, let Briley feel Selena's death. Let her process what it means. Where is the body? Where is the body?"

They begin to chant "Where is the body" over and over and Taffy jerks on the floor and coughs and coughs. I close my eyes and listen deeply and I hear a heartbeat, thump, thump, and I think live, live, live, and I think, live, Selena, call me, you stupid twat. I start to tremble and it feels like an earthquake until I realize that Taffy has braced herself against my chair and is rocking me back and forth. When they stop we all sit in silence.

"Yes," Denay says finally. "Dead."

"I saw fields," says Lacey.

"I saw dark," says Taffy.

I am the only one who didn't see a thing.

The day before Selena left we had gotten froyo. We sat outside and I felt giddy about Kevin. I wanted to just tell her everything, that he was coming that night, that she was going to be so in love, he was so hot, he was everything she would want. Like a movie.

"Just tell me the surprise," she said, mouth full of vanilla.

"I can't," I said. "But you'll know it when you see it."

"I hate surprises."

"Come on, what's the matter?"

"Daddy Marc and my bitch mom said they aren't paying for city college."

"Maybe you won't need to go to school," I said.

"Of course I have to go to school. I can't depend on a man to get me out of here, I've realized. I'm smart. I can do this myself."

"I guess we'll see." I drove her home.

"Bye bitch," she said.

"Bye bitch," I said back.

The box is gone now. The email account is deleted. I sweat all night and I have lost more weight. Mother comes into my room, wearing a long house dress.

"Geary called me up," she says. "While you was in school."

"And what?"

"Wanted to know what I knew."

"He tell you any news?"

"He wanted to know about you," she says. "Says they pulled a man over up the I-5 for speeding and in his car they found Selena's purse."

"Her purse," I repeat.

"He's just figuring you know more than you're saying," she says. "And I tell him, 'Geary, my girl and that Selena, they speak their own language.'"

"Why are you telling me this?"

"I know about your emailing, and all your flirting with that man, and I thought nothing's to it, but then Geary said that, and I can put together two and two, Briley. That man from the internet took her."

"Yeah, to his place in the city." I stand up, pace around.

"I told him it's a damn shame all this sex trafficking. That is the God's truth."

"What was the man's name?"

"Angel," she says. "Something like that. They threw him in jail. Figured you heard already on the news."

"No," I say. "His name is Kevin."

"That's what he told you."

"Well, yeah."

I felt sick then.

"And you believed him?"

Well, yeah.

Did I know that Selena had emailed a stranger she met online? Did I know she was engaging in a romance with a man involved in a street gang? Had she ever mentioned Angel? Did I know that usually they don't find the girls the gang picks up, that she could be anywhere at all right now? That they could have put her on a plane and changed her name?

No, no, no, no, no, no. No, I tell them. No, I did not know.

"You girls shared everything, right?" Geary asks me again.

We are in the station. They have announced to our town that they know who took Selena.

"Why can't she just have been kidnapped by him, and now you go find her?"

"When are you going to tell us that you made all this happen?" Geary smiles.

I say nothing.

"Not sure why you're keeping it secret," he says. "Unless for some reason you're feeling guilty about it."

"She wanted me to do it," I say.

"Why did you dump that nice box with all them pictures of her?" Geary smiles wider.

"Have you been following me?"

"Figured if you all were as close as you've said, you'd lead us there eventually."

"I never meant for this. This is crazy! His name is Kevin and he lives in the city!"

"We doubt you meant for this," Geary says. "Just a one-thing-led-to-another kind of situation, am I right?"

"This is just a mistake."

"You kids. You're so damn stupid. You think nothing matters. What you learn when you get old like me, is that everything does."

Selena's mother gave a statement to the news and they play it every ten minutes. She has tears pouring down her face, and she is asking Angel to please, just break his silence, and *say where she is, just say where she is.* He sits in a jail cell claiming over and over that he left her in the Bay Area, and he ain't seen her since. They have him on camera, and he smiles a tiny bit, and a small dimple can be seen. I feel shocked at how different from Kevin he looks. I have the urge to email the real Kevin, to tell him what happened. To see if he can help. My brain can't accept any of this. Angel says, "That was a beautiful girl."

I drink a pint of Mother's special strawberry vodka and call Daddy Marc.

"You messed with her, don't think I don't know."

"Listen close," he says. "They're gonna put you away for what you done."

"You mean what you did." I start crying and realize the line is dead.

The news prints a story about the mysterious twist. The friend and the emails and the box recovered in Tent City. And they show a picture of us together, one I took, my arm outstretched with the camera facing in. Selena looks tiny, her chin down, big eyes up. And people begin calling in from all over the country saying they've seen Selena at the bus stop, walking down their street, outside Carl's Jr. My mother has taken our phone off the hook because it won't stop ringing. Angel will not say anything new. Denay writes me a letter that says she and the girls are praying for me, but they need to keep their distance. Geary comes by and tells me to hold on to my britches, that it won't be long now, just a few more kinks to iron out. I ask Mother if I need a lawyer, and she says, *We can't afford that.* She turns her program up and brushes the ringlets of her baby doll, counting strokes under her breath.

I put on Selena's denim skirt and old T-shirt to wear to court. They fit me great now. I smear on her lip gloss, a shade she said was good on me. I set out the gold eyeshadow she loved, the nice bronzer. I can see her beside me in the mirror. There's glitter in a line above her dark lashes, perfect. Hair parted down the middle, cowlick-free. There's the way she would bump her hip against mine without saying a word and it meant everything. How right now she would turn to me, shaking her head. *Oh, Colt.* She'd wipe away the bad makeup job I'd done. *Here, let me fix you.*

Cowboys and Angels

I had me a cowboy once on a hot steam Friday night, on a hot go all the way time, just us together in his truck with old "Angel from Montgomery" playing way turned up. I wanted that cowboy but he had eyes for another, some slack-jawed Sally from the next town over, daughter of the dairyman. Me, I'd been out turning grapes as far back as I could remember but by then I was fixing to marry and I had long red hair down to my waist and I was one sunburn away from old age. After our first intimacy I wanted that cowboy to come to his senses and I decided he had about a week to do it before I'd tell his future bride all we'd done together, how he'd kissed me each and every place and we was one before the Lord and in the eyes of God we was already married and she ought to step aside and abide by our blessed salvations evermore.

When I met him I was working a shift at the feedstore, standing there with my tongue hanging out like a dog in the desert. In he walked, short as myself, strong legs in tight thick-cut denim, an ass high and proud as a horse. Boots of turquoise, hat to match. A rhinestone belt and a flaming pink, pearl-buttoned shirt. His eyes were glassy lavender. I'd never seen purple eyes on no person but there he was. He walked right up to me and I straightened, thinking, What on earth is this clown doing in here? I was used to men in overalls and no shirt, straw hats with no grace. But then he smiled. Lord. The teeth on a man always did me in. Those little crooked fangs crammed into each other. The overall impact of them was sacred. His face was unfreckled and pale, shaven clean. His nostrils had no wily hairs poking from them and his eyebrows were plucked even and he struck me almost girlish but for his voice. He said, "Lady, I'd like to be with you somewhere other than here."

Now I was of course waiting for my wedding day before becoming one flesh with a man but this cowboy told me all I wanted to hear. I said, "I'll need a white dress." He said, "I can imagine you in white now." I said, "I ain't got no daddy to marry me off," and would you believe it, he said, "I'll be your daddy."

I left the feedstore saying I had an emergency. Ten minutes later I was in his truck panties off and his tongue was up *there*.

Only after all that did he tell me about his Sally up the road. How he planned to marry her in an arrangement situation. "So you see I can't skip out on her, honey."

"You a real cowboy?" I asked him, weak over those teeth. I had never kissed a man on account of suffering alopecia in my younger years and keeping to myself. By the time I'd bloomed a desert rose all the boys had turned into gut-slinging men and were married right up. Now the Lord was rewarding my patience, and I could see my God-given future up ahead.

"'Course," he said. "My daddy owns the biggest cotton plant in the west."

Money, I thought. Money was colorful and so was he. God spoke to me then, let me know a man like this wasn't an everyday occurrence and I ought to act. "Well, you're gonna be with me," I told him. I wasn't one to ignore God.

He laughed. "I couldn't love you, honey."

I eyed the pair of diamond-studded dice hanging from the rearview mirror, classy as all get out. I knew he wanted a woman of big money because that's all he'd known.

"I could love you." I was breathless.

"You and me, we're on different tracks."

"Seemed to be on the same track just a minute ago."

He got stern with me. "Get on now. It ain't gonna happen."

"See me again, will you? Then decide."

"I've got big business up at Sally's all week. Can't be bothered."

That's what he said, but I thought different. I watched him tear down the road until I couldn't see his taillights anymore. I felt I had been changed. The Lord gives you challenges, my mam always told me. So this was mine.

I set off on a plan to convince him I was rich. I wasn't rich at all. My daddy sold the family raisin farm when his alcoholic tendencies became a full-time job. After that I worked in the fields for pennies. That's why I had a second job at the feedstore and a third job Saturday nights where I was a telephone operator of the sensual variety. All these jobs enabled me to keep my hair shiny and buy myself enough fine fabric to make one new dress a month. My flair for presentation alone would show him I was a worthy bride. Yes, I'd convince him I was rich and by the time he found out I wasn't he'd already be in love with me and I'd probably be pregnant.

The sensual hotline was called The Diviner's, a Lady on the Line. My mam's best girl friend growing up, Daisy, was low on women and begged me to work for her. I said, "Daisy, you ain't never respected me and my mama's twang," and she said all high and mighty, "Don't worry, there's a pit for every peach." After four years taking calls I could do it in my sleep. Now being a Christian I did feel shame, but I made up a fake name and kept my hand firm on the Bible while I took the calls, and I am sorry to say that I still felt a brushfire fairytale in my own knickers while talking the bliss to the men in Daisy's big ole house, but that was only because I was nearing thirty and still chaste. It was me and two others, some pretty dumb thing named Louise who walked around starry-eyed in love with one of her customers, a common but disastrous mistake, and D'Andra, who brought in Chinese chicken salads from Applebee's to win my friendship, but she was playing a dead hand: I couldn't be friends with a phone sex operator. I ate those salads, though, imagining my real life going on somewhere else, out of the valley.

But once I met the cowboy I saw my life turn dreamy before me and so next day I quit The Diviner's. I told Daisy that I was getting married and she said "hell's bells hallelujah" without so much as looking at me. D'Andra hugged me like we were next of kin, her sloppy tears dripping on my new raw silk shift. I was happy to never see another Applebee's salad again. It would be fine dining from here on out. Steak and mashed potatoes.

The cowboy didn't give me a way to contact him after our first love encounter but I knew his Sally lived in the next county over in the big dairyman's mansion. I borrowed a car from our neighbor Wayland, a lazy old fixture on his front porch, no excitement in his life other than my brief passing-bys. "One day you'll hafta kiss me for it," he grunted as I walked on past. "Kiss my dust," I muttered as I took the keys.

"Huh?" he said.

"I said next time I'll give you a real smacker."

I'd need the cowboy to think I had a nice car, and this car was nice by my standards in that it had four wheels and fabric on the seats. I gussied myself up and used the purple eyeshadow that went with the red of my hair and I wore two push-up bras for luck. I looked at my sun-spotted hands nearly headed toward a spinster grave and I said a thanks aloud to the mirror. "Dearest Papa God, a husband you have delivered at last and saved me!"

My younger sister Beulah hovered around, sensing I was taking off toward uncharted places. She was stick in the mud boring and didn't like to leave the house aside from running the pig races every year at the town carnival. All she had to do was pull up the hatch on their gate and call out the winner, but the town loved her like some kind of prize. "It ain't a hard vocation,"

I'd told her and she'd said, "Yeah, Vangie, you're right," which made me burn with anger. She was always doing that, making me mad by agreeing with me.

In any case, I knew she'd be fine alone. She could cook soft white rice and brown a beef tongue from Mike's Meat Market, delivered by Mike himself who always stood around too long talking to her. "On you go, Mike," I'd tell him. "We get it." Once Beulah told me Mike had asked her for a date to the movie theatre all the way in Fresno, suggesting they eat French fries afterward, and that's when I met Mike at the door and told him we'd taken up vegetarianism. "I'm to be wed before you, little sister," I reminded her once he was on down the road, and she said, "'Course, Vangie."

Now I looked at her staring at my beauty. She was wearing one of our dead father's shirts and worn Levi's, her fine blonde hair in its natural swoop.

"Beulah, we always knew it was coming to this moment, didn't we?" I said. She moped at the kitchen table while I packed a bag. "I'm the marriage material of us girls. Daddy always said that."

"I don't remember him saying that," she said, holding her pointer finger up. "I remember him saying to keep our knickers on and our hands in prayer."

"My husband's arrived and you'll just have to understand. I can't be around here to pet your head all the night."

"You real sure, Vangie? Maybe we better write down the phone number of this husband?"

I didn't want to tell her I didn't have it, let alone know his Christian name. Who was the idiot here? Not me.

I drove Wayland's car to the dairyman's house, where I knew the cowboy was likely getting ready to bend down on one knee. *Big business.* I would tell his Sally to step aside and make a case for myself—some exaggerations about my robust savings account and perhaps a feigned pregnancy if it came to it. Mostly, I assumed things would take the natural course of miracle. That he would see me next to her and understand that I was to be his rightful bride. He'd think, my oh my, a single girl in the country with her very own vehicle. Love's recognition would set in. I'd brought my recipe book, prepared to show him everything I could cook and what sort of mashers and cranberry sauce he could come to expect. I hadn't washed since I'd seen him and I could still smell him on me. It was something like the herbs my mother used to rub on a freshly killed chicken, and I knew this was a cherishable thing, loving deeply the scent of another.

As I parked, my hands shook with excitement. I was going to have a husband. And not just any, but one who could afford to take me far away and to a place with its own swimming pool, I just knew. I didn't have a swimsuit but soon I'd have a closet full of them. Of course, living poor my whole life had made me resourceful and he'd hardly notice my spending, just needless me, no hungrier than a mouse. I let out a long breath. It was exhausting being poor.

Sure enough there was the cowboy's truck, shiny and black, lifted into the air by four huge tires. Not a scratch on that paint job. I could have licked it. I checked my reflection in the paint and I stood extra tall. For the first time, I would get what I wanted. I walked to the front door of the house and opened it. Who had time to knock, not me. Keep me strong in Your will, Amen.

The house was something else. I stood in an entryway large enough to be its own room with a dresser and a metal basket on top used only for mail. Who puts their clothes in an entryway, I wondered, counting the drawers. There were family pictures on the wall, one featuring Sally all alone in her cheerleading outfit, silver braces a-gleam, her blond ponytail in one huge curl coming from the top of her head like a lasso. I couldn't remember if she was out of high school or not, but who cared about youth? I felt that high school was just yesterday for me and people always commented on how young I looked and acted. I could compete is what I'm saying.

I walked into the living room where there was a plump blue couch and cooking magazines spread across a clean glass table. The air in the house was still. It was cool. They had air conditioning. I lifted my arms and let my sweat dry in luxury.

Now I've always been real tight with God, and I liked to think he gave me special previews of things to come, but when I saw the dairyman's bare feet poking out from behind a big La-Z-Boy chair, I uttered aloud, "What in tarnation?" I rounded the chair and saw him lying there, shirtless with kiss-sized welts all over his body, quivering. He didn't see me on account of his blindfold, but he sucked air in a desperate fashion through his nose. I bent down and tried to pull the ball from his mouth but boy it was in there.

"Sir," I said. "This is Vangie Herd from up the road. I'm looking for a cowboy, maybe you've seen him?"

He grunted, almost a cry.

"Thank you for your fine fresh milk," I went on. "My mam always let the fat rise and then ate it off like frosting." He was still. I bent closer to his ear. "No need to be embarrassed, sir. I know all about your type. At my workplace I have all number of men who tell me they want to be hung up by the ankles. I'm not here to judge you, just looking for your girl to set her straight. Seems she thinks she's gonna be with my cowboy and it just ain't so."

I looked at the red and strained skin of his stomach. He shook his head back and forth like I was slapping him around. I thought of the cowboy's lavender eyes, how I missed them so strongly in just a short amount of time.

"I'll go have a look myself seeing as you're busy."

I stood up and as I turned to go down the hall it all went black, a gunnysack over my head, arms dragging me down a long hallway, my heels bouncing along.

As I went, I thought of Beulah waving sadly from the door as I drove away. I had poked my head out the window and said,

"When I'm settled, I'll call for you." The last thing I'd said to her was a lie.

The arms set me up against a wall and I heard a door shut. I remembered my mam once telling me about a story where a carjacker came to her window the first and only time she ever drove around Fresno alone at night, and all her mind could muster up was "Oh, brother." She said everything was happening to her and she had no choice in the matter so she let herself go soft as he pulled her onto the hot street. She told the story in a numb voice but it still terrified me. "Vangie, quit your crying. If something like that's coming your way, it's coming."

The sack was pulled from my head. It was my cowboy. He shook his head like he was disappointed to see me. "Here you are involving yourself." My heart flickered.

"I won't run," I said, and he dropped the coil of rope in his hand in total trust and belief in me. His lavender eyes were red. I could see he was tired. My heart ached for my tired husband. "You need a glass of water," I told him, imagining the name of our firstborn son. *Ras July*, I'd already decided.

"Welcome to the show," he said and that was when I saw Sally in handcuffs with a rope tied round her neck like a leash, her ankles bound, slumped in the corner like a down and out doll.

He dragged me closer to her so we were sitting side by side and then he walked to the corner of the room and messed with a small radio. "I think he's going to kill me," she said to me, her voice a scratch.

"Well, why'd you get involved with him anyhow?" I hissed. This is exactly what happens when you don't follow God's plan, I wanted to tell her.

"I've never seen him before in my life," she said.

Here she was denying their arrangement when it was plain to see that their arrangement was the thing keeping him and me apart. We could be elsewhere but we were here, a true inconvenience. When the cowboy turned back toward us I gave him the eye. He could tell I was on his side with whatever was going on.

"Until she can tell me where her daddy keeps the money," he said. He poked Sally's nose like a pup with his finger. "Then this will just go on and on."

He stripped off his shirt. A snake tattoo wound its way up his arm and down his chest. I hadn't noticed that during our consummation. A country song streamed from the radio. He danced with himself, wrapping his arms around the paleness of his long torso. He didn't have a muscular stature. He was straight with a little paunch belly. Sally sobbed quietly next to me but I was enthralled by him. All my hours listening to the men tell me their deepest desires over the phone had equipped me for just this moment. I wasn't scared of anything.

He pulled a jar of peanut butter from his rucksack and opened it. He began to spread it across his midsection with a bread knife, stopping occasionally to eat some. Then he told us it was our turn.

"I'm allergic to peanuts," Sally said.

"Another reason she ain't gonna be the bride of your dreams," I said. "Imagine giving up peanut butter cookies the rest of your life." The cowboy gave me a half smile.

"I'm aware of the allergy," he said. "I've been watching her for a while now."

Sally looked at me as if we were on the same team. "Do you know this person?"

"We made love like in the movies," I told her. "Like you've probably never known."

She looked real young to me then. I let my eyes trail over her. "I was a virgin when he had me," I went on. "We're married already if you really get down to it. You still a virgin?"

"There's no money in this house," she said to him, ignoring me.

"You like your daddy of the alive variety?" he asked Sally.

"Here, she wants to marry you," Sally said, her tone changing into a child's. "I bet she has the money you're after. Why don't you leave me and my daddy be and get with her?"

He looked me up and down. I imagined myself crawling up to him and licking some of the peanut butter off his stomach, just showing him my dedication.

"I can't marry a girl like this," he said. "She talks like a hillbilly."

"There ain't no hills around here," I said.

Sally scooted toward the door. He closed his eyes and put his hands together under his chin like a prayer.

Where was Sally's mother, the woman from the photos

with teased hair two inches off her head and string of pearls around her neck? Wasn't she bound to come home? I thought of my own mam and how she'd died only a year ago but most days it felt like she was still alive, just waiting for me to come home so we could smack our gabs about the sinners at church. Beulah and I had left my mam's earthly body in her bed for just under one month before calling the authorities, that's how sad we were.

"My mam would think the size of this house is ridiculous," I said to Sally and she squinted her eyes at me like she was staring at the sun. I knew she was thinking the cowboy was crazy. That is what an unspiritual person would think, but I was not that way. I saw a man willing to do whatever it took to get what he wanted, and that was an attribute that could not be invented in a person. Here it would be all about the taming, and I was up for the job.

I felt all the strength of the Lord in me until I noticed a pistol on the floor in the corner. Fear touched me then like a rolling wind. I'd seen a gun before. I'd handled one, sure. I'd shot a rabbit in a field and felt little to nothing over it. I'd fed it to Beulah and me and we were thankful.

Lord, keep me, I thought. I closed my eyes and prayed and when I opened them I felt more alive than I ever had: The cowboy was wounded internally in a deep and hellbound way and was acting out in a cry for help. His salvation was mine to give. This was what I'd been waiting for all my years turning grapes, all my days at the feedstore counter, on the phone saying *Come now, come.* This was the payment the good Lord was finally re-paying for the years of suffering I'd gone through.

The song changed. Iris DeMent. I knew all the cowboy's songs because they were the same songs my father loved. You only have to hear a true cowboy song once for it to brand you. Whatever was on the radio these days was anyone's trash. I walked up to my cowboy and dragged a finger through the peanut butter on his stomach and wiped it across my lips like lipstick. I danced slow to Iris's high voice. He looked at me confused for a moment and placed a hand on my waist, but then dropped it. Stomped his foot and turned to Sally.

"I'm done going round in circles," he said. "I'm here for the money!"

"I'm rich," I said, standing between them. "You should understand."

"Richer than this girly here?" he said.

"'Course," I said. I looked at Sally who was pressed into the door. It was like she was barely breathing, making a horrible wheezing sound. It seemed dramatic.

"My daddy was the Sun-Maid raisin man of all the world," I said. "I got jewels and rubies in my rightful house. My sister Beulah guards them day and night."

His hardness softened, and he looked at me and only me. Said low, "I don't want to be nice. I've been nice for a lot of my life and I don't know it's gotten me anywhere. How can I trust you?"

"You can."

"No. I can't trust no broad. You're probably in on this to-gether. I ain't getting nowhere in here."

He pushed past Sally and his boots clomped down the hall.

"Come on," she said. She got up and hopped to me and grabbed my arm, the rope leash trailing behind her. "Let's get out the window."

"You think you're better than us don't you, in your nice house? Well, him and me are gonna have a house even bigger than this one. Paint the walls sky blue."

"What's wrong with you? We need to get out now. You're acting like you half like him or something. You're crazy!"

She gagged as she made her way to the window. She reached her handcuffed hands up and tried to open it. The window was high and we both knew she wouldn't be able to get out without my help.

"You know," she said. "I saw my life flash before me there on the ground. I never done anything wrong, believe me. I've been a good girl and this is what I get? I don't believe it. And here you are, a nightmare woman, no help to me at all."

I didn't appreciate her talking to me like I was beneath understanding, but when a loud pop came from the front of the house, I saw fear become her and I felt for her, I did. Sally crumpled to the ground and tried to lift her hands over her head. "Daddy," she whimpered.

I imagined the cow slaughters of my youth, the ones my daddy would take me to at his friend Beagle's. We'd watch the cows be shot and then gutted upside down while the froth of them poured out and I never felt strange over it because that was my life.

"A gunshot wound don't always mean death," I told her, comforting. Red hives had appeared on her mouth. "My cowboy wouldn't hurt a fly. I bet it was nothing more than a startle shot."

She started coughing and sputtering a storm. She was saying "Jesus take me now," over and over. I felt annoyed she seemed to think she had a hold on Jesus too.

The cowboy came back in white as a sheet. The small pistol in his grip looked unnatural like he'd just discovered such a thing could be used. "Can you believe her daddy won't talk? Even when I showed him this? I didn't mean for it to go off but it did. It wasn't my fault, I'm telling you." His eyes looked through me and it gave me the willies.

"Let's be on our way," I said. I got myself together. "Already ruined things with your potential father-in-law, I'd say. Imagine, with me, you won't have no in-laws to concern yourself with."

He bent down near Sally, shaking. "Give me the goddamn money. Now."

She gasped for air. Her face had turned a dirty purple. "There's no money," she pushed out.

The cowboy looked at me as if I knew something I wasn't telling him. "I was told by a very reputable source there was money by the millions hidden in this place." The father moaned down the hall. "He's alive," the cowboy said, nodding to himself.

"I bet the neighbors heard that shot, honey," I said. "Let's be on down the road to our destiny."

He looked at Sally. Glanced nervous out the window. He was a smooth operator but not then. He was showing me his shakes and worries.

"I'll take you to my place," I went on. I took the gun from his hand and he let me. He was once a little boy. "I'm telling you. I'm an heiress to a raisin fortune."

"Why you wanna give me all your money?" he asked.

"What's yours is mine, of course." I said. The metal hard in my hand. "I keep trying to tell you." I stuck out my chest.

The cowboy showed me his slanted teeth. "You're growing on me. This might work," he said. "And that man in there's still alive. Everything's gonna be just fine."

"Let's leave this place. We can come back if you're unsatisfied by what I have to offer. Sure, we can always come back."

He put his clothes on and hurried me out of the room by the hand. I tucked the gun into my raw silk fabric belt. We were practically skipping through the house until we came to the dairyman lying face down in a pool of red. He wasn't groaning anymore but breathing in short little rasps. "Oh no," I said. "What did you do?" The dairyman's feet were perfectly fine, plump and pale, black hair on the toes. I was glad I couldn't see his face then.

"It just went off," the cowboy said. "You believe me, don'tcha?" He got on his knees and hugged my waist.

My body froze and I felt like all my years walking God's

earth reached back and slapped me. I remembered the nicest thing my daddy ever said to me which was *Vangie, you're pretty but you're stupid.* His voice was a siren going off between my ears and I knew I'd never seen a man dying this way, for this was surely what he was doing. I'd seen my dead daddy, sure. Soft as a plum in the end, lying in bed with a wool blanket on a one-hundred-degree day. But that was a death that had taken years and years. The dairyman had been fully alive moments before and now perhaps didn't have long. I felt the Lord come into me. Keep moving, He told me. In what direction? I asked in my head. I knew Sally was probably on her way to meet Him, too, if I didn't find her some help.

"He's alive," the cowboy kept telling himself.

I yanked him up. "Let's go," I said.

We walked past Wayland's car. It looked cheap and I didn't claim it. The cowboy's truck had looked so beautiful before but now it just looked like a hearse. We peeled out of the driveway and sped down the dirt road. I couldn't take him to my house. Beulah was there and she was an innocent. What had she ever done wrong? And Sally, Sally needed a paramedic.

"Take a left," I said.

"You seem different," the cowboy said. "Where's your sparkle now? Here I am giving you just want you wanted."

"Oh, I know, honey," I said. "Think I'm just hungry or something."

"Now you said you didn't live far from here. I don't see no houses."

"You done something like this before?" I asked, slow and steady.

"Like what?"

"Like with that Sally back there. You know. The gun."

"I'm a traveling man," he said. "I was just having a little fun with her. Turns out she wasn't no fun. Not like you. And that man is still alive."

"Take a right here," I said.

We neared the main strip and the police station. I would just alert them to go to the dairyman's and then I'd feel fine. I was certain God didn't intend for two to die along my path of salvation. His truck slowed to a roll. "I told you not to take me through town." I tried to open the door. His arm shot out and held me in.

"I shoulda known not to trust a hillbilly," he said and he pressed the accelerator. I thought we were going to sail through the main strip, past the feedstore, past the post. Everyone would see my hair flying out the window. They would think wow, Vangie's really going somewhere and they wouldn't know I had failed at my one life and trusted a cowboy who was no cowboy at all. Goodbye town, I thought. Goodbye men on the phone. Goodbye grapevines and raisins.

In the distance I could see old Mrs. Evers holding a shopping bag at the crosswalk. She had a stooped back and no peripheral vision. We steamed forward. Her life would be over, too.

"Stop," I said. "You hit her, imagine the fury. Imagine the

cops hightailing behind you. Right now you're clean. You're free like a bird. Just nice and easy. You killed a man but you can leave it here."

He slammed on the brake and we jolted to a stop just a foot from Mrs. Evers, who turned her whole body toward us and leaned back to look. She showed her middle finger and the cowboy wrung his hands together.

"I didn't," he said slow, "kill no man."

It was time, I decided then, for the truth. I'd saved Mrs. Evers's life and I felt high. I felt God right there in that truck with us. "I'm going to tell you how this will go," I said.

He hit the steering wheel and grabbed my collar. I felt my precious handmade dress strain. "I ain't got time for this."

A horn blared behind us. "Attracting attention," I said. He let go of me and rolled on.

He was back to looking like a boy then, like he wanted to cry. I saw all his sins before me.

"My buddy up in Sacramento said you country folk down here are dumber than a bag of hammers. Farm rich, storing money by the millions under the floorboards. That's why I came, see."

"We ain't dumb," I said. I pointed to the town bank. "That's where the money is."

He grumbled and sank in his seat, pouting. Yes, he could be tamed. And something new became clear then. A greater purpose perhaps, my own abilities finally apparent to me—I was the smarter of the two of us.

"Now listen," I said. "I didn't like that stuff you did back there. That ain't no way to do it."

"What do you know?"

I looked to my left down a long dirt road that would run into Daisy's hotline, where I could waste my life away. I saw the feedstore up ahead where I could scoop pellets into sacks until I croaked. "What you need is a sharp mind and a slow hand on the trigger," I said. "I could help you."

"I'm in no mood for settling down," he said.

"We could do banks," I said and smiled, for it was certainly God who had planted the bank before me, showing me the way. "And you can't do a bank alone. You'll need someone with a foot on the gas. You'll need me."

He looked at me and the red was all drained out of him.

"Husband and wife," I said.

A long moment passed, our many possible destinies swirling around us. Finally he nodded, muttered "fine," and all faded away but our one true future.

"I need to make two calls and then we'll go and never look back," I said to him. I put a finger on his teeth, felt the ridges. He let me do it.

I led him to the feedstore where I walked inside and let myself behind the counter. I picked up the phone and dialed 911. "Head to the dairyman's," I told them. I paused. I considered that I could tell them everything and they could pick me up a victim, but Sally was bound to throw me into the sawmill. She wouldn't be rational at all. I'm on your path, Lord. I hung up. I called Beulah. "I love you but I ain't coming home," I told her. "Vangie, are you in some trouble?" And I said, "Call up that Mike. Go to that movie and when you close your eyes at night imagine me riding into the sunset toward the biggest city you ever seen."

"What you want for dinner tonight?" she asked, no belief in me at all.

"Goodbye," I said.

I opened the register and took out the cash and jammed it in my pockets. I took one last look at the town as I hitched up into that big black truck and I spread the money over the bench seat between us. My husband smiled at me. The Lord shined down. I had saved two lives, maybe three, and now I'd save the cowboy's. I'd bring him to faith, I would, and we'd get rich along the way. We rode off and I got a new name and dyed my hair bleach blonde and the cowboy fashioned his in an inky pompadour and grew a beard down to his belly button. I was the keeper of the pistol and we slept in the back of that truck in the wide-open plains alongside highway after highway, riches like tall cotton.

And that's how a cowboy became the husband of a traveling robber, Amen.

Fact of Body

We lived for a time in a car, my mother and me, alongside a slow-buzz highway that led to a toxic beach. We had come from the valley to the coast with new plans of making our way as clam diggers. I would spend the summer eating ice cream on the boardwalk, and we would take in a stray dog to keep as our own. My mother said living in the car was just until her dream catcher business took off, and that it would be fine. No, better than fine. It would be fun.

In the car on our first night, my mother slept soundly but I laid awake, keeping watch. At fifteen, it was unspoken between us: I would take care. The next day she woke with vigor and crafted her tiny dream catchers one after another. I had drawn a sign for her business that read MAKE ALL YOUR DREAMS COME TRUE and I held it up while she waved to cars as they passed and talked in loops about manifesting her number one destiny: that a documentary filmmaker would discover her and they might fall in love and he would take us into a new stratosphere entirely, her specialness leading the way. You have to be specific, she always told me. So the universe can hear you.

We sold one dream catcher keychain to a woman who had stopped only because she thought we were in trouble, and my mother felt it was time to celebrate. We walked down to Seashell's, a little shack bar at the foot of the power plant that had leaked the year before, cracked open in an earthquake. I grew quiet then.

"Bobby, don't get judgmental," my mother said. She looked at me and I watched her cross over into the bad way. It hadn't always been like this. I remembered her picking me up when I fell as a small boy, kissing the hot red bump under my chin. Carrying me around on her shoulders like a little prince. Singing *He's my one and only, who could ever have a boy like this? Me me me me me.*

Inside the dim bar, I sat in a corner booth drinking plain soda water and soon enough, as she always managed to do, she made a friend. She had promised me no Seashell's situations would happen in this new toxic town, but now. Well.

I walked over to them. His arm was already around her shoulders. She seemed surprised to remember I was there at all. I looked at the man.

"She's a thief," I said to him. I knew better than to try and convince her to leave. I'd have to convince the man.

"Bobby," my mother whined. She looked at the man. "Excuse me for a minute."

She got up and led me back to my booth. "You wanna eat tonight?"

"No. I don't want to eat. I'm fine not eating."

"It's one time and then never again."

I shook my head. I felt like crying. But I didn't.

Sure enough she ended up in the blue lit bathroom with him and then back in our car, where his heavy sequined blazer shed stars over the dark fabric of our car seats. She normally never brought anyone back, but she said this one was special, which just meant she wanted more money. While the small car shook in the familiar way, I pretended to be asleep in the trunk but of course I could hear them and life was closing in. I felt it in my chest, sharp heart pains and little heart skips. I couldn't breathe deep enough. That night the man told my mother what a boy my age could make at Seashell's and I heard her mind spin with this new information.

I spent the next day alone at the beach dreaming, pushing away what the man had said, floating in the condemned waters on an abandoned raft, letting the sun bake my skin, thinking about the school my mother said I would attend in the fall—maybe I'd make friends, maybe there would be a girl who liked me. Maybe my mother would find meaning in joining the PTA. I was being specific.

But as we walked to Seashell's again that night, she reminded me it wasn't her fault the world ran on money. When I said no, anything else, she said, "You want me to leave you on the side of the road? 'Cause I will." That was my first night working.

After that night I could no longer afford the fantasies we kept up, that my mother was different, uniquely talented, and that someday soon a filmmaker would show up to change our lives forever. She would say to me all the time, "Bobby McGee, imagine the feasts! Dungeness crab for days." Once I'd asked, "Why a filmmaker? Maybe you could just get a job at like Denny's or something." And she'd scowled. "I am a creative, Bobby. How dare you suggest I work like a basic person? Who raised you?" And she'd sort her remaining pills, the ones that kept her up in one pile, the ones that put her down in another, then shove them back in her pockets all mixed together.

Once I started working at Seashell's, my mother became more affectionate, treated me like a friend, perhaps, comrades finally in the great toil of life. She liked to imagine that I was like her, that I forgot the days as they happened and woke each morning with no memory of us or the things we'd done, but that's where she had me wrong.

The reason I tell my story is this: while I had stopped believing in miracles, and stopped believing anything my mother told me, what came to pass that summer on the loneliest highway in the world still sits with me as a kind of intervention that could have only been constructed by angels. It is why even on my darkest days, I must revere the possibility of magical fate, of protections beyond imagination.

Because my mother was right. A few weeks after I'd taken up servitude at Seashell's, a documentary filmmaker did come. The sight of his car parked next to our beat-down Fifth Avenue pulled me from my depressive fog. The filmmaker told us he was on his way to the toxic beach to see if things were as bad as everyone said, and maybe he would shoot a film about how the community had abandoned the beach instead of fixing it. There was a young woman with him and she stayed in the car looking at her phone, and then at her pretty self in the mirror, applying pearled gloss. The young man said he had passed us before during their reporting trips and wanted to know why we were here.

"We're traveling artists," my mother said.

She said it as if it explained something, our filth for instance. We didn't shower, but instead wiped down with paper towels in the Seashell's bathroom. My mother wore her hair in a matted bun on top of her head and with time it had grown large and larger until it was nearly the size of her face. In it she stored feathers and shells, sometimes a pen. She wore a full face of makeup every day, layering blushes and foundations over each other. I never knew if the drugs came before her mind collapsed, or if she took drugs because of it. I wish I could say she was beautiful, but she was not.

The young man said he was in school for documentary-style art, and his girlfriend was in school for journalism. The beach story was their senior project. He said maybe we could be part of it, to show the world who had been displaced by the nuclear waste spill, how the government had let a mother and son slip through the cracks. I didn't stop him to say we hadn't been displaced by any force other than my mother. We hadn't even been here when the earthquake shook the town into a terror. We were hours away, living on a raisin farm in the Central Valley where we turned plump grapes by hand, letting them shrivel and die on trays, another life my mother had ruined. We never stayed anywhere longer than six months.

The mother and son by the highway, the young man said, would add a human element to his piece.

I watched my mother's eyes fall in love with him. The girlfriend squinted at us as if she couldn't bear the full view.

Their names were Andrew and Jean. My mother and the filmmaker shook hands.

I woke early the next day to a camera outside the car window. My mother snored on. She had celebrated the night before, eating uppers a client gave her at Seashell's, and wouldn't be awake for at least a few hours. I didn't know if I should pretend to be asleep or get ready like I normally did, take my piss in the heavy ocean air, brush my teeth with my finger. What did Andrew want to see? I got out of the car.

"Hey, Bobby," Andrew said. "Just act natural."

"Are you going to interview me?" I asked.

"Uh, sure," he said, like he'd just thought of it.

"Of course we are," Jean said, holding a notebook. She stepped in front of Andrew. She was different than the day before, suddenly present and attentive. "We're just getting some footage of, you know, the situation."

The situation: my still-sleeping mother, me eating stale

cereal from a box with my hands. I saw my knees, scraped and dirty, and then ran my fingers through my hair to find it was somehow past my shoulders now, matted with sea grease. I'd grown out of my clothes and I spent most of my time shirtless, shoulders peeling and burnt. A mysterious bruise on my rib had turned a muddled green. Sometimes I wore my mother's floral blouse, but that day I wore only too-large boxers that had appeared from nowhere months before.

My mother was so still when she slept that I imagined her dead each morning and I played a game, wondering what I would do if it were true. She had threatened me my whole life with her death in one way or another, using it for everything. If I didn't work at Seashell's, she wouldn't have money for her pills, and do you know what happens if you abruptly stop taking medication? You die, she said. Do you want me to die? I did not want her to die. But in my imagination, I let myself go high and low, feeling the boil of panic and then, shamefully, the welcome cool relief.

I tried to wake her and she swatted me away. "God willing and the crick don't rise," she muttered, still in dream. When she saw Jean and Andrew she sprang up and shook into a manically efficient version of herself.

"Howdy!" she said.

For a few hours they filmed my mother telling them her whole life story. She spoke of a beauty pageant she won as a teenager, how she'd dressed as a pineapple and tap-danced and the glitter from her hairspray stayed on her scalp for weeks, how her mother had stapled her evening dress shut in the back because a zipper broke at the last moment. She smiled up at the cloudless sky to show them the face she'd used when they placed the crown on her head. Maybe she had won the pageant, I thought for a moment, taken with the story myself, but five minutes later she told it again. In the new version she was a runner-up kiwi and her mother hadn't even shown up. Tears streamed down her face. I saw a flicker of annoyance pass over Andrew as he lowered the camera.

"Let's try again," he said. "Just tell me what it was like being in the earthquake. How did it feel?"

"Come 'ere, Bobby," my mother said, and I stood by her. She shook my shoulders hard back and forth, laughing. "Like that."

"Were you scared?" he asked me.

My mother squeezed my arms and tossed her head back. "He's my boy. He doesn't scare."

"Terrified," I answered.

Jean pulled me aside as they were leaving and asked how we had any money. Her eyes speared me. It was clear Andrew was there for himself and his social media, excited to be holding a camera, but not really engaged with us. But something about Jean's intensity made me nervous.

So how, she wanted to know, did we have any money to speak of?

"I can't tell you," I said.

"Don't want to get Mom in trouble?"

"I'm almost a man." I thought of the guy I'd been with the night before who kept saying that to me like a song, *You're almost a man, aint'cha? You're almost a man.* I mean I was, wasn't I? Only three more years until eighteen.

"If you don't tell me what's going on, I can't help you," she said. She said it easily, and I imagined us inhabiting two entirely different worlds. In hers, there was help to be had. In mine, there was only my mother.

I wanted to grab her thin wrist then, for her to take me with her, but I couldn't bear her recoil, not wanting my filthy hand on her, looking at me like people sometimes looked at my mother. With disgust.

"I don't need your help," I said.

They drove away and all day I imagined myself standing on a crumbling stone ledge overlooking a swelling sea. I could just jump.

My mother decided she needed new clothes for the film and so I stood outside the men's room at Seashell's and waited for the signal, a needful person walking past who would tap his pointer finger three times on the door before he entered. I'd wait a few moments before following him in. No one cared what went on in the bathroom, but the ceremony felt like something sacred to me, a small bit of respect. I waited while my mother crushed pills on the bar top and sucked them up through her nose, before lighting a spiced vanilla cigarette. She wasn't opposed to working herself for money, it's just that boys did better on Tuesdays, she explained, stroking my hair.

"How come you didn't tell Andrew and Jean to follow us here tonight?" I asked her.

She smiled at me, put her arms around my waist. We were the same height.

"The dream catchers are our real job, honey," she said. "The metaphysical arts. This is only the beginning. Soon we'll have people following us around, wanting what we have. We'll be teaching them all our ways. Andrew said I was like a female Jim Jones, the way I talk. I mean, he gets me."

"Who's Jim Jones?"

"Well, he meant the good parts about him, not like the making people drink all that Kool-Aid stuff."

A man walked in and did the signal. "This is our real job. Right here," I said.

"When you get like this, I just can't connect, Bobby. It's like you leave the spiritual realm and you're just all about reality. I hate it."

I made fifty dollars and gave her forty, saving ten for gas, something she could never remember to do. We went to the Goodwill situated in a small cluster of shops a few minutes down the road, and she blew it all right away, buying several stretched-out and crisped bikinis, in case they wanted to show us on the toxic beach, and a boxy yellow cardigan and green

patent leather loafers she said would make her look profes-
sional. Then she picked out a mug with Donald Duck on it
that said YOU'RE A QUACK! to give to Andrew as a thank you.
She let me buy something with the remaining five dollars and I
chose a pack of pens and a book of postcards of old California
missions. Maybe I'd write a plea to the God of the toxic sea,
send it sailing in the radiation waters.

I didn't think Andrew and Jean would come back but they did.
Every day for a week my mother wore the yellow cardigan over
a bikini and every day she told more lies about her life, as well
as her ideas for the commune she would start once she had her
following. But I started to notice the truth slip in. She told
them stories about being a girl, dreaming of the beach. About
my father and the concert where they met and how the herbal
blend her witch friend made had not worked on the pregnancy,
here I was, and she was grateful. "Bobby and I have traveled
many lifetimes before this one. There wasn't anything that was
going to stop him from coming into the world." She told them
in a stammer of gestures and clouded phrases about working at
Seashell's, how she sold true connection, something most people did not have these days, and Jean finally said flatly, "Are you
a prostitute?"

My mother paused for just a moment, her eyes glancing
at me.

"No," I said before she could answer. "She's an artist."

My mother smiled. "Bobby gets me."

"What is she doing to you?" Jean asked, looking at me, and this time my mother stopped. "Why are you defending her?"

"You said you were here to make me a star," my mother said.

"Come on, now," Andrew said, glaring at Jean. "Don't make a scene."

"No, I think it's important, right, like what is going on here? He's just a kid."

I looked at my mother and saw her fade. I jumped in quickly. "Did she tell you how I had shark teeth across the bottom when I was little? Two rows of teeth."

"Usually people with spiritual giftings have crazy teeth, it's true," she said sweetly. She pulled back her lips and showed them her loose front tooth. "This will be gone soon."

"We're good for today, right, everyone?" Andrew said. He packed away his things and Jean stood there staring at my mother. My mother smiled back at her so purely. "Bobby," she said lightly. "I think Jean here wants to buy a dream catcher."

When they drove away from us, I figured I wouldn't see them again.

After the days with Andrew and Jean, my mother fell asleep early, her body reclined in the driver's seat, feet on the dash, toe prints on the window, but I felt wired at all hours and would go for walks to the beach and listen to the water pull and push. I could stay there all night, the moon a headlight, and feel outside of myself and wonder if the things that happened to the body could fade away easily and on their own, or if they were facts meant to be carried forever. The touch of a person. Did it ever leave you? It didn't seem plausible that as humans geared toward survival, as every animal was, that we could be so broken by the movements of others over us. It didn't seem practical.

On their last day of filming, Jean brought me a brown bag lunch of pasta and salmon, sliced apples, and almond butter. Organic protein bars. She pulled me aside. "It's not right, you living out here. She's abusing you."

"This is so good," I said, shoving the oily pasta in my mouth.

"Bobby," Jean said.

"Things have been hard for her."

"Think about this," Jean said, poking my chest. "You have one life. One. That's it. Don't you want it to be something great? It'll never be great with her. You've got to believe me. I'm older than you, I know."

I looked over at my mother dancing in front of the camera that Andrew had set up on a tripod. He talked on his phone, but her eyes were on him, crooning *Oh, won't you stay, we'll put on the day, and we'll wear it till the night comes . . .*

"It's temporary," I said, hearing my mother's voice run through me.

"I've heard what goes on at that bar," she said.

My heart pains started up, and a new fear I couldn't name covered me.

She handed me her notebook. "Why don't you just write me a letter?"

I thought of how my mother always said that if I tried to tell anyone from the outside about us, they wouldn't believe me and I'd end up worse off than I was before. I drew a picture of a waxing moon and Jean sighed.

"There's a million other ways to live," she said.

I was quiet and ate.

"I can't sleep at night thinking about you out here."

I smiled. "Imagine being out here."

"I'll have to do something, you know."

I didn't say anything.

When the filmmakers didn't come the next day, my mother refused to believe everything was over so easily. She wanted her fame to bombard us. She wanted to see the film. She wrote Andrew notes on napkins, confessing her love to him, offering herself to him for free. She buzzed around cleaning the car, moving our stuff to the trunk, asking herself questions about whether or not Andrew would like her to read his palm, or if he was more into astrology. She scribbled numbers on strips of paper and hid them under the seats and in the glove box so she could be surprised by them later. She was obsessed with angel numbers, any triple sequence of the same number. 555 was her special one and she said it meant life was handing over a significant change. We saw 555 all the time on billboards for Little Caesars Pizza, on other license plates. It seemed to me utterly ordinary.

"Bobby, Bobby," my mother sang as she wiped dust away with a pair of my underwear. "Who knew we could be this happy?"

She pressed me to her and we twirled next to the car, sometimes bumping into the hot steel of it, and she laughed. She pulled me down with her and we lay on the sandy ground and everything was clear. Her speech sharp, her eyes steady. Maybe it was good the filmmakers had disappeared, maybe they'd forget what they'd seen. Perhaps this was my mother at last, the one I'd waited for.

"Probably need to get registered for school soon," I tried.

She squeezed my hand. "I always knew someone would find us and tell our story," she said.

"What's our story, Mom?"

"We're gonna be eating filet mignon every night, just wait."

"Mom."

She dropped my hand and got up, went back to her tidying. She held a strip of paper up to the sun. "Bobby! It's my angel number!"

"I don't want to go back to Seashell's," I said.

Her face shifted. "Riches are on the way but until then you have to work."

"Please," I said.

"All the things I've done for you," she sneered and crumpled the angel number up in her hand.

"And all I've done for you," I said. She looked sad then.

"Aren't you happy you aren't ordinary? At least you can say, my mom—she was never boring."

"Jean's gonna turn you in," I said. "You might go to jail."

My mother scoffed but I saw her fear. "You would let them do that to me?"

"I want things to be different. I want you to have help."

"You want me to be in an institution, but I won't go. You want to be ordinary, you go ahead. But not me."

It was a slow night at Seashell's, the regulars on barstools drinking cans of Bud while two women, one old and one young, stirred cocktails in red cups with long pink straws and stared at one another, tired, waiting for a client. I sat on the stool on the far side of the bar and the bartender set a Shirley Temple filled with maraschinos in front of me. I wanted to be done but not yet. I needed money my mother didn't know about. I needed money to leave.

"You look just like that mama of yours," the bartender said.

"I look like my dad," I said, though I knew my mother had given me her exact face. Our relation was a simple fact of body.

"Where she's at?"

"She's home waiting on something."

"Tell her she don't come she loses her spot."

A short man in pressed flared jeans and an aquamarine buttoned shirt walked in and ordered a small glass of whiskey. He eyed me from under the brim of a stiff white cowboy hat while he darted a narrow tongue at his drink and then walked to the bathroom and tapped. I glanced at the women and they showed no signs of moving. The toes of his boots shined, his clothing clean. He probably had money. I finished the Shirley Temple and followed him in.

He sat on the toilet with his head between his legs. He had removed the hat and I could see his scalp shine through stiff combed black hair.

He stood. "My wife loved me, but she didn't really know me." He reached in for a hug. His hands spread across my back and it took me a moment to realize he was crying.

"How do you want this to go?" I asked.

"Say you love me," he said. "Look in my eyes."

I started undoing my shorts but he pulled my hands up to his face. "My wife is dead," he said, I think to make me sympathize with him but instead I wondered if he had been the one to kill her. I couldn't read him. I pictured Jean's face and I stepped back.

"Just pretend to be her. It's all I want. I'll pay you just to stand here and hold me," he said, and tossed a rubber-banded wad of bills at my feet. I picked it up. I could leave. My mother wasn't on the other side of the door.

"Please?" he begged. But I ran out the back door of the bar and down to the beach, and as I ran I returned to a secret and comforting thought: that if I looked hard enough I would find my mother's real spirit. That it was lost somewhere searching for her body and I alone could reunite them. I alone could fix her.

I let the ocean touch my feet back and forth and wondered what parts of it were toxic. Was it the sand caught between my toes that would poison me, was it the air, or the water? But of course, one could not be harmful without the other. They were all one. How long before it would be clean again? How many years would have to pass and what would need to be done?

Back at the car my mother was gone and her things were strewn around on the floorboards. I put on her yellow cardigan and sat in her seat, my feet on the dash. My body wouldn't run. My body would wait. She was off finding our next opportunity. We would become clam diggers like she'd promised, in the next town up the highway. And what could Jean have meant about a million other ways to live? She didn't know. This was my only. My mother, my only.

Keep Her Down

Baby sat on her rickety twin bed and rubbed petroleum jelly into the deep-cut wrinkles around her eyes. She could hear Jan down the hall clanging around in the bathroom, reciting her grievances. "I've cared for Golda my entire adult life, for Chrissakes," Jan said. "Who else was gonna do it? No one. Me. I stepped up." It was morning and the women were gearing up to tend Jan's sixty-five-year-old sister, Golda, who was shrunken as an elf with the lifelong mind of a child. Baby had helped out for nearly fifteen years, but still, it took all of her nerve to get Golda up each morning, something Golda was physically capable of but refused to do. "Bad Jimmies under there," she would say, pointing to the dark space below her bed. And Baby would slur that there were no bad Jimmies, whatever a Jimmy was. "She's as good as a chastity belt for a lonely woman," Baby heard Jan say. A drawer slammed.

Jan and Baby were both ex-wives of Pretty. Ex-wives weren't meant to live together. Anyone understood that. But after Pretty left Baby and her drinking got worse and worse, the courts took her nine-year-old girl away. She was mowed down by the list of things she would have to do to get her back, like attending rehab and then holding a job, and she had found herself thinking of Pretty's first wife, Jan. Though their previous interactions had mainly consisted of Jan flipping her the bird from her car window when she dropped Pretty's first set of kids off for the rare weekend, she secretly felt a connection to this woman who had also loved Pretty, who had also been dragged through the mire of her own devotion, then scorned, beaten, and spit on. Betrayed. On those difficult nights, when she felt the most hopeless, Baby had wanted to call Jan for help or guidance, but she never picked up the phone on account of her pride.

Once her pride was gone, though, once her child had been taken, there was nothing to stop her from walking out of rehab, buying a fifth of vodka, and speeding toward Jan's small foothill town with one eye closed to keep the lines on the road straight. By the time Baby showed up she was drunk enough to beg, and Jan sat her down on the porch and slapped her. But Jan didn't turn her away. And after some time, as the evening grew darker and their respective substances took hold, they considered the truth of the matter. They had both been madly in love with Pretty. They should be closer than sisters, considering what they'd gone through. And they both had lots of life yet to live, didn't they? Still in their forties then. He hadn't taken everything. Baby told Jan about the time Pretty had thrown her headfirst into a dumpster outside FoodMaxx, and Jan said, "Me too!" Yes, Jan decided, it could work. Baby had leaned forward to hug Jan, celebrate the two of them against the world, the unlikeliness of it a temporary high, but Jan held up a hand. "Hold it," she had said. Baby could stay, but there was one condition. Much to Baby's relief it had nothing to do with her drinking.

"Hello," Jan called from the bathroom, pulling Baby away from her memories. "The old gal's not going to change her own diaper, is she?"

The deal was that if Baby moved in, she would have to help Jan with Golda. She would be useful, her mornings spent securing Golda's wispy white hair back in a tiny clip, changing diapers, spooning porridge and beans with a wooden spatula, whispering little fables that came to her about tree fairies and good witches, and usually Golda would give her the thumbs down sign and push her bowl to the floor. At the start, and sometimes even still, Baby imagined a secret camera watching her tend to Golda, proving she was a fit mother after all. Her daughter was grown now, it was all too late, but tending Golda felt like she was proving something day in and day out.

The later afternoon was for Baby's drinking and Jan's smoking, and they would shut Golda in her room with her television stories and a box of cheddar crackers. At first Baby felt bad when she could hear Golda throwing a tantrum, reprimanding herself, "Bad Golda, bad Golda!" Acting out the shows of her mind: "He's not your boyfriend, Golda!" But Jan said, "Get over it. She ain't an actual baby. Give her some respect and leave her be." Baby thought of the many times she had left her daughter to herself, had let her be. How that was not okay. But she let the urge to check on Golda fade, and relaxed.

Morning duty with Golda was the hardest. Golda always woke feisty with hunger, ready for mischief. Now, Baby paused at the door and took a breath. She would need all her wits today because lately, to make matters worse, Golda had been hiding poop somewhere in her room. Baby could smell the old and drying shit, but she couldn't locate it. Baby walked in just as Golda fished a fresh piece from her diaper and flung it across the room, where it landed behind the television. "No, I didn't," Golda said, smiling. She jostled her dollies, of which she had fourteen in various states of rigor mortis.

"Lord a-mighty," Baby said. She was still drunk from the night before. "Jan, you had better come here."

Jan walked in wearing an orange spotted one-piece pajama with cat ears sewn on the hood. It was zipped all the way to her chin. She had picked up several pairs with different prints at the Dollar Disco and wore them all the time. She had been proud of the find—finally a comfortable sleeper that could take her from night to day and back to night again. Underneath she wore only old Hanes panties, which bagged out at the crotch from a decade of wear. She used to care about the state of her appearance. Baby had seen the old bombshell photos that Pretty had refused to get rid of: Jan leaning against his old Road Runner wearing a paisley swimsuit, smoking, her hair parted down the middle. Jan smirking at the camera, red-lipped. Baby judged Jan sometimes for the way she neglected herself now, the lank hair and colorless cheeks, the way everything about her seemed to droop depressingly, though she knew she was no different. She looked down and realized that she too was wearing a onesie, the cow one, and underneath, who knew? Jan stood next to Baby and they surveyed what looked to be about a three-inch high mound of dried poop pellets behind the TV.

"Really pulled the wool, dincha, Golda?" Jan said, shaking her head.

"I swear I looked everywhere," Baby said to Jan, wiping the sweat off her forehead. "Just been back here all the while." In truth, she hadn't looked very hard. Not hard enough to push the TV back a little, and she felt ashamed of her laziness, of the voice that sang in her head, *Out of sight, out of mind,* as she had glanced around the room. They looked at Golda. She was in a cotton doily nightgown, the same one she'd always worn. Some days they would just leave it on her. It was easier. Suddenly it looked dark and sallow and Baby felt the peculiar feeling that some kind of God was looking down upon them, very displeased.

"Let's go into town today and buy her a new one of those," Baby said. Baby felt like she was going to be sick but she'd be sicker if she didn't care for this one basic need right away. "Come on, now, Janny. Perk up. Golda's bored. Let's take her out. Maybe she'll stop, you know, flinging the shit."

"Offered her one of the animal suits, didn't I? She's refusing it. Got too much dignity, ha!"

Baby wanted to at least do this one job right. Just one job

right. To see Golda through to the end of her life. How else could she expect to worm her way into heaven? After all she'd put her daughter through, this was a last chance if she'd ever known one. And if she could see Golda through to the end of her long prattling life, she had to admit, she could perhaps end her own life finally and go sit with God in heaven and this misery of her mind could stop. But the joke was on Baby. Golda just kept on living far past what any doctor had ever expected. A true modern miracle.

Jan smoothed Golda's hair down and reclasped her pink baby bow. "We're gonna fix you all up, my sweet champer damper."

"You're a good sister to her, Janny." Baby's stomach was rolling in on itself. She remembered how the first time she saw Golda, she smiled and said hello but had to excuse herself. The sight of Golda had set off a sense of alarm. She had truthfully never seen anyone like her. Golda belonged in a movie, Baby thought, one where the children fear her strangeness, but in the end, she winds up saving someone's life unexpectedly. Baby feared Golda, but she was fine living in fear. There was no other way to live that she knew of.

Jan stared at Golda as if contemplating her deeply. "Maybe some old fashioned pin diapers," she mused. "Maybe a disposable, then a cloth over it. I don't know. She needs psychological help like the rest of us."

"Bad birdy," Golda chirped, looking at Baby.

"Why does she call me that?" Baby said. She edged around the doorway. Golda seemed to see something in her no one else could, and it wasn't something wonderful, like strength and re-silience or an innocent inner child. Golda could see the darkest parts of her heart, the parts that had felt relief when her daughter was finally taken away. The parts that relaxed just a little bit and thought her daughter was surely better off. Those were the parts she hated of herself the most. Golda seemed to look at both Jan and Baby with wise, mystical judgment.

Jan pressed her mouth up to Golda's ear. Golda was hard of hearing, according to Jan, but Baby wasn't so sure. "Gol-Da!" Jan screamed. "Why. Do. You. Call. Baby. Birdy?"

Golda smiled and looked out the window. "Bad birdy," she said again.

They set off for town with Golda in the backseat. Usually the two women would do errands during Golda's long afternoon naps and Jan would chortle that, unlike an actual baby, they could lock their big baby in her room and leave her home alone. But today they resolved to take Golda with them to Town De-partment, and on the way home they would treat her to an ice cream cone.

"She hasn't been out in years," Jan said, driving too fast around the bends in the curvy road. "People probably think we've been two crazy ladies poking at a corpse all this time."

"Used to take her out a lot, didn't we?" Baby said. She re-called her first night after coming to stay and the weird celebra-tory steak dinner Jan had taken them to at Ned's Family Valley

Dining, how Baby had anticipated thick soft meat, potatoes with butter, heavy with salt. She had her mouth set for blood, but what arrived was rubber, hard and brown through the middle. Jan gnashed at hers like it was her last meal and Baby stifled all future hope for her life right then. The arrangement was supposed to be temporary. A place to get back on her feet. When she ate that steak she knew she would probably never get custody of her daughter again. She had tried feebly to help Golda select something healthy from the menu, maybe like she would have helped her daughter, but Golda ordered macaroni, and macaroni was what she got.

"She's my sister," Jan said, glancing at Golda in the rearview mirror. "And so I love her. When she was a kid they put her in a home! They didn't know what to do back then. If you were different you went straight to the bin. My mother said it broke her heart. They didn't know no other way. But still. God a-mighty, have you ever heard of anyone like her living this long? I used to get checks in the mail for this. Where's my checks now? I tell them, com'ere and see her for yourself. Alive as ever. She's gonna outlive me."

"I wouldn't doubt it." Baby looked back at Golda. "Golda," Baby screamed. "Are you enjoying the ride?"

Golda stared into Baby's eyes and slowly shook her head side to side. *No.* Then she winked.

"She winked at me," Baby said.

"She don't wink." Jan chuckled. "She probably didn't hear you. You really have to get on top of her."

"She just winked."

Jan gripped the steering wheel and Baby looked at the speedometer—70. That was too fast. It seemed to Baby that Jan had almost forgotten how to drive.

At Town Department, people stared. It was a small town and everyone was interested in the two ex-wives living together with the old woman. Well, the three old women, really. The ex-wives had not aged as well as they could have. When Jan was very small her mother entered her in pageants because she looked like Shirley Temple. Baby had been beautiful, too. She once won a bicycle at the Central Valley State Fair and someone took her picture for the paper.

Baby was just a sad alcoholic, according to Jan, while she likened herself to a salt-of-the-earth type of woman, living off the land, smoking the marijuana she grew in the backyard. Her two kids were grown, one of them dead, and the other a mother of four children whose names and ages Jan often lost track of.

They went to the lingerie section and Golda skipped up ahead to a mannequin, pulled its black lace panties down, and pointed to its crotch where an asexual mound was exposed. "Where's the puss?" she demanded in a deep, roving voice. "Where's the puss?"

"Golda," Jan said, clapping a hand over her mouth. "Who taught you to talk like that? Not me. Not me. Jesus, Golda, you'll get us kicked out. This is a nice day on the town. A nice day."

"Should we let her pick her own night dress?" Baby asked. "That might be special for her. Give her some purpose." She was skimming the sale rack of teddies. She tried to imagine her young self in them and felt nothing. Gone, she supposed, were the days where thinking of a sexy thing caused her to feel a rush. She felt dry as the mannequin.

"We can see if she goes toward any one thing, I guess," Jan said in a huff.

The ex-wives watched Golda, expected that she would try to escape, but she didn't. She held fast to the mannequin, seemingly very attached to it. She was petting its leg. The head had no face. It was wearing a black wig and had baseball-sized breasts that sat with an unnatural perk.

"Did you breastfeed your girl?" Jan asked Baby.

"No, I wasn't good at none of that," Baby said. She remembered how her breasts had ached and swelled after her cesarean surgery. Her own mother had told her to just ignore the engorgement, get on with life. She did what she was told. And that was best. She had given up breastfeeding and filled herself a mug of wine and took very small sips throughout the day while she fed the baby girl like a gerbil, holding a bottle of foul-tasting formula while the child sucked. More than once she looked over and realized she was holding the bottle just out of reach of the child's mouth. Sometimes she couldn't hear the child cry even if she was sitting right next to her.

"Me neither," Jan said. "I was no dairy cow. Some are and

some ain't. Myself, I find it disgusting. I did try, and as soon as the child latched I would have to vomit."

Golda was not leaving the mannequin's side. She was hugging its long trim leg, playing peek-a-boo. She started chanting, "Mama."

"Well, what the sweet hell is this?" Jan asked Baby. "This is why I don't take her nowhere."

"Golda," Baby screamed. "Pink or white?" She held up two identical cotton shifts. They could not be any more basic and utilitarian, nothing pretty to admire. Baby wanted to leave the store now that she had slipped three pairs of panties in her bag and was feeling antsy. She had one Sutter Home wine cooler she had planned on drinking in the dressing room but now the lights were burning the top of her head. *Get out get out*, they said.

"Mama," Golda said. "Mama mama mama."

"Let's go," Baby said. "Just buy her this one." She held up a brown shift.

"Not a bad idea," Jan said. "It'll stay clean looking."

Back in the car, Baby pulled out the stolen underwear as well as a pair of Calvin Klein sunglasses she had clearly swiped. She had no specific memory of the action. Golda had caused a scene coming out of the store, sobbing and reaching toward the mama mannequin as Jan half dragged her, screaming, "Stop hurting me!" Everyone was focused on her and so perhaps Baby had taken the opportunity then. She felt happy wearing the designer sunglasses, even though they did not flatter her face and pinched the side of her head. She looked at them again. They were children's glasses, something she might have bought for her daughter, or would have wanted to buy. She remembered how a few years ago she'd excitedly sent her daughter a box of treasures she had found at the Goodwill and received a note back from her stepmother to stop sending things that smelled of smoke and were four sizes too small. *She's not the same age as when you left, Baby. Wake up.*

Jan grabbed the glasses. "That's nothing," she said. She pulled out a rolled-up lace nightgown from her bag. Then another. Then another. The same one in three different colors. "One for each of us."

"Well, we bought something, at least," Baby said.

In the back Golda had calmed down but was still forlorn. She was bearing down and grunting.

"She's trying to poop," Jan said. "Can you believe her? After all I've done for her, she's trying to shit so she can throw it at me."

"You don't think she'd try for it in the car, do you?" Baby said.

"You'd be amazed at what she'd do," Jan said, as if Baby didn't already know. "Only man I ever dated after Pretty, well, she scared him off. Got up in the midnight and came to his side and whispered 'boo.' Now who taught her to do something like that? Well, he was gone by morning, wasn't he?"

Baby opened the wine and drank the small bottle in one go. The lurid taste was so familiar it was like walking back into her childhood bedroom, getting into her sweet bed, climbing under the down comforter, and falling into uninterrupted sleep. The kind of unworried sleep only a happy child can have. The wine was like that.

They pulled over at the general store to get ice cream cones, but Golda refused to get out of the car. Jan stroked her fine hair and promised her a pistachio cone. Golda had pooped, or so it smelled. They weren't going to lay her across the backseat of the car and change her. She wasn't a baby. And it wasn't right to take the smell inside. So the ex-wives went in without her. Baby had a sweet tooth if she wasn't drinking enough, and she wasn't drinking quite enough today, being on the town. She bought another wine and a mint chip cone. Jan bought herself a rainbow sherbet. They would buy Golda's on the way out so it wouldn't melt. It was a hot day, but not that hot, they agreed.

"Let's eat inside and really enjoy ourselves," Baby said. The windows of the car were cracked and they could see Golda's head. "She'll be fine out there."

"More than fine," Jan said. "We treat her like a queen."

"Well. I'm not sure we're so good at taking care of her," Baby said quietly.

"You speak for yourself," Jan said. "I take care of her fine. I've done it for years and I can do it until she dies. I'm the only one in my family to step up. Once the checks start rolling in again it'll all be worth it."

"It's getting to be too much, ain't it? Even with all my help? She seems . . . unhappy."

Jan cocked her head and Baby knew she was going to say something cruel. She reminded Baby of Pretty in that way, how he always knew the very meanest, soul-crushing thing to say. All things considered she was lucky to have Jan and so she braced herself for the blow.

"Your help? You've got to be kidding me," Jan said. "You left your baby girl like it was nothing, so don't tell me what I should do with my very own sister."

Baby nodded. Jan wasn't wrong. She had left her girl. She had watched it all unfold as her daughter called her grandparents to finally tell them what was going on—that her mother hadn't fed her in months, that she'd been stealing and hoarding food at school, that Baby would leave for days and days and then return only to hibernate in her bedroom. She struggled with her daughter for the phone, but didn't fight very hard. It seemed that eventually this was the exact thing that would happen. And what could she say when the truth was right there for all to see? She was unfit. Eventually she fell back onto the couch and watched the nine-year-old sob and scream into the phone, finally refusing to cover for her mother. It was like watching a movie. Like she was only barely there. Well, she was very drunk. Things had continually happened to her and she had ridden the tides of those things like a passive sailboat, and here was one more. It seemed life was determined to keep her down.

"I think she had a good childhood," Baby said finally to Jan. "Better than what I could have given her. I always knew that deep down."

"Well of course Pretty never stepped up. Ha!" Jan slapped the table. "He only showed up in time to sign her off to your parents. Look like a hero in court. Just like him. He never loved you, and that proves it."

Baby took another drink. "Well, he had to work." She finished the small bottle and felt better. "He was looking out for our girl at least."

"Why don't you save yourself the trouble and buy a big one?" Jan asked, poking Baby's wine. "Who you trying to impress?"

"You ever wonder what Pretty's health is like?" Baby said. "An angry heart don't fare well."

"Winnie says he's got pulmonary trouble and liver trouble. Passing out mid-sentence on account of the highs and lows of blood pressure. Go figure." Winnie was Jan's daughter who lived a few miles away but only saw Jan once a year, at Christmas, when she brought the children. "This is what you don't want to become," Winnie had whispered to her daughter on their way out last Christmas. Jan's ears were as sharp as ever and later Baby had to listen to Jan's rendition of the whole night over and over.

"I loved that man more than I've ever loved anything," Baby said. "Really broke me when he left. That was the beginning of my end."

"I thought I loved him, too," Jan said. She finished the cone. There was hidden chocolate at the bottom and Baby noticed how the discovery lifted Jan's eyes for a moment and she felt warm toward her again. "But the thing was, and maybe we both know this even though we've never said it, that that man wasn't equipped to love women."

Baby considered what Jan meant for a moment, but drank more instead. It was too hard to consider all the ways Pretty was ill equipped to love her. "I think I'd go back to him if he wanted me," Baby said, the wine washing over her heart.

"If that happened I'd kill you both."

The women laughed. Then Jan said, "That's the long and short of it."

Baby felt hot from the conversation and looked out the window. There was the outline of Golda's head, but she couldn't see much more. A man working the register had been glancing at her and she imagined having stand-up sex with him in the bathroom. It might be nice just to be knocked around a bit. Jan must have sensed her train of thought and said, "Keep to yourself."

When they returned to the car, Golda was napping. Her head was slumped forward and the car's heat had amplified the shit smell. "Best get this sleeping beauty home," Jan said, licking Golda's ice cream. Baby laughed. She found Jan funny sometimes. Jan drove fast around the bends in the road and Baby toyed with her new sunglasses, trying to bend the wires so they might fit. When they got home Golda was still asleep.

"Good for her. Needs the rest." Jan slammed her car door.

Baby felt a strange feeling go up her spine, but she figured it was nothing. Just time for her next bottle.

The women decided to put on the new nightgowns and watch some soaps. Jan pulled out her old nail file and polish and painted her fingernails. Baby tried her best to paint her toes but kept getting red polish on her skin. Hours passed while they watched episode after episode of a show about women who killed their husbands. Baby drank quite a bit more than usual to make up for the wine she hadn't drunk at the department store, and she whooped and shouted with loud confidence when the man was fairly killed in each episode. The sun started fading behind the trees and stillness spread over the land. The coyotes were quiet, the road was quiet, and it was then that Baby remembered they had left Golda in the car. All this time she had pictured Golda in her room as she usually was. They never went into town all together and the change had really thrown her off.

"Jan," Baby said. "What about Golda?"

"Christ," Jan said. She got up, knocking over the tray of polishes. The red spilled on the carpet. "Would you get that," Jan said, "while I get her?" Baby wet a rag and rubbed the red polish deeper into the carpet, watched the stain set. She braced when she heard Jan scream.

"Oh my dear Lord, Baby! Oh, no, oh no. Oh, no. She ain't moving!"

Baby stumbled outside. The world was hazy. She peered in on Golda, who just looked asleep. She thought she even saw her stomach rise with a small breath but couldn't be sure.

Jan leaned against the car wailing about what they were going to do now. "It's the end," she said. "The outing killed her. It was too much. I try to do one nice thing and this is how I'm repaid. Why, Baby, why?"

"You sure she ain't just sleeping real deep? I think I saw her breathe."

"Don't get things in my head. She's dead clear as day. You can't tell cause you're nothing but a useless drunk."

"There's gotta be someone we should call." A swirling memory of the prenatal first aid class Baby had taken came to her—how to resuscitate an infant. She had breathed into a plastic baby doll's mouth and snuck cigarettes during the break with a classmate who furiously ate M&Ms from a large satchel. Beyond that she didn't remember anything helpful, and besides, Golda was no infant.

"No," Jan said. She held Baby's arms to her sides. "Golda wouldn't want strangers' hands all over her. She'd want me to be the last to touch her. To say goodbye."

"But maybe someone could revive her," Baby said.

"Now just let me think." Jan pulled Baby inside by the arm and slammed the door. She zipped her cat suit on over the nightgown. Baby mirrored her and put her cow suit on. Surely if she just did the things Jan did it would pull her into sobriety and she could make sense of everything. Jan made some instant coffee and sat at the kitchen table chewing the grits. A long while passed and Baby concentrated on tearing all her cuticles away, drinking water from the rusted tap. Prayer was a distant thought. "We gotta take her to her resting place," Jan said finally.

"I don't know," Baby said. She ate a piece of white bread. If she could just soak up some of the booze. She just needed to get to that happy place where her mind was sharp and her body brave. But how to get there? She took an expired vitamin from the cupboard and swallowed the metal taste. "I think we better just let someone else handle this."

"Get in the car," Jan said. "You're not going to crap out on me now. You're as much at fault for this as me. Maybe more."

"People's gonna find out she's dead," Baby said.

"No one's looked in on her for years. I want my checks again, goddammit. I want to be paid for all this toil. They find out she's dead now, I'll never see another cent."

The ex-wives got in the car, Golda in the back. It was night now. Baby decided to keep on drinking. It seemed things were already going one way. She wouldn't be able to change any of it. Jan started the engine. She drove fast around the curves. Baby gripped her seatbelt. As they neared the small urgent care, Jan slowed down. Baby thought maybe she'd come to her senses. They would just take her there and they would fix her. They would hook her up to some IVs and she'd be fine. But then Jan sped back up. "Nope," she said, deciding something alone in her mind. "Nope." A few miles later she pulled over.

Jan dropped her head to the steering wheel. "My own sister. She's dead, Baby!"

"Go back to that urgent care. I told you I swear I saw her breathe." It seemed to be just a little heat stroke to Baby. Maybe all she needed was water. Yes, that was it! Once, her daughter had been dehydrated and she had taken her to the urgent care and they fixed it all right away.

"You didn't see anything," Jan said. "She's dead and we both know it for a fact."

"I'll take her in," Baby said. "You can drop us off and I won't bring you into it."

"Listen to you slur. You can't even get words out right," Jan said. "I can't trust you like this. They're going to arrest us for elder abuse, you dummy."

"We thought she was napping!"

"You're the one who said to leave her in the hot car," Jan said.

"I never said that," Baby said, though she certainly didn't remember whether or not she had.

"Sure you did," Jan said. "I swear to God. You made me think it was alright."

Jan looked past the guardrail hugging the curve of the road to the trees beyond. Baby looked in the backseat at Golda. She just seemed asleep, but very asleep. Extremely asleep. It seemed that her skin had lost color. But it was hard to see in the dark. She put her hand on Golda's chest to feel for a heartbeat but her hands shook so bad she didn't know what was what. Baby turned back and threw up wine and white bread onto her lap. She let out a sob.

"Get it together." Jan got out of the car. "Help me now."

"What are you doing?" Baby asked.

"In the wild, when a member of the family dies it's up to the rest to place the body in its rightful place."

They carried Golda's body down a steep slope. Baby kept tripping and cutting her legs over and over on branches and rocks. The strain was almost too much. She felt the wine weigh her down. "Here," Jan said, and they dropped her in the leaves and Jan and Baby sat. Jan pulled out a joint and lit it.

"I never imagined it ending this way," she said.

"I never imagined it ending at all," Baby said.

"Sure you did," Jan said. "It don't make you a bad person."

I think it does, Baby thought.

Golda did look serene in the leaves. Baby half expected her to start flapping her arms making leaf angels. Jan kissed her forehead and crossed Golda's chest like a Catholic. Baby wondered if Jan was in shock, but she seemed fine. She seemed clearheaded, still thinking primarily of herself. Golda's eyes fluttered and her hand twitched and Baby gasped and pointed. Jan shook her head. "That's just her spirit leaving her body."

"But," Baby said. "She moved."

"Leave it," Jan said, stern like a mean mother, and steered Baby by the neck back up the hill and to the car. Baby tried to squirm out from under Jan's pinch, but Jan had a strong hold on her.

"Let's get some sleep, and how about we just don't talk about this?" Jan said, driving. "We'll lay low and before you know it the snow will come and nature will just pull her right back into the earth."

"I'd like to talk about this with someone medical. I think she's alive," Baby said. "I'm feeling real bad over this."

"Well, I'd feel bad, too, if I was you."

As the morning light fell into the window, Baby realized she had never actually fallen asleep. She looked across the room at Jan snoring in peaceful slumber. She turned so she couldn't see her and let her thoughts stay on Golda and how they had left her to rot like an animal. Of course she was dead. Jan was seeing clearly, and Baby wasn't. She felt a deep pain she had felt before. It was close to the pain she felt when she lost her daughter, but this was worse, because this was her last chance at heaven and she'd obviously failed. She loved Golda, it turned out, and she hadn't understood this love until it was too late. Golda saw through to the very blackest part of her heart, into the sour center, sure. But it was more than most people could do.

She would turn herself in. She would spend the rest of her life in a women's prison. This was her destiny. Once a psychic had told her she was a very, very young soul and at the time she had been annoyed—wasn't it preferable to be an old soul?—but now, imagining herself in prison, she felt relieved. She was very young in this life, and there would be time yet to learn more.

Baby went to the bathroom and drew a bath. She brought in a box of wine and drank from the spigot while she soaked and looked at her body through the water. Her shoulders slumped forward and her feet were warped like the snarled roots of old trees. She wondered if the other women in prison would want anything from her body or if she would seem too old and sad, even for them. It might be nice to be touched by another person, she considered. Jan opened the door.

"The cops just pulled up," she said, smiling like a jackal, red in the eyes. She looked in the mirror and applied some of Baby's lipstick. Baby could not remember the last time Jan had worn makeup.

"Get dressed," Jan said. "We'll just say that she must have gotten out in the night and wandered down the road. Golda always loved the outdoors. It's something she might have actually done."

Baby nodded. She knew Golda hated being outside, complained about getting rocks in her old clog sandals and swatting at tiny bugs. "Buckies! Buckies!" she would scream as she hit the air. Besides, there was no way she was physically capable of walking that far along such a narrow road. Surely she would have been run over before she could have traipsed into the forest and taken a nap. But Baby nodded anyway. She imagined herself on a cot in the women's prison wearing the same clothing as everyone else and the thought was not horrifying. She had already been doing it, hadn't she? Jan pulled on a fresh animal suit, a giraffe this time.

"Aren't you sad?" Baby asked Jan.

Jan looked at her with disgust. "Of course I'm sad, you twit. But there's no time for that now."

While Baby got dressed, she could hear Jan flirting with the cops, or Jan's version of flirting, which was really just talking loudly and laughing and coughing. They all sat down in the kitchen and Officer Geary crossed his legs and stared.

"What can we help you with, then?" Jan asked.

"Haven't you noticed Golda's missing, ma'am?" he asked.

Jan gasped and clutched her throat, choking herself. "My word, no. She sleeps in is all. Come see, sleeping like a baby in—"

"Golda had been pooping and flinging it behind the television," Baby blurted, interrupting Jan. She knew immediately she shouldn't have mentioned it but things were just happening now. "It was getting to be too much."

"No need to embarrass the old gal," Jan said. She touched the knee of the younger cop. Baby started crying.

"Now, now, what's the matter?" Officer Geary asked.

"I didn't mean to do nothing wrong."

He looked at her. "We all do things we aren't proud of in this life," he said. "But I want to talk about Golda, and the next step. I think it's clear she belongs somewhere with a little more structured care. Now, Jan," he said, "no one is implying you ain't done your damnedest with her, but she's on in years and so are you. We got a call from Sandy down at Town Department and she was in a tizzy about piddle on the floor and stolen undies. She had a right to complain, even though we all feel bad for the gal. It's just, we think a facility would be best for everyone."

Jan spit her coffee into her hand and then wiped it on the leg of her suit. "Facility?"

"Twenty-four-hour care," the young one said.

It was like someone was banging together two cast iron pans hard and fast near Baby's face.

"Golda will be fine there. In fact, when we asked her about it she smiled up to the sky and hugged her own self," Geary said, wrapping his arms around himself. "I'm telling you she won't know the difference."

"She did what now?" Jan said. "She was moving around?"

"This morning we found her wandering the highway. A car almost hit her. Who knows how the hell she got all the way out there." He shook his head. "Let's hope no one helped her. Some don't mind taking advantage of the feeble-minded, if you can believe it."

"Give me a minute," Jan said. She got up to go to the bathroom. Baby could hear her retching.

"We thought she was dead," Baby said to the floor.

"I'm sure it was a real scare," the young cop said, putting his hand on Baby's shoulder. "But she's okay, just scuffed up a bit." Baby fiddled with the leg of her animal suit, remembering her own scratches from the night before. She caught Geary looking at her sideways, as if he knew, but then his expression settled to neutral again. If he knew he didn't want to bother.

The ex-wives followed the cops to the station and there was Golda covered in dirt and leaves acting out a play to the concrete of the holding cell. "It's all over now, baby blue," she said. They watched her for a while and then Jan turned to Geary.

"I don't think I'm ready to be rid of her," she said. "I had deep thoughts last night and I swear some great animal came to tell me that Golda was special and that she was my special job. That's got to mean something, don't it?"

"She is special," Geary said slowly. "But imagine. If she had proper care you could start over. You could date even. And of course you'd visit her."

"Who would I date?" Jan said.

"You're not dead," Geary said. "You could get online or something."

Baby thought of the story Jan liked to tell of the time she heard Pretty reading a child's story softly in Golda's room. How she stood in the doorway and watched Golda calmly listening. Jan said she felt good about life right then. She felt she had found a good man in that moment and she had kept the memory dear to her ever since.

When Golda finally saw them she paused, then ran to the bars, pressed her face out, and kissed the air.

"Golda, I'm so sorry," Baby said, sobbing. "We didn't mean for any of this."

"It's all fine," Jan said, nudging Baby out of the way. Golda began chirping louder and louder. "Who cares what she does? She's ours. You're coming home with us, Golda." But Golda looked only at Baby. She said, "Birdy, birdy." So Baby went over and hugged Golda through the bars and when Golda pressed her soft cheek against hers Baby thought, She wants me. Someone truly wants me.

"Well, look at you two getting on," Jan said. "Yes, we'll take her on home now."

Baby nodded slowly. She liked that idea. Total acceptance. Entrance to heaven, a debt paid for leaving her daughter motherless. Golda released her from the hug and when no one was looking gave her a nasty sneer and whispered, "Bad birdy."

"Did you hear that?" she asked Jan.

"Shut up," Jan said, signing some papers.

Baby stepped back and looked at Golda's ice-cold eyes and her pinched nose. A chill ran through her, and she heard the mean voice of her mind. *You thought she liked you? You thought she loved you? No one ever will. No one!*

Jan took Baby's arm and led her back outside to the car. Baby felt awful, maybe worse than she ever had. It would take so much wine to get out of this feeling. Jan got in the car and started it.

"Aren't you getting her?" Baby asked.

"We ain't taking her home," Jan said. She looked at Baby. "Just wanted her to think we were. I wasn't going to have a scene."

"Shouldn't we tell her we're leaving? She understands everything, you know. She can hear just fine."

"Get online and date," Jan said as she squealed out of the lot. "Fooey."

"Go back. We need to tell her."

Jane slammed the brakes. She turned the ignition off and squared herself to Baby. "Decide now. You gonna go forward and forget about her? Or wallow in the past worshiping all your ghosts? Me, I'm moving on. You coming or not?"

At home, they watched television in silence and every so often Baby would weep. What would she do with all her hours now? She was scared. But Jan seemed filled with a youthful exuberance. She was on the phone with Winnie asking about computers and how to obtain one. She was practically radiating joy. It seemed she was finally released. Baby wished she could feel the same, but she couldn't stop imagining Golda lonely in a new place, wondering how they could have abandoned her like that. She saw her own daughter's face, felt her own daughter's wonderings. She drank more and more.

"What do you think Pretty's doing tonight?" Baby asked when Jan was finally off the phone.

Jan considered the question. "You know. I don't want to play that game anymore, but I hope wherever he is, he's eating fried oysters and catsup," she said. "Always had a fondness for oysters if you remember."

Baby closed her eyes and imagined herself making them for him, holding their baby daughter in her arms. Then she imagined bathing Golda, a task she had never loved but wished she could do one last time. The smells undiluted, the cleaning a feat. But it was the only time Golda was nice to her, playing with her soap and moldy rubber ducky. Sometimes she would smile up at Baby with a true, wordless appreciation. Now that was over and what lay ahead loomed lonely before her. Baby took in more wine. Perhaps she could find another person to look at her like that. Perhaps anything was possible. At least tonight she could sleep well, knowing she was no murderer after all. It was a bright sweet truth against the hell of life.

Lyra

When my little sister Maple was setting to leave the ranch, she begged me to come with her. Said everything that happened with Mama was all over and buried and that I should move on. As if such a thing was possible. She couldn't understand the strong force that kept me here, that keeps me here still, some twenty years after everything. Mama's spirit most likely, punishing me from where she lies. Or perhaps I stayed because I knew one day someone would come sniffing around, and I would be the exact right person to tell the story. And now, I see it all before me, full of meaning. Because just like I sensed, the world turned over again and a young PhD student from San Francisco, interested in all kinds of gore and whore, came to the ranch, hands shaking but brave-faced, wanting to know about Mama. She used the word *trauma* a lot as she explained herself. I smirked, said, "trauma for your mama." But Merriam wasn't after jokes. She was writing a dissertation, she said, on unspeakable acts of violence toward rural women.

"Sounds specific," I said. I kept the door open a crack.

She nodded. "Very."

"Are you interested in finding who did it?" I asked her.

"Not really," she said. "More after, you know, examining the effect of it all."

I looked her up and down. After working so many years at the ranch, I had a near perfect intuition about people. She was alright. And something else rose up in me. Call it curiosity.

"Okay."

Now Merriam was staying with us, uninterested in the motel the next town over. She wanted to be *immersed.* She stood out from the rest of my girls, taller than most men who came through, with double-jointed fingers and hips that entered the room first. I couldn't help but size her up. Men usually liked a little girl, unless they liked a tall girl, but then she couldn't be too tall. I was like a livestock judge at the county fair. It was about the facts. Merriam's hair frizzed right in her eyes and her skin looked brushed by a Brillo pad, yet there was something soft about her, the way she wore a muted floral dress that looked aged and worn, had perhaps been her mother's. I asked her if there were any forlorn suitors upset that she had left them to come live at a country cathouse, and she said she had a boyfriend for five years and he wouldn't lick her puss, so then she had a girlfriend for a year, but she wouldn't lick her puss either. She had given up on love.

I said, "Hon, maybe it's you."

She shrugged. "Probably."

Later I felt bad and I re-explained myself. "What I meant," I said, "is that maybe you aren't presenting it right."

"I have a full bush." She said it like it explained something about the situation. "Maybe that's not popular around here, but I feel really good about it."

"It doesn't matter how you decorate. You have to lift it up to them like you're offering the king's dessert. You have to believe in it."

She looked at the wall. I was making her uncomfortable. "Well," she said. Paused. "I guess I don't believe in it, then."

She'd never experienced the darkness of life firsthand, she told me, but had read almost every true crime book ever written and so she carried a great deal of heaviness in her heart with nowhere to put it other than her dissertation. I poured her a brandy and she cried from the weight of all that reading.

"Why do you suppose you do this to yourself when you don't have to?" I asked. "You could write about something else. Anything, I bet. Or why write at all? You could just go to Costco and watch a lot of TV. Many people enjoy passing life that way."

"Your mother," she said. "The way it must have been. Just imagine her fear."

"She's an easy one to feel bad for," I said. "But you have to remember, she made choices, too."

"That feels kind of victim-blamey to me."

"Maybe I don't see her as a victim," I said.

"I can't imagine the kinds of stories you've had to tell your-self to get by. I hope I don't seem judgmental."

"I don't need anyone feeling sorry on account of me," I said.

"Yes you do," she said. "We all do."

Merriam wanted me to show her the last place I had spent time with Mama. We sat on the swing bench out back and let the sun burn our shins.

"What kind of woman was she?" Merriam asked. The girls crowded the window and watched us but we ignored them. They knew if they weren't working they were supposed to be cleaning or studying, but once they got comfortable here they only half listened to me. Merriam had her notebook with her but didn't seem compelled to write too much. I felt nervous about the pad, but as we spoke, I found myself enjoying when she would look away from me and start scribbling. I might have even embellished a little to get her to write faster and more.

"She could be creative," I said. "Named me Nevaeh, which if you spell it out, is Heaven backwards. Never met another per-son named that, but I also haven't ever left. Mainly, though, she liked to look out at the horses. There used to be about ten horses here. They were all big lazy things. No one rode them. Mama liked to watch the way they walked around, how the flies landed right on their eyeballs. She had a lot to think about to-ward the end."

"Like what?"

"Well, toward the end she was concerned over being revived, you know, religiously."

"Do you think she was ever revived?"

"I suppose that's not for me to say," I said. "But I doubt it."

"Did she want you girls to be saved, too?"

I was quiet. Now here she was poking the exact sore I didn't want poked.

"Oh sure," I said. "She took up with a real zany pastor. He has lots of ideas about how women were meant to live. She was into it lock, stock, and barrel. It was like a switch went off in her brain for God."

"Do you think she knew her kidnapper?"

"It's always someone you know."

"I can't imagine that," Merriam said. "Some man you saw regularly and thought was a good soul."

"What makes you so sure it was a man?" I looked in my cup. Brandy gone, mouth on fire.

She shook her head. "A woman isn't capable of something like that."

I patted her knee. I almost told her then, feeling high on our camaraderie, our easy connection. The way her kind face took me in with such sweet regard. But I was no dummy. I didn't say any more.

Things are about the same at the ranch now as they were when I was a young girl. I was fifteen and Maple was only eleven when

Mama got desperate for a place to live and brought us here. She talked it up the whole bus ride over, saying how it would be a communal place, a place where women helped women. That we would love it. That we would be safe, at least.

"You might even like having boyfriends," Mama had said as the crops ticked by out the window. "Boyfriends bring you stuff to show you they like you. Like those Coke freezes from the gas station."

"I can get my own Coke freeze," I'd said to her.

She'd let out a big nervous laugh. "Well, either way, Nev. I told them there'd be two of us working. I can't be the only one. It ain't a daycare." She looked so young to me then.

"I'll figure out another job there," I said to her. "You'll see."

I learned a hard adult lesson my first days at the ranch, which is to say, I didn't figure out another job. But I enjoyed being around the other girls. I felt like I'd come into some sort of backwards boarding school. We traipsed around in bikinis and boxer shorts, shifting in and out of bedrooms, eye makeup in clots. We chewed on candy necklaces all day, the string rubbing the corners of our mouths raw. Sometimes we crowded into a kiddie pool in the backyard and braided each other's hair, cracked imaginary eggs over each other's heads. *Now you've got the shiveries . . .* I vowed to keep Maple from the work even if I hadn't been able to keep myself from it. Even as Mama spoke of us needing more money.

"Money for what?" I asked her. I felt ready to fight, imagining my little sister in the same way as myself. "We don't leave. What do you need to buy?"

"Well, if we had more money we could leave."

"You said you liked this work. You said I was doing a fine job."

She looked at me, disgusted. "You idiot. This was supposed to be temporary. I never wanted this for us."

This for some reason hurt me more than anything else she'd ever done. How I'd believed her, that this was for the best.

So I told Maple to look busy, and she made sandwiches for the girls, played outside climbing tall trees, writing in her notebook. I pulled one over on everyone and we had two twelfth birthdays for her in a row. Maple knew what went on in the rooms, of course, she was never dumb. But she knew it at a distance. She couldn't possibly know what went on in the mind, how it was surprisingly easy to feel fine about it, to feel like what you did didn't matter from one day to the next. But I didn't want her to feel the other way I sometimes felt, like my spirit was tying itself in an unwindable knot.

As Mama's spiritual exploration ramped up, she took on a strange intensity. She seemed suddenly sure of the rules of the universe, how God worked, and what He wanted. She told me all about her plan one lazy afternoon, well really it was the pastor's plan, that we would all come to live with him. We would all be his wives. Me and Mama and Maple. She had had too many wine coolers. I thought she was joking. But when I finally saw she wasn't, it made me dizzy.

I kept the truth about it from Maple. I bit my tongue when Maple got excited by Mama's ideas, said she looked forward to maybe having a right daddy and moving off the ranch. I didn't want to tell her the ugliness of what was becoming. The specifics I knew to keep to myself until I had a plan of my own.

But Maple pestered. She combed Mama's hair and asked all about our future life and Mama smiled and hummed. Lied right to her face. Mama's eyes were gone by then, of course, little spinning stars of love and God. She couldn't see us anymore, if she ever had.

"I can't wait for our new house," Maple said. She really believed in Mama then.

"White with a golden bathtub," Mama said.

"You've never seen a golden bathtub in your life!" I slapped the table with my hand. "I won't let you do this to us."

"The ungrateful will inherit nothing," Mama said.

I told Maple what Mama was planning that night in bed. I whispered to her clear that we had no other choice: the only future we could trust was one without Mama in it at all.

Maple cried, soft baby. "So let's leave, then," she said. She got up and started feebly packing a sad bag of dollies and underpants.

But I felt pressed down and rooted. "I'm too angry to go."

"What do you mean?"

"It's time Mama learns a lesson." Now this surprised even me.

"What kind?" Maple asked. I heard her shifting around in the covers. She was feeling nervy and I wanted to comfort her but where was comfort when I needed it?

"The hard kind."

Understand, I was a girl coming into my own. I was realizing that what my mother had thrown me into at the ranch wasn't good but that now she was fixing to do me one worse. At least at the ranch I felt safe. I knew I could bide my time until I turned eighteen and then something new could unfold. What that would be, I had no idea, only that it would be made up of my own decisions. But now nothing Mama had planned for the future took Maple and me into consideration. It was time to say goodbye.

There was this one guy I saw a lot back then who liked me to pretend to be a famous fashion photographer and he'd tuck his stuff between his legs and model, naked, of course, sprawled every which way and I would direct him with a twangy, high voice. Then he'd go into the closet and close the door and do whatever he did to himself. Usually he would just leave without acknowledging me at all, but one day he told me to sit down.

I sat on the bed and he sat next to me and I could see clearly then that he was probably someone's father. This was the way he would sit next to his own daughter to give her advice about college, or tell her about the intentions of boys before her first big date.

He said, "I could get you out of here if you wanted."

"We ain't supposed to let none of you fall in love with us," I said. I pulled thread from the quilt.

"I'm not in love, honey. I'm just worried for you. You're real young and haven't you imagined a real life?"

"My mama says this is where we are right now."

"Your mama's put you on the slow road to nowhere."

Before Mama's new plan, I'd always thought it was just hard old life that was giving us the bad luck, just forces beyond our manipulation, but not my own mother's choices. But I saw it then so easily as if he'd pulled a curtain back on a painting, the way she'd used me. The way she had never made one decision that was for my benefit, and now the awfulness ahead. I kept seeing myself through the man's eyes. It all looked so sad. I felt a new anger crawling under my skin, one that I couldn't shake. And my anger couldn't withstand my mother's new religious plans, I knew that then.

"So what do you want to do in life?" he said.

My brain was scrambled. What did I want to do? "I don't know."

"That's your first homework assignment then. Figure it out."

A few weeks into her stay, Merriam insisted on being given a job, so I put her to work as a secretary. She signed the clients in and she chose a girl for them. She asked what they were hoping for, even though most have no idea. They all say something like *a real nice one*, or if they're bold, *brunette, huge knockers*. Asking them helps them think they're in control. But usually we just assigned them to whoever was freshest.

Merriam would then go to the TV room and let the girl know to go into the bedroom and get ready. Then the man would go in and occasionally Merriam would listen on the other side of the door, expecting to hear fireworks. Expecting something real original. I could have died from boredom listening to the sounds coming from the rooms. Most of these men seemed so confident at the desk but when they were finally in front of a naked woman they started babbling. Or they went soft and quiet. We saw it all. Tears, childhood memories, role-played apologies to dead parents. The emotional labor was backbreaking. Me, I always preferred a take-charge sort of guy so I didn't have to do any mind work.

Around then Merriam entered a very emotional period. One day I caught her leaning against a door frame, weeping.

"Why're you in such a tizzy lately?" I asked her.

"Listen," she said. "Really listen."

I put my ear to the door. The bed creaking, the girl saying oh, ohhhh.

"What?" I whispered.

"She's singing." Then she went back to the couch to write it out while sniveling and taking big gasping breaths. Sometimes I wanted to ask her what she would have done, if her mama was ready to sell her off as a sisterwife to some cult pastor. But my shame kept me from it.

Most of the girls didn't really interact with Merriam much, just looked at her strangely, but some had warmed up to her. Later that afternoon as Merriam ate two bologna and mayonnaise sandwiches at the table with them, Kat pulled out her suitcase of makeup and began going to town on Merriam. Quizzed her on what she did at her fancy school. I stayed in the hallway. I listened.

"It's a lot of reading," Merriam said. "So sometimes I just want to be in the world, you know, experiencing it."

"Here's the world," Kat said, gesturing around the room. She wore what she always wore: an oversized Raiders jersey she claimed was her father's, but I had my doubts. Most of these girls had never met their daddies.

"I have some novels you might like," Merriam said.

Kat tapped her nails. She laughed. Said, "When I open one of them, will money fall out?"

Merriam wanted me to go deeper with her, but I couldn't tell her that a few years ago some men had come knocking, and of course I thought they were coming round for servicing, but no. They had questions about Mama. A young one and an old. Henry and Rivers. They said they might have found the guy who did it. Seemed he'd been on some kind of spree up the I-5, making stops from here on up through Oregon and Washington. Lots of similarities. An obsession with submission and keeping the women in small spaces. They suggested that whoever had done it wasn't really a murderer, just a hobbyist, and that Mama had died by accident when no one found her in time. She died from starvation to be exact, but not cold-blooded murder. The way they said "accident," I'll never forget it. It hit me as a kind of relief.

I said, "Well, that man must be too old to still be at it."

"Not really," Rivers said. "If he had been in his twenties when he kidnapped your mam, a strong young man, he would only be in his forties or so now, plenty able."

"How about a name?" I said to them. "Give me the name of this guy so if he walks in wanting one of my girls I can steer him right out." They said they couldn't do that, no, and then Henry, the nicer-looking one with the soft body and wispy hair, looked back and smiled at me in the very way I hate. Pity is unmistakable.

Before the ranch, Mama and Maple and me used to live in Fresno with Mama's folks. Me and Maple got two different daddies, both of a bad nature, according to my grandma, who insisted we call her Elvira. She said we were not authentic relations to her, as Mama was never rightfully married. Elvira wanted Mama to do some honest work and check groceries at the Pac 'n Save and come home and care for us girls and not have any sips from Grampa's bottles at night.

"Lyra," she said to Mama. "You are a disgrace to these two girls. And I care for them, I do, don't act like I'm some witch, but if you don't get yourself together, it's out with all of you. I wasn't put on this earth to hold back disaster."

Mama would shrug, and I knew it wouldn't be long before we were out again, back at the shelter. I had hoped it would be a different shelter, maybe in another town. I had felt nervous at the Good Samaritan ever since a woman knifed my cheek for using her toilet paper.

I tell Merriam all this and she gets funny again and she reaches out and touches the scar. "You should have been protected from that," she said.

Then she said, "You ever take a lover, Nevaeh? Like not a client, but a real lover?"

"Never," I said. "I ain't been with nobody for better of ten years."

"Why?"

"Someone's got to be the mother around here. Ask any of them and none of them's got a decent mother. How else they get here?"

"I bet you could do other kind of work," Merriam said. "I bet you could have a real family if you wanted." I notice she's wearing Kat's blue eyeliner, a neon pink bra under her white buttoned-up blouse. A real family. Other work. She was so simple and yet the world had deemed her so smart.

"What makes you so sure this isn't a family?"

She smiled. "You know what I mean."

"What's your paper about again?" I asked.

"It's coming along."

"Don't I got a right to know what you're saying about us?"

"I won't know what I've written until I've written it."

Since Merriam came around, I've nearly stopped sleeping. I go over and over it all again. How maybe things were not my fault. That the real trouble was born with my mother and then set to flame when that Pastor Vern started coming around. He'd come up that long dirt drive, rhinestone cross standing a foot tall on his dash. He was a shorter man with heavy sunspots who wore pure white dungaree overalls with nothing underneath and a white cloth choker round his neck and a cheap-looking polyester cape. He came bursting in one day asking who was ready to be taken. I remembered how Twila, the manager at the time, pointed straight at Mama, who was eating string cheese at the kitchen counter in her tiny shorts and a cropped shirt with no bra. She had beautiful long blonde hair that hung down her back in waves, and she was long-legged and bird-skinny. Her teeth were crossed and punched in, but she had a nice way of smiling when she wanted to, with her lips almost closed but not quite.

"Take her," Twila said. "To funtown, right? Hon, we've heard it all."

He looked around like he wanted a reaction from us, perhaps some fanfare over his outfit, but it didn't impress us girls. My mother, however, perked right up.

"Can't hardly breathe but for the smell of sin in here," he said with a smile. He turned and opened a creaky window, letting all number of horseflies in.

Mama waved and smiled her good smile.

I watched him look at her. He stared a good long while as she struck different poses, pouted her lips, and bent forward showing a small press of cleavage. "She needs me," he said finally. She walked toward him, the candy necklace in her mouth, toes tipped in like a girl. Something in my stomach knew it was all wrong.

"Mama," I said. "I thought we had that thing to do. In town?"

"Huh?" she said, then ignored me.

"How about an hour?" Twila said.

"I only need fifteen minutes," he said.

But he didn't take fifteen minutes. He howled in there and mama cried and gasped for well over an hour. When he came out I was standing there nervously eating rope sours one after another and he looked me up and down. I could see Mama through the open door on her knees and she was praying.

"You of some relation?" he asked me.

I kept silent, chewing. He walked over and placed the Bible on my head like he was giving me some physical balance test. I didn't let it drop. I looked right into his eyes.

"She said she got two daughters," he said. "Of marrying age."

"What's it to you?" I asked. Unlike Mama I had sense.

"It's everything," he said. "I'm building a kingdom here on earth."

The other girls had gone quiet. "Well, we have a kingdom right here. And it's going just fine."

"In time," he said and walked on out. "In time, you will see."

Mama came out from the room lovestruck and smiling. Her clothes didn't look like they'd been ripped off and put back on. Her skin wasn't a brushfire of beard burn. She looked untouched, in fact. "That was God," she said. "He pulled my demons out and they flew out the window. I saw them go right away from me. I'm free!"

Well God saw Mama once a week after that, then once every few days. Then he started coming around and Mama would get in that awful car with him and leave and never tell us where she'd been. She'd return hazed and glazed, smelling like Chicken Man, grease still on her lips. At the ranch we ate TV dinners and I hadn't smelled fresh fried chicken in a good long while. My stomach writhed with both desire and anger. How hard would it have been for her to bring some back for me and Maple?

"He wants me healthy," she said. She pressed a hand to her mouth, then her heart.

I stormed away and sat in Twila's office staring out the window at the farmland.

"If that mama of yours is courting some romantic relation, gonna have to cut you all loose. We don't do that here," Twila said. "It's just a rule."

I nodded. "I'll bring her back around. Just give me a chance."

But then Mama explained Vern's divine plan. He wanted us all. And weren't we lucky? Mama and I disagreed.

I didn't tell Merriam that Rivers and Henry kept pressing for more than I was willing to share. They kept coming by at odd hours, surprising me, like they were trying to shake loose my repressed memories. It got my girls skittish thinking there was bound to be a bust, but that wasn't at all what they were after. I told them what I could tell them, which is that as soon as Vern came into our lives I feared getting kicked out of the ranch and what would happen to my little sister and where we could go that wasn't already worse than where we were.

"Did you suspect that Vern killed your mother?" Henry asked.

"Coulda been," I said, even though I knew it wasn't him. He wanted her aliver than alive. He wanted her ascended to the fifth dimension of holiness. I lit a cigarette. "See," I said, "after it all happened he came round just weeping and weeping and hugging on me and crying like a damn baby. He was in love with her. Said he was gonna take her down to Peaches County and marry her and spend forever and ever under the keen eye of God."

I didn't say the part about how me and Maple were supposed to go too. How he pressed that Bible on my head and tried to convert my mind.

"Just because he showed remorse don't mean anything," Rivers said like I was an idiot of the worst kind.

"Maybe it don't matter too much who did it," I said.

"Is that right?" Rivers said. "Hear that, Henry? It doesn't matter."

"We know this isn't easy on you," Henry said. "But you might be able to help us catch a dangerous man. Save innocent lives."

A fluster fell over me and I nearly gripped Henry's nice arm and told him Vern's wishes. How he wished for not just my mother in marriage but for Maple and me as well. His plans for what he liked to call "Whole Heart Living." But I didn't.

"I believe that's enough for today," Henry said. "You take care, Ms. Nevaeh."

"And keep this place in line," Rivers said. "Looks like a lot of underagers in here. Would only take one call to raid this place."

"These girls don't got nowhere else to go. I take good care of them."

"We define care a little different," he said.

Henry nodded and closed the door slowly behind him.

When they were good and gone I found a phone number on a small piece of paper that Henry had left in his empty mug.

I woke to Merriam standing over me. I sat up. There was a gun under my bed. The image of it came to mind.

"You sleepwalking?" I asked.

"I want you to let me participate."

I didn't know what she meant right off. I had been dreaming of horseback riding and now I was pushed back into my real life. Dread settled over like normal.

"Let me have a client. I'll do it for free," she said. "I need to know what it's like."

"It's not what you want."

"I need to get closer to this."

"To what?"

"To your mother's life. To your life. To their lives." She waved her arm toward the rest of the house where the girls were asleep, piled together like sister pups. "Why should I get to be so lucky? So unpunished in this world?"

"I'm thinking this is all getting to be too much for you," I said. She got under the sheets with me. My body went rigid.

"I wouldn't let my own daughter do it," I told her quiet. "I tell these girls I would, but I wouldn't. This is the last house on the block for them, but not for you."

"I'm not your daughter," she said.

"Even if you did it once, you still wouldn't know what it's like. You're educated. You're older. To you it would be knocking boots with a stranger. You could have that experience on any bad night out."

She seemed dejected and young. Her eyes closed. I spent some time looking at her. Her long nose and bucked teeth. Her wild hair. Someone's smart little girl. I felt proud of her and confused over it all at the same time. I wondered if my mother ever watched me and Maple while we slept. Did she feel any special way toward us? In my deepest place I know she didn't. At best she thought of us as her friends. I could never figure out who was supposed to be taking care of who.

The shame of imagining myself a bride alongside my mother was different than any I'd ever known. Imagining Maple's life changed forever. How trapped we would be. Of course he'd want us pregnant with his flock right away. I could see it all so clearly and it froze me with fear. Three brides in white, stomachs pushing out like broody hens. And shame, I was to learn, could drive a person even further than anger.

Maple was with me when the sheriff finally found Mama's body in the shed of an elderly couple a few houses up the road. The couple's son had found her when he came over to clean out the house before sending them off to a nursing home. The couple never went in there. I was told by police that Mama was wearing a white nightgown. When they said that, I said, "I know." And they said, "How do you know?" I kept my mouth shut after that.

Maple looked at me with tears down her face and I knew then that she finally understood what had happened.

My last memory of Mama before she died: I got into bed with her and held her waist and begged. I was not above it. I was still her little girl. I cried into her hair and asked her to please leave us out of it. Just leave us at the ranch and go on with Vern and marry him but leave Maple and me alone. She said Vern's kingdom didn't want her without us girls. The wedding day was already planned. "We should cut your hair before then," she said, looking out at the moonlight. "Vern said all that long wiry hair makes you look dirty."

It was her or us, can't you see?

◆

I went into town for the weekly supplies and when I came back Merriam was sitting bleary-eyed on the couch wearing a maid outfit three sizes too small.

"Don't hate me, Nev."

"Did he say the house safe word?" Since I had become manager the house safe word had been my mama's name. "Did he say *Lyra?*"

Merriam buried her head. "He didn't like my outfit. He called me dumb."

"He hit you?"

"He didn't want to do anything. He just yelled at me for a little bit. It was horrible."

"He yelled? That's it?"

She shrugged. I started to laugh. I couldn't stop. Merriam sniffled and then started to laugh with me. We cackled like that for what felt like the course of the afternoon.

"This costume hurts," she said eventually.

I helped her take it off.

"I don't know if I can write the paper anymore, Nev. I just don't know."

I always kept the TV on at the ranch as a way to keep us company, and the other night a reality show about some Nevada bunny place with a pole and girls in all kinds of fancy lingerie with toys and fake titties and dyed hair came on.

"Why ain't we like that?" Rhanda, my twenty-something that had been with me since she was fifteen, said. She was keeping clean at the moment but had a habit of finding drugs.

"I want me a show name. Rhanda Panda," she said.

She stood up and shook herself around in her bikini top. She leaned her boobs on Jade's head, the youngest in the house at sixteen, and laughed. "Jade the Spade," she cooed.

"Those girls bring in way more money than this sad lot," Jade said. "That's why they're so fancy."

"Hey, Nevaeh," Rhanda whined. "Why don't you ever get us a pole or nothing?"

"This ain't that kind of place," I said. "This is the kind of place where a man can come and be respected and go home with some of his week's pay still in his pocket."

In my head I thought of what I really knew of the place. That more than a brothel, it was a refuge. I didn't take in no flashy wannabe actresses on their way down to Los Angeles. I took the ones who came from the dark place. I could tell who they were because they looked like me.

After Mama was discovered, the big police from Fresno County drove up and investigated and wrote detailed reports about the way she looked and fictional little stories about what they imagined had happened. I wonder still what Mama must have thought Maple and I were doing to her that night. Maple had kept watch outside the shed. She didn't notice how I'd gotten Mama to drink half a bottle of brandy so by the time I was tying her up she was already half asleep. I tied her real tight. Over the years I've had to ask myself the hard questions and I've settled here, on this, and I hope you'll believe me the way I've come to believe myself: I imagined Mama would be able to break free. I figured she'd wake up and have a struggle, some time to think and come to her senses, and then she'd stumble back to the ranch overcome with a new vigor for motherhood. An awakening of love.

On our walk back to the ranch Maple said, "Are you sure about this?"

I turned to Maple and told her that I was sure it would be good for Mama to spend a few days alone to consider what she was doing to us. That a few days would be long enough for Vern to give up on her and stop coming around. I reminded Maple of Mama's plan over and over, and let her cry it out until I believed she understood Mama deserved a punishment. Until I believed she sort of understood what we were doing, but not quite.

Then the days trickled by and it started to feel normal not having Mama around. I even started to imagine that Mama was off with Vern and living her life, happy as a lark without us. That perhaps we had all won.

◆

When Rivers and Henry came by for the last time, I fixed some lemonade and we sat at the picnic table.

"Well, we have some news on your man," Rivers said.

I stood up and sat back down.

"We don't think he's related to your mother's death, unfortunately, but we think he was a copycat. We think he liked what he read about it and wanted to recreate it or something."

"What's this got to do with me?" I asked.

"We're wondering if he maybe stopped by recently to check out the ranch, get a feel for the place, see where the first victim slept at night. Something of that nature," Rivers said.

I tried to think of who had been in, a name I could supply them. But nothing came.

"I can't think of no one unusual," I said.

"We need you to understand," Rivers said, "that just because you didn't sense or intuit a bad boy around, doesn't mean there wasn't one. Some of these guys are real good at working around a women's intuition, in fact, that's how they're so good."

"He just means you shouldn't rule anyone out," Henry said.

"We found your sister, Maple," Rivers said. "She said we were barking up the wrong tree by asking you anything about it. She said, 'My sister did nothing but right by everyone.'"

My pulse beat in my neck. I tried to imagine what Maple looked like now, but I couldn't. All I wanted was for her to be okay, great even. To make it all worth it.

"She happy?" I said. "She alright?" Tears came to me like they rarely did.

"She seemed good," Henry said. "Got herself a couple kids in school. Nice house."

"Nice house," I repeated. "Good good. That's really good." I cried a little in front of them. "She leave me a way to contact her?"

Rivers shifted his eyes. Henry said, "Well, no. She wasn't sure that was such a good idea. She seemed to really care for you though. She kept saying that."

"Some have boundaries," Rivers said, looking around.

"You know, sir, I may talk like a hick, and that's cause I am a hick and I don't pretend to be anything else, but I can read you pretty well and I know when you're being snarky. And you don't have reason to be snarky with me. Maybe you're getting off on it or something, but it sure doesn't make our time together very nice."

Rivers smiled. "I think you're holding back on telling us things, and I ain't sure why. Maybe someone like you is bored and likes us coming round, especially Henry smiling so sweet at you like a goddamn fool. Or maybe you're playing with us. Maybe you're messing this whole thing up for us. Maybe it was you who led your mama in there. Maybe Maple was a little girl and didn't know what was going on, but you did, didn't you?"

"Come on, man," Henry said.

"Well look at you, smarty," I said. "You've solved it."

"It still shocks me that she starved to death in the end," Merriam said as she packed her things. "It just seems crazy to me."

"I might miss you after all," I said. "Maybe I can come visit you sometime." I was surprised to hear myself say this but when I did I realized it was a hope I'd held deep down since she first arrived. I imagined the lights of the strange northern city, I saw a brick apartment building swarming with different lives, and I thought maybe I could disappear into it. Crazier things had happened in a life.

Merriam paused, looked at her feet. "Sure, Nev. Maybe after the term is done."

I smiled, biting the inside of my lip. I knew I'd never see her again.

Years passed and I didn't hear from Merriam aside from occasional letters that addressed the whole house, saying basic things like how cold the weather had gotten where she was, and how she thought of us often. We never wrote back. I had one picture of her standing by the fridge eating from a brick of Colby jack, stoop-shouldered and grinning. I kept it by my bedside and looked at it most nights.

Then, when I thought she'd forgotten us completely, a large envelope came. The dissertation. She scrawled on a Post-it— *Nev, please read this over and let me know what you think. A big publisher is interested, but I want your blessing first! Also, I'm sorry if anything offends or simplifies. It was not my intent.*

I had to lie down for a while before I looked. I worked on the bookkeeping a bit. I chewed out the girls over attracting ants in the kitchen. I finally read it when the sun went down. It was very long and hard to get through, but I read it carefully, dictionary by my side. When I was done my hands were shaking. I imagined Maple coming in and sitting at my feet.

Did she figure us out? she might ask.

I would put my hand on Maple's head like I always used to. Feel the pulse of her fear. "Of course not," I would say. "Of course not."

Women and Children First

Lisa was forty now with no job and hadn't seen her daughter, Wonder, in two years. Two years not seeing your own child was a lifetime. All that could happen in a mere two years. Lisa had stopped mailing letters. With no response it was hard to keep writing. Now her daughter would be eleven years old, a stranger.

She had named her daughter Wonder because she had wondered why God had allowed her to become a mother. Some things were simple. The rest of Lisa's life hardly ever seemed simple and right now she was focused on finding a shelter for the night or a boyfriend, whichever worked out first. She had her wine from the corner market where Shelley knew her and took care of her. Shelley was a kind-faced old woman with most of her teeth knocked out. After Shelley had caught Lisa stealing, she took her hard by the arm and said, "What's your story?"

And Lisa started crying right there in the aisle for the first time in so long, and she told Shelley how her daughter had been taken by social services and placed in foster care and no one would listen to her side of anything. How she was trying, every day, she was trying. But they expected her to fight an addiction she'd had most of her life with little to no resources and do it while caring for a child at the same time. Some days this seemed like something she should have magically been able to do, will herself into sobriety. But some days, most days, she was crippled by despair knowing the limits of her capabilities. Her need was immense in two opposing directions: she missed her girl, but also, desperately, she needed a drink. After she lost her daughter, she felt her shame confirmed: she must be a horrible person.

Shelley understood. From then on Shelley kept a bottle of wine for Lisa to come collect each day, no more and no less, and the two women smiled at one another because they were of the same cloth in one way or another. It hadn't occurred to Lisa to ask Shelley what her story was.

Lisa had been to Women and Children First many times. They wouldn't be happy to see her again. They said they never wanted to see the same woman twice if it could be helped, but they wouldn't turn her away. She never caused problems, and sometimes she even helped out, picking up trash and reporting fights. But they wanted her to get a real life. To get better. But their service was about immediate safety for the night and then goodbye in the morning. Maybe they had given her the numbers of some rehabs, maybe they had tried to connect her with a social worker who could help, but Lisa needed someone to dial the number for her. She needed someone to hold her hand like she was their precious daughter and take her in and admit her and then be there when she got out, but that was not available. It seemed like for most of her life people were there to tell her to change, but never how to change. *It's a God problem*, she'd heard before in her meetings. But was it? If God was so big, Lisa thought, why couldn't he relieve her of the itch to drink? He had given her this mind after all. Why couldn't he just make things better for her?

But enough with God, because right now she needed some money. She needed to make something out of nothing. And no, there were no bootstraps for her to pull even if she wanted to. She took a few steps backward and sat on the bench to collect herself. Sometimes a man would drive up looking for a panicked woman who hadn't made the shelter cutoff, who was liable to make a poor choice for the night, and Lisa was not opposed to this as there was always the possibility that she would be able to steal a wallet, or some cash at the very least. She didn't have any love inside of her anymore, so sex had nothing to do with love, if it ever had. She didn't feel she was giving anything away and she only felt shame late at night when she closed her eyes and saw her daughter's face, but if she drank enough, the sweet amount, she wouldn't see anyone's face, and that's how she liked it.

She closed her eyes now and saw her daughter. Everyone said Wonder looked like her father, but Lisa could see a bit of herself inside the girl. She'd seen it when the girl laughed hard in the passenger seat of the car. She'd seen it when the girl cried at her feet. She was hers. And where was the father anyway? She hadn't heard from him in years, though sometimes she remembered him in injuries—the time he'd pushed her down the stairs and the time he'd given her a concussion by banging her head into the counter. She opened her eyes and standing before her was a man tilting his pelvis in her direction.

"You ain't got no money," Lisa said. "I've seen you around here begging like the rest of us."

"Suck me off for ten bucks," he said.

Lisa considered it. Ten bucks was ten bucks. She remembered this woman who spoke once at a rehab about the body collecting pain, storing it. The woman irritated her. Couldn't things just happen and then those things were over? Why did everything have to mean something? Why did everything need to be "processed"?

The door to the shelter opened. "You coming in?" It was a younger woman Lisa had never seen there before, probably a college intern trying to get some real-world experience, as if that could really be gleaned by volunteering at a shelter once a week before going home to her dorm and boyfriend and nice laptop computer and spiced lattes. "We have one spot left, better claim it." Whatever, Lisa thought. She had a place to sleep.

"See ya later, sucker," she said to the man. He shrugged. She watched him walk down the street in a crooked and stumbling pattern, yelling abrupt vulgar things to people as he passed them.

Lisa had almost nothing with her. She'd found a pink child's backpack left outside a school and kept everything inside, which wasn't much: a few crumpled math tests and some broken pencils and a dirty fleece hat, now mixed in with her cigarettes and the wine Shelley gave her. She had a small wallet with her ID in it, which she had miraculously managed not to lose, and a little picture of Wonder. Sometimes, tears would spring to Lisa's eyes when she caught her reflection wearing the backpack. Her true self was horrified by the current state of her life. The self that had sat on her father's lap as a child as he sang Swedish folk songs and bounced her on his knee, the self that had been a really good swimmer and freakishly strong. By seventeen she could pick her father up and throw him over her shoulder where he would dangle like a doll. It was like a party trick and everyone would clap and cheer. Mostly that self was buried though. There was no room to carry it around alongside the wine.

Lisa could imagine what Wonder would think of this shelter. Somehow her girl had come out smarter than her, more intuitive. She seemed to sense danger before it arrived. Wonder would lean in close to her and say, "Don't talk to that one," or "That woman's trouble." She was always right, and Lisa always found this out the hard way.

The trouble was in front of her now. A teenage girl perhaps, or a small-headed adult woman, with a face that looked like it had never been loved. A meth head most likely, Lisa thought, and felt superior. At least, *at least*, she hadn't become that bad. Her old sponsor had told her she could add *meth addict* to her list of *yets*, but Lisa knew she would only ever be an alcoholic, that alcohol was her love and her blood force, and she needed nothing else. She shook her head at the tweaking woman who was sitting in a ball on the floor shivering into her knees. Her eyes darted all over and she swatted at the invisible flies that landed on her sweat-slicked skin. A shame, Lisa thought. She straightened. She walked closer to the woman and was shocked to see a small pair of feet poking out from a blanket next to her.

"Lord, tell me that's a baby doll under there." Lisa said. "Gonna suffocate it under that blanket, don't you know that?"

The woman looked down at the feet and then she looked at Lisa confused, as if she had forgotten there was a baby there at all. She pulled the blanket off and Lisa was relieved to see the baby was awake. It let out a cry.

"He's fine," the woman said. "He's fine."

"You know, they took my girl away," Lisa said. "They said I was endangering her. You better be careful or they'll do that to you."

"You got anything on you?" she said.

"I didn't come in here with drugs up my snatch if that's what you're asking. I have some self-respect."

The girl sniffled and scanned the room. Got up and sat back down. Got up again. "Can you watch him for a few minutes?" the girl said. She looked up at Lisa and for a second Lisa could see the true her. The original girl was still somewhere in there but very deep down. Could this happen to Wonder? A chill came over Lisa then. No, her daughter was different. She would never be like this girl no matter what. Lisa looked at the baby. She had loved when Wonder was a baby and she could take her anywhere she wanted and there was no talk back and no judgment. She had even been sober for various lengths of time while Wonder was tiny. She liked babies, she remembered. They were only themselves. "Sure."

Lisa sat down next to the baby boy who was on his back, helpless, and probably only six months old. He wore a thin and dirty white onesie, and his diaper was leaking out down his legs. The smell seemed too putrid for someone so small. She lifted him by the armpits and saw that the poop had spread up his back and had crested the collar of the onesie. Jesus help me, Lisa thought. She gagged and felt the wine rise in her throat. Her buzz left her and a headache crept in. But the baby needed help. She stood and carried him to the bathroom which had always reminded her of a prison situation, though she couldn't confirm this, as prison was one of her *yets*, but there was no privacy to be had, just toilets in open air with no barriers from each other, and a big silver sink basin you could practically take a bath in but was meant for handwashing. An old woman with a braid down to her butt rifled through a large makeup bag seemingly full of only receipts. She lifted her gaze to Lisa as she walked in with the filthy baby and Lisa almost started explaining the situation to her, but then she went back to her receipts. Another woman did her business on a toilet near the wall, picking her fingernails with a pocketknife. A sudden fear washed over Lisa that one of them could at any moment pull an alarm, be so disturbed by the sight of the dirty baby, that they would recognize her as unfit. She wanted to say, "This isn't my fault, I'm just fixing things," but there was no alarm and no one cared. They were in their own worlds of relative misery.

Lisa held the baby out away from her while he shrieked. She couldn't get poop on her sweatshirt. She didn't know the next time she'd be able to get clean clothes or wash this one and she didn't know how on earth she would care for a baby in a place like this, but then as if by magic, there, next to the woman on the toilet, Lisa registered a Koala Kare changing table bolted to the wall.

"Gotta use this," she said to the woman on the toilet and the woman obliged, putting her knife away. Lisa had forgotten how people couldn't very well argue with the cause of a baby.

The woman flushed and stood up. "Cutie," she said in a singsong voice. "Take care of yourself, mama."

Mama. *I'm not the mama*, Lisa almost began to say but then she stopped. A thrill ran through her. "I will."

She laid the baby on the changer and saw that the shelter had supplied diapers and wipes and a bin of donated baby clothes right there next to it for the taking. What a great shelter, she thought. At last, something was as it should be. She peeled off the baby's onesie and threw it in the trash. Wet a paper towel and cleaned his skin gently as he cried. His eyes were pinched shut in agony. The receipt woman left and now they were alone, which felt tricky because on one hand no one could judge her, but on another being alone was terrifying because she was liable to do something wrong. Was he sick? she wondered. She felt hatred for his mother begin to unwind in her and alongside it a fresh-born love for this child. His mother didn't care about him, that much was clear, and yet she had custody. But not Lisa. Lisa had never left Wonder with a stranger lady at a shelter. She never laid her on the dirty floor and forgot her. But there had been no gray area. *Unfit, unfit.*

She took the baby over to the sink and let the cool water stream over his body. It was too cold for a baby but these were desperate times. She did it as fast as she could and dried him with one of the muslin blankets in the donation bin. She put cream on his immense diaper rash, the red and raised welts covering his skinny butt and balls, crawling down his even skinnier legs nearly to his knees. "I know it hurts, baby," she said to him. Her own voice surprised her. It came out sure and smooth. Kind. "Almost done."

She diapered him and dressed him in a little one-piece pajama with elephants on it and put a fleecy sweater that looked brand new over that. Socks for his feet. A little cotton cap. That wasn't hard at all, she thought. What was wrong with his mother? She imagined herself in the courtroom confirming his mother's failures. *I was no saint,* she might say, *but I wasn't nearly as bad as her.*

By now he had stopped crying and looked up at Lisa, open and clear. The red splotches on his face had calmed down and she admired his big brown eyes. A head of dark hair. Olive skin. With his thick bushy eyebrows that nearly met in the middle, he reminded her of the Italian mob bosses from the movies she loved. "Who are you?" she asked. "What's your name?"

He gurgled. She felt her true self right there at the surface and it was almost like a tingling in the spine, crawling up through her bones asking to come out. It was definitely time for more wine, she thought, but. But the true self needed to take care of this baby, needed to be better than his mother. *Look how sweet he is*, the true self said.

She pulled the baby to her chest and cuddled him a little. He didn't smell great but he didn't smell bad. What was this mother feeding him? He wasn't plump like a baby should be. Wonder had been very plump and loved her milkies. She'd never gone hungry no matter what the court documents said. She remembered how Wonder testified at only nine years old that Lisa would leave her alone in their apartment for weeks at a time. That she set her own alarm clocks for school, figured out the bus, stole food out of lunchboxes. That their neighbors would leave her takeout leftovers and she'd eat them on the floor like an animal. Well, Wonder hadn't said it like that. They'd asked her, "Where do you normally eat your meals?" and she'd said, "On the ground."

Lisa emerged from the bathroom with the baby and walked around the cots to the front where a secretary of sorts sat talking on the phone. "Who's that?" the secretary mouthed at her. They knew she didn't have a baby. "Food," Lisa said, pointing at the baby, and the woman handed her a brown paper bag and said no more. Inside was a six pack of formula bottles and a nipple. The nipple simply screwed onto the bottles and it was ready to go, no mixing or fuss. Mothers had it easy these days. She dropped and spilled the first one, her hands nervous and shaking now, and then took out another. She wondered how long it would be before someone came by and asked her more specifically about this baby in her arms. Perhaps they would take the baby from her right there, seeing as she had zero authority over him. But the counselors who recognized her were off tonight, which seemed like a sign of something new. She sat on the floor and the baby boy sucked the bottle down quick. She gave him another and then burped him. He barfed a little on her shoulder but kept most of it down. "There it is," she said to him. "Fed, washed, happy. What more could you need?" She realized then that she had bypassed the idea that the mother would return for him. That it was the mother who could simply pluck him out of her arms.

He smiled at her. He had a single dimple.

It was now dark outside and Lisa had changed him again and fed him again, and she was beginning to feel her own needs surface in a roar. She settled on a cot on the floor in a sea of other women, some passed out, some talking to themselves. A few young and scared-looking women were doling out saltines and pink popcorn to small and surprisingly well-spirited children. The woman next to her was moving erratically and whispering to herself, "I'll get the salt and you get the pepper," over and over. The key to get through the night was to pretend nothing existed, Lisa knew. She would just focus on the baby. But she needed a drink from her backpack or she needed some food. She needed both. She couldn't remember when she'd eaten last and she felt lightheaded. She didn't want to go through the food line in case they asked questions, and she didn't want to drink her wine while she held the baby, and it would be awkward to do that anyhow, the baby perched on her lap while she crouched in the bathroom. You couldn't just drink at the shelter. She had enough respect for the place to hide it.

She debated in her mind how the mother's return would go. She imagined making the mother feel inadequate and rubbing in the fact that she had taken such great care of her son. How functional she was. *Maybe,* she imagined saying, *you should just give him to me. He'll be better off.* Hadn't they said that about Wonder? *She'll be better off with her grandparents. She'll be so much better off.*

But when the mother finally came in she was slow. She scanned the room in a daze. She'd taken some kind of tranquilizer, Lisa guessed, could even be deep in a K-hole. She could tell this mother was the kind to take anything and do anything. Lisa looked around, wondering who would stand up for her if needed. But then the mother took the baby from Lisa's arms and walked away without saying a single word. Lisa sprang up.

"Hey lady," she said. "You might want to know that I washed him and fed him. He was all dirty. You know they have supplies for him in there. Hey, what's the matter with you?"

The mother turned around and said, "Fuck off, bitch. I don't know you." She held the baby boy like a lifeless doll with one arm on her side. His head flopped. She laid him down on the cold linoleum and made a heap of herself next to him on the cot while he cried. They were two distant islands.

So that was it? Lisa thought. Fine. She went to the bathroom and drank all her wine, knowing it probably wouldn't be enough to really conk her out for the night. If she ate something she'd be even worse off, even more sober by morning than she'd want to be, but this was her life. *Acceptance is all we can take comfort in,* she remembered from her meetings. She accepted this night and ate a flat hamburger patty and a slice of white bread and lay down on the floor and closed her eyes and listened to the baby cry. But then the baby stopped crying and she shot up. What was wrong? Had that mother smothered him in her delirium, putting that horrible blanket on his face? She had saved that baby today but what about tomorrow and the next day? When Wonder was a baby Lisa had a real bassinet for her. She had been working at Marie Callender's and she saved up to buy it new. She was so proud of it. She rocked it every night before Wonder was born and she would fall asleep just waiting for the moment her own baby girl would be sleeping peacefully by her side.

She crept up on the mother. She remembered once in elementary school having a school-wide sleepover and everyone brought sleeping bags to the cafeteria and laid on the floor and this was like that but with adult women who were scared or crazy or numb, crying and shaking and speaking to ghosts. The lights were dim but it wasn't dark. It rained outside and at least she was dry. She felt strangely alert. The mother was still passed out in the same position she'd been in hours before. She didn't look well. The baby had scooted away from her a bit and had rolled to his side. Lisa felt panic. Was he dead? She bent down and pressed a hand into his stomach. She felt it rise and fall. His skin was cold.

She nudged the mother and she didn't move. Lisa held a finger under her nose. She could easily die in her sleep, depending on what she'd taken. But there was breath. For now, at least.

She walked over to the night guard in the little office who was on a computer, dazed looking and in deep hatred of his job choice and life.

"There's something going on out there," she started. She had come in to report the baby all alone on the floor. She had come to report the baby all alone on the floor, the unfit mother. *Take that baby away!* She was all set to tell them. But then. Something else came to her.

"Huh?" the man asked. His nightstick was leaned up against the desk.

"Yeah, some junkie chicks are fighting out there. Goddamn meth heads. You know at least I'm not that. They're over there by the cafeteria lineup." Lisa's throat went dry with the lie.

"I'll come take a look in a minute. You hens are always squabbling. Break it up now, break it up later, it don't matter, you'll all be back the same."

Lisa hurried over to the baby and crouched near him. She watched the night guard's head turn slowly toward where Lisa had directed him. She picked up the baby and kept her eyes on the man's back. The mother didn't move, not even when the baby was a few feet away from her. Her internal mothering alarm was deactivated. The baby whimpered but sort of pressed his face back into her chest. *That's right,* Lisa thought. *It's me, the woman who took care of you before. The woman who loves you most of all.* She pulled her jacket around him.

Then she was blocks away. She was running and then walking, catching her breath and running again. The baby was still with her and yet, no mother. The mother was not following. She turned around. No one was. The streets felt totally empty. Hardly any cars and Lisa wondered if this was real. Was this a new life she had just walked into? Just like that she was a mother again? She laughed and the baby slept in her arms like a little koala and Lisa just kept walking and walking, until she surprised even herself with a plan.

She used to work at Shimmers as a dancer and her best friend at the time, Jolene, still worked there. Jolene had cut her off when Lisa had slept with her boyfriend but she was the only person Lisa could think of to ask for help. She stood outside the strip club. Her arms ached from holding the baby boy and she wanted to set him down so bad but no. No. No setting him on the floor like that trash head mother of his and no drinking with him. Not this time.

She walked in and no one noticed her at first but then the hostess came up and said, "Oh no. We don't have children in here, state law. Get on out."

"Jolene here?" Lisa asked. She held the baby's head in toward her chest.

"You wait out there. I think she's on her break in a few minutes."

Lisa stood outside and breathed in the cold air. "Glad we got you that little sweater, huh? You'll need a nice warm coat soon. I'll find one, don't worry. I'm really resourceful."

She reached behind her to pull the pink backpack around and see if she had a cigarette, but the backpack was gone. Her heart fell. She had left it there on the floor of the shelter. Had she left it right by the mother? She couldn't remember. It was somewhere there. She'd soon need a bottle for the baby and the remaining bottle was still in the backpack. Lisa had meant to give it to the mother, but she'd walked away so rudely. But her little wallet with the ID. It had taken her days to get that ID, maybe months even. Gone now.

Jolene came out in a fake fur coat. "Oh shit, had you another one? Thought your ass was too old."

"It ain't my," Lisa started to say but stopped. "Look, we need help. I need a bus ticket or something."

"I don't have no money for you, honey," Jolene said. She lit a cigarette.

"Please. I've got to get out of Reno. I've got him now."

"What's his name?" Jolene asked blowing her smoke away from the baby.

"Can I have one?" Lisa asked. "Left my backpack somewhere."

Jolene handed her the cig she had been smoking and lit a fresh one. "Shouldn't smoke around a baby," she said.

"Just one before I quit."

"He ain't got a name?" Jolene asked again, leaning in close to see his face. Lisa shielded him, bouncing and swaying back and forth in the cold. She saw an anti-abortion sign across the street floating above a quickie mart. *Psalm 139—For thou didst form my inward parts; thou didst knit me together in my mother's womb.* The words were in white under a photo of a child bathed in heavenly light. An angel of a baby asleep and beautiful.

"His name is Psalm," Lisa said.

Jolene looked at her funny. "Is that so," she said. "Gone all Christian on me too now?"

"Can you help me or not?"

Jolene smashed her cigarette on the ground. She handed Lisa five dollars and told her to get the baby some food. "That thing looks hungry. Don't your tits work?"

Psalm woke up as if offended and shrieked into Lisa's chest and sort of beat his head around. He was hungry. That's what Wonder would do to Lisa and she always had a bottle ready.

She had clean bottles with fresh formula. She'd tried to breast-feed but gave up after Wonder clamped down on her nipple the first time. Formula was a loving option for both of them, but Lisa knew it was probably just one more thing someone might hold against her.

She walked under the abortion sign to the quickie mart to buy the formula. She needed a drink and her hands were starting to shake. She'd once had a boyfriend who called this "earth-quaking." They were only in their early twenties then. This was before Lisa was forced to reckon with her alcoholism. It was still hidden under the guise of partying too hard, even though she blacked out most nights and woke with mysterious injuries. Even then she drank in the morning as if by instinct, not because she'd ever seen anyone else do it.

"Whatever happened to that guy?" she asked Psalm as they entered the bright store. The lights stunned him and he looked up glassy-eyed and quiet for a moment while she chose the formula.

She took her time in the warm store, walking each aisle, imagining she could fill a cart to the brim and pay for it all. She was sure that she'd never approached a checkout line without a buzz of fear, either because she would have to put some things back or because she had stolen several items and was waiting to be caught.

She bought the formula with the fiver and the man asked how her night was going.

"If you've got someone that can help me get out of here, my night would be going real well."

"Might be able to help. It'll cost of course."

Lisa understood.

She strapped Psalm to the changing table in the fluorescent-lit bathroom and he cried and writhed, and the man stood, gut out, waiting. He put his pigly hands on his hips in a child's stance of impatience that Lisa might've found funny in a way, if she hadn't been sweating hard from withdrawal and some old familiar feeling of failure. Here she was already exposing Psalm to the ugliness of life not hours into becoming his mother. This wasn't how she planned it. This was life, it was not unimaginable. Psalm wouldn't remember it, but she would. She would always know it had occurred and maybe that was enough to transmute to Psalm so that once he could speak and talk and be a member in the world, he would smell it on her and not respect her and leave her.

"Can't you make it sleep?" the man asked. "I got to get back out there, you know. Who else is gonna run this place?"

"Why don't you just stand there, and I'll give you a handjob? Keep your back to the baby."

"I think more is in order."

"What kind of person are you?"

He grumbled. He unzipped himself and sort of leaned against the wall and Lisa let her knees hit the tile. She couldn't see Psalm but she could hear him, his high-pitched wailing, and she knew his wailing was making him out of breath, his cheeks bright with discomfort. She spoke to him with her mind. *This is for you, just once then never again. I promise. Just to get us out of here.* "No mouth," she reminded the man, and before he could object she began pulling him off, watching his face as if a distant observer, his eyes on the ceiling with two fat fingers plugging his ears. It occurred to her he was once a baby boy like the one strapped to the table but it offered her no goodwill toward him.

He came and it pulled her back into the room. It had gotten on her sweatshirt. "Fuck," she said. She wiped it with a paper towel but it would crust and stay all the same. She held her hand out to him. She should have gotten the money first, what had she been thinking. "Come on, I got to move on now."

He wrestled up a twenty from his back pocket and she looked at it. It didn't seem to match the moment. "I got a baby, man. Can you give me a little more?" The man now looked horrified to be alive, sweating and glancing around like he'd woken from a nightmare. He thrust two more twenties in her hand. "Just get on." He hurried out. Lisa felt elated. Sixty dollars. She picked up Psalm and held him to her and he calmed immediately. He wanted her and he needed her, that was all that mattered now. It was all that was in front of her.

The night bus would take them to Fresno, where Lisa had grown up, an eight-hour trek that would cut a straight path through the Central Valley. Sometimes at night before she fell asleep, if she had enough awareness, she would take herself there, imagining the long expanse of orchard rows, the perfect symmetry of them and the way the flatness was a comfort. She loved the predictability of the valley. She hadn't been back in years, though now the little farm church she had grown up attending beckoned to her, it would save her. It was so simple and so pure.

She would go to the church and the church would care for her. She had Psalm after all. A church wouldn't turn her away with a baby in arms. Especially a woman like her, seeking salvation. What sort of salvation didn't matter.

Psalm slept against her like the most natural thing as the bus churned along. On the way out of the quickie mart she had stolen another canister of formula. She wanted an ice-cold Diet Coke but settled for the formula instead. She had asked herself what a good mother would do in that moment, and then she had acted accordingly and she had to admit that it had given her the spark of a high to do the right thing. It seemed the world was opening up, offering solution after solution, and for the first time in so long she had hope and it fluttered around her, danced before the bus as it lurched down the highway like a sparkler, the baby on her body. She kissed the top of his warm head. She imagined herself confessing the story to him one day, telling him how she had saved him from squalor like a guardian angel. But then no. She wouldn't need to. They could forget the hows and whys. Being his mother would be enough for both of them.

Cadillac Flats

Cadillac Flats was a slum at the edge of town, a danger zone, a place where the walls were coming down, where the people drank sewage water and babies crawled around snot-nosed and crying, in charge of their own days. Old, rusted Cadillacs were lined up in front of the squat houses and trailers, making a dividing line: the flats against the world. The Cadillacs rode low and the front ends looked like twisted jeering faces. It was a no-go zone. At least that's what Pretty's father, Roger, said about it when they would drive past on their way home to their simple two-story with the square of green grass in the front, flowers in white planters under each window.

But his older cousin Jackie Herd told it different. Pretty was fourteen and Jackie Herd was nineteen and for Pretty those years made the difference between two spinning planets. Jackie said that real men smoked cigarettes, men got their due from whatever woman they pleased, and men went to Cadillac Flats to dance. No sock hop bullshit. They dirty danced. He said that Caddy Flats was the only place to be, a neighborhood really, where at the center was a party that raged all night. They knew music, they knew fun, they had spirit, and they could move. Jackie had said, "You can sweat it out and no one cares. Hell, you can take off your goddamn shirt and it don't matter."

Pretty begged Jackie Herd to take him along, and finally Jackie decided the night was right. Pretty and Jackie drank Roger's beers in Jackie's truck on their way there, throwing glass bottles out the window. They parked far away and walked through the cars, some with tires so flat that their iron bellies pressed to the ground. Pretty was shivering though it was a hot summer night. He'd never been so excited. With every step, his body alerted him, *something different. Something new.* They stepped over a few sleeping bodies on the ground and Pretty was amazed that Jackie did it so natural. He thought they ought to see if the sleeping people were okay but Jackie charged ahead into the center of things, toward a long rectangle building bursting with sound and a sign that said COMMUNITY CENTER. "Don't make a big deal of yourself and no one will make a big deal of you," Jackie said as they slipped inside.

Pretty found that the music was different from anything he had ever known. Roger listened to country, and so Pretty listened to country. But this was alive in a different way. Saxophones and velvet voices and deep beats. Hot sweat poured from him and he flew up and out of the town away from Roger, up away from Jackie and all Jackie's ideas about how to be a man. The women knew the words to the songs and danced with the same vigor as the men, who would lift them up over their heads, skirts flying. The two cousins blended into the dim lights and

Pretty found he could make noise as if for the first time in his life. He could scream and no one could hear him. Maybe Jackie was talking but it didn't matter because the music drowned him out. At some point Jackie disappeared and Pretty pretended he had come alone and it was heaven. Jackie was concerned with all the girls there, so many girls who didn't know him yet.

Pretty made one friend at the flats on his first night. His name was Hodges, and he was seventeen. Pretty had been leaning against a wall out of breath. Hodges had gone up to him and said, "You gotta dance, or they'll getcha." He grinned.

"I need me some water," Pretty said. "I'm just catching up here."

"I'm kidding," Hodges said. "You'll be all right."

"You live around here, then?" Pretty asked.

"'Course," said Hodges. "But that ain't all. I just picked up some shifts at the Tastee-Freez in town center. I've seen you, have you seen me?"

Pretty had never seen this boy before in his life. But then maybe he had. He couldn't be sure of anything. "Yeah, I've seen you, that's right."

"Come on," said Hodges. "I'll teach you to walk the dog."

Pretty followed him back into the center of the people, and they danced and Pretty raised his arms above his head and thrust his hips like he hadn't before. He looked at the sweat on Hodges's forehead and surprised himself. He wanted to put his mouth there. When they walked from the dance floor, he wanted to grab his hand.

It only took Pretty one time at the flats to recognize the king. Chilly Willie cruised the narrow streets in a midnight blue Cadillac, exchanging handshakes. "Is he like some kind of landlord?" Pretty had asked Hodges as they watched Chilly get out of his long car and walk slowly up to the community center. Pretty and Hodges had been getting some fresh air, and Hodges stiffened when Chilly strode up. "I steer clear. I'm not into no drug game. Like I said, I have me a job."

Pretty knew nothing of drugs, nothing of how one man could have so much power over a place. Or maybe he did. Certainly he and his mother never crossed Roger. Certainly they flinched when he moved too quickly, held their breath to see what mood he was in when he came home in the evening. Chilly looked them up and down. A toothpick hung from his lip. He twirled keys on one finger. He was wide, a box set on two stumps. His hair was close shaven save for a skinny braid that grazed his mid-back. His biceps reminded Pretty of the red and swollen meats at Mike's Meat Market. Slabs upon slabs. He thought of shopping with his mother, the grand display of chopped dead muscle, how once he had said aloud to her, "I want to roll across it."

"Ay Chilly," Hodges said, his eyes on his shoes. Pretty looked at his own shoes, too, not sure where else to look. Chilly didn't say a word, just disappeared into the building. Pretty thought of Jackie then, loud and boisterous, probably trying to get fresh with a girl inside, trying to sniff out trouble where there wasn't any. A trail of fear ran down his spine. "That Chilly dangerous?" he asked Hodges.

Hodges smiled. "What do you think?"

The next week Jackie Herd snuck through Pretty's window after a night of dancing, jumped onto Pretty's bed, and woke him. "That Chilly Willie don't want me around there no more. You believe that? He said for me to stay out for good."

"You went without me?" Pretty said, wiping sleep from his eyes. He felt irritated that he had missed an opportunity to dance with Hodges again, but he couldn't say that. "What'd he do?"

Jackie was shaking, smelled of sweat and breath. He pinned his arms on each side of Pretty, looked down on him, their noses almost touching. "The question is, what am I gonna do?"

"I wouldn't mess with him if I were you," Pretty said, rolling away from Jackie. Now that he was wide awake, he wanted Jackie to leave so he could check on the white suede shoes his mother had dyed blue that were drying in the laundry room. Soon he would have shoes just like the Elvis song and he could show them to Hodges and maybe they could dance some more. Maybe they could even catch a movie after one of Hodges's shifts at the Tastee-Freez.

"Half a mind to put your daddy's guns to use," Jackie said. In the dark of Pretty's room, in the cloud of Jackie's beer breath, Pretty didn't take him seriously. An image of Roger's guns in the garage flashed before him, how they hung in a row like prizes. "Give Chilly Willie a little scare."

A few days later Pretty and Jackie Herd walked down to their spot near the old canal. It was about a mile from Pretty's house, and even though they knew the canal was dangerous, and local children often drowned there every summer, they got down to their underpants and swam in it. Then they lay out in the sun smoking stolen cigarettes. Pretty was getting better at smoking all the time, even though he didn't particularly like the way it made him feel, headachy and buzzing.

"I stayed up all night thinking about that Chilly," Jackie said. "The way he looked at me. Boy you shoulda seen it, like I was a speck of dust. Like I was nobody at all."

"What he say exactly?"

"Didn't say much," Jackie said. "Didn't have to. It was the look in those eyes, like a bull about to charge. Think he's worried I'll steal his girl. Real pretty thing, I'll tell you. She had a smile for me, Lord."

"You try to steal his girl?"

"You know me, Pretty Boy baby. I'm smooth. I don't have to steal what's already coming toward me."

"I'd leave it alone," Pretty said. "Hodges told me all about him. He could kill you with his bare hands."

"I ain't gonna sit back and let no man make me feel like shit on a shoe. No Big Chilly scares me. It's time for me to make a name for myself around there. I ain't going to college like your fancy ass. I'll be taking over Pop's vineyard. I'll be here my whole life."

"Let's just forget it," Pretty said.

"Forget it?" Jackie said. "This is what we need, man. We need excitement. I'm going goddamn crazy cooped up in this shithole town. I can't let it go."

"Let it go, man. Don't ruin that place for us, alright? I like it there."

"Yeah, yeah, ol' Pretty likes to dance with the boys. I saw you. Shy as hell. Won't go near a girl, not you." Jackie got up and shotgunned a beer. "I might be unappreciated round here. But not there, man. No one knows me over there. Not really. I can be anyone I want."

Pretty thought of how Jackie's deep-set acne scars were softened in the low light of the community center, how he did seem happier at the flats. But also how most of Jackie's pursuits were reckless and momentary. "Chilly's going to have a day with you," Pretty said, standing up next to Jackie.

"No one's having a day with a shotgun down their throat."

There were times when Pretty got angry. And it sometimes had to do with Jackie, but more often to do with Roger and what happened after Roger hit the whiskey. Pretty's mother was a kind and a soft woman and to see a woman with such small bones get beat the way Roger did it, it incited a rage in Pretty. When he felt this way, he went to the garage and pretended to shoot. He pictured Roger's face at the end of the barrel, firing off to save his mother. For his mother had a beautiful singing voice, and Pretty knew he would die if he never heard it again. "No one has a day with a shotgun down their throat!" Pretty imagined himself yelling like Jackie would. But it was hard to imagine, and afterward he sat in his room and watched the day turn from light to dark out his window.

There were things in the family's past that troubled Pretty. Troubled him, yet no one spoke of them. He knew his father had fought in the war and now he walked with a limp and his heart was purple. He knew Roger saw Haldis for the first time working at a hot dog stand and he went right up to her and said, "I'm gonna marry you," and he did. Other than that, Pretty found things out in other ways. Like the box of pictures in the garage. Pictures of babies he had never seen. A small baby in a carriage in front of a house, another one in his mother's arms, her hair blown back by the wind, a small pregnant belly. On the back it said 1944, the year Pretty was born. He showed it to Jackie, and Jackie said that Roger and Haldis had two babies that burned up in a house fire.

"Then they started over, and all they got was you," Jackie said, smirking, like it was all a joke.

"What house fire?"

"My ma said something blew up while your mama was out changing the laundry on the line. House went up in flames."

"They're my—" Pretty paused. He couldn't tell if the babies were boys or girls.

"Don't cry about it," Jackie said, brushing him off. "Not like you ever knew them."

"Jackie, ask your ma to tell you their names."

"Alright, I'll wait until she has a few drinks. Make her tell me the whole sad story."

The next day Jackie reported that their names were Johnny and Jane.

*J*s, Pretty thought. *I can remember that.*

Jackie waited for Pretty to get out of school and they walked over to Billy's Gas 'n Stuff where Jackie liked to shave his face over a metal basin in the bathroom. Pretty sat on the toilet and watched. He tried not to think about Hodges but it was no use. *I've seen you, have you seen me?* Now all Pretty wanted was to see him.

Jackie maneuvered the plastic razor around the sharp hollows of his cheeks, even though he only grew patchy hair under his bottom lip. He stole razors from Billy's, used them once, and then threw them away. It seemed Jackie was always doing things just to see if he could. Pretty sipped a warm root beer Jackie had snagged on the way into the bathroom.

"With all plans like these there's the leader," Jackie said. "And that leader calls the shots. You don't plan too far out. No need, because the leader has it all up here." He tapped his forehead.

"How will I know for sure what you want me to do?" Pretty asked. "What if I don't want to go through with it?"

"You're about to be a man," Jackie said. He turned to Pretty. Blood trailed down the side of one cheek. "This is the stuff I'm always talking about. Man-making stuff."

Roger had often said he became a man in the war. He said it accusingly as if Pretty should have already found himself a war and enlisted to fight.

"You're just going to scare him, right?" Pretty asked. "Nothing crazy."

"Would it be crazy, Pretty Boy?" Jackie slung an arm around Pretty's neck and he could smell Jackie's deep odor, like sourdough warmed in an oven. "No one's gonna find out it was us, first off. And second off, who needs some Big Chilly, anyways? Worthless piece."

"Hodges said Chilly doesn't mess around." Hodges had not said these words, but Pretty could see this was true by the way Hodges had bent his head down when Chilly had passed. He resented Jackie then, for making him remember his night with Hodges only as it related to Chilly, when in fact there was so much more: the way their fingers had brushed, the way he felt panicked almost at the thought that anyone would ever know that he had never once felt this toward a girl before, and now didn't even want to try. The way Hodges waited for each song to come on and when it burst forth he would clap one time and say "alright."

"Sure on about Hodges, huh? If I didn't know better I'd think you had a crush on the guy." Jackie snorted like it was the wildest thought in the world. Pretty's neck burned.

"Knock it off, now," Pretty said.

"Listen, I'll be needing your old man's Smith and Wesson. Just wrap up it up for me nice and have it ready."

"Roger'll kill me."

"Roger's two sheets to the wind half the time."

"Exactly."

"Just do it."

They parted ways and Pretty went home. He stood in the kitchen and listened to the hum of the refrigerator and tried to imagine what it would be like if Jackie pulled the trigger of his father's gun, but there was no telling if Jackie would actually do it. Really, it felt like all of Jackie's plans: half-baked and stupid. Something they would just talk about for a few weeks while drinking by the canal. Pretty knew he should do all he could to keep Jackie away from the flats, but he also needed to see Hodges again. It didn't seem like a choice he was in charge of anymore.

"There's beef loaf in the oven," Haldis said. Her face was puffed around the eyes.

"Not hungry, Mama."

"You got the spooks?" Haldis said. "What's in ya?"

"Can you tell me about Jane and Johnny?" Pretty asked.

Haldis paused and opened the cupboard and stared at nothing. "Talking to that Jackie Herd too much, now?"

Pretty waited for her.

"I said there's loaf in the oven. Help yourself."

"Why wouldn't you tell me about the house burning, Mama?"

"You in a fever?" She touched a chilled hand to Pretty's forehead.

He looked at the soft tuft of dander around his mother's ears, where her baby hairs grew. He just wanted to feel her hair against his cheek, be soothed by her breath, the two of them alone.

"Your daddy said never speak of it again, and I think he was right. God gives each of us a road to walk, and that was mine."

"That's a rotten road."

"I have you."

"Where's Roger?" Pretty asked.

"It's a bar night," Haldis said. "He's anywhere."

"Maybe I am in a fever," Pretty said. "I should sleep."

"Unless you want to dance," Haldis said quietly and lifted her shoulders so her night dress rose a bit above her small knees.

"One song."

Haldis put the record player on, and they danced slow, and Pretty rested his head heavy on Haldis's shoulder, though he was taller than her, and to do this he had to bend halfwise, rear stuck out.

"I love you, Mama," Pretty said. She smelled like talc and rose.

"There something on your mind?" Haldis asked. "Roger's been rough on you lately."

"Yeah, maybe that's it," Pretty said. "I want to do right."

"You do right all the time, son."

They finished their dance, and then Haldis did what she normally did on bar nights and poured a large jar of wine and turned on the television programs Roger did not approve of. Pretty watched her for a few minutes from the darkened hall, and then he walked down to the basement and retrieved the shotgun and the bullets.

The next morning Pretty put on his blue suede shoes and a quiet yelp of joy escaped him. They were perfect. They were all he had hoped they would be. In these shoes maybe his life would take an alternate course. But then he remembered the gun under his bed and how its presence there felt like another body in the room. He thought of what Roger would say if he knew the gun was wrapped in two Town Department white undershirts under his boy's bed, ready for Jackie Herd. Maybe I don't care what he thinks, thought Pretty. Maybe I don't care what anybody thinks except Hodges. Was this what love was? he wondered. Imagining what someone thought about you all day long? He wanted to imagine Hodges might think him brave helping Jackie scare Chilly, and that Hodges would see him in the way Pretty wanted him to. Strong and unwavering. A man newly born.

It was hard to tell what made a man. He wondered for the thousandth time that day if Hodges was thinking of him at all.

It occurred to Pretty that Roger might be proud of him and Jackie for taking the piss out of Chilly. Maybe they could scare him real bad and he wouldn't come back. He'd hit the road and they could clean up the flats and maybe those people sleeping on the ground could sleep somewhere inside. For a moment, he enjoyed the image of him telling Roger the story over beers, laughing.

When Pretty went to the kitchen for cereal, Roger was sitting at the table in his undershirt and jeans, staring out the window.

"You know what," Roger said, not looking at Pretty.

"What, sir?"

"You don't respect me," Roger said.

"Of course I do," Pretty said. He felt his body begin to brace. His throat constricted.

"No." He paused. "You don't."

"What do you mean, sir?"

"You thought." Roger laughed. "You thought you could take my gun?"

"No, sir."

"Do you know what I should do to you?" Roger asked.

"Sir, let me explain."

"Get upstairs, and get your mother out of bed so she can see this."

"No, sir, please." Pretty backed into the wall.

Roger went to Pretty's room and Pretty was amazed that his father knew right where the gun was. It was so simple. He reached under the bed, and there it was. Roger walked to Pretty's desk and with the butt of the gun smashed his model wooden ships, the ones he had built and loved so dear. Pretty looked at his blue suede shoes. Please, he thought, don't let him take my shoes.

"Haldis," Roger called. "Get in here."

Roger pointed the gun at Pretty and then pointed it at the bathroom. Pretty went inside. He wanted to kick the shoes off in case they got wet, but there was no time.

"Get naked," Roger said.

Pretty removed his shirt and Roger pressed the gun into his back, between his shoulder blades, pushed him to his knees.

"Confess."

"What is it?" Haldis said. "What in the hell's going on?"

"Tell her, son. Tell us all, Lord watching."

Pretty was out of breath and could not talk properly. Would his father shoot him? Certainly he was trained to know how to shoot and not kill. Roger grabbed Pretty's hair and forced his face into the toilet. While Pretty was under water he felt scared, but somehow better, because he knew this would end and when it did, things would be fine. He was only in the peak, and it could only peak for so long. Roger might even feel bad and treat them to ice cream sundaes. He pulled Pretty up and he gasped for air.

"Now?" Roger said.

"I took the gun."

"Why ever?" Haldis said.

"I wanted to clean it for him."

"Liar." Roger fired the gun in the tub wall and for a moment Pretty thought he had been shot the sound was so loud. Roger walked away. Haldis followed, whimpering, and Pretty was alone.

✦

After school, Jackie Herd picked Pretty up and they headed toward the Tastee-Freez. Pretty looked in the mirror and borrowed Jackie's rat-tail comb to push his thick brown hair into a smooth wave.

"Don't worry, Pretty Boy, you're the prettiest boy I ever seen," Jackie said, tousling Pretty's hair. "Those are some nice shoes you got there, too. All dressed up."

Pretty looked down at the shoes. "My mom made me wear them," he lied. He took another glance in the mirror, nervous. He had never been this nervous before, not in this way. He both wanted nothing more than to see Hodges, and at the same time, it would be a sweet relief if he was not there.

He walked in with Jackie and Jackie did his thing when he entered any place, which was to sort of open his arms like an airplane and take a jogging lap around everyone, as if to say, *I've arrived.* Pretty saw Hodges putting fries onto a tray but he pretended to be looking at the menu.

"Yeah buddy!" Jackie yelped. "Your friend here can hook us up with some free grub."

Hodges looked up and registered Pretty. He smiled. "Hi friend," he said. "How's the day?"

Jackie placed a wild order of just about one of everything, and then headed off to use the pisser, as he called it.

"We aren't buying all that. Just some fries and shakes," Pretty said.

"Sure thing. So you coming around again, or once was enough?"

"Yeah, yeah. I've been wanting to come back. Hey, Chilly around tonight?"

"Well, that depends," said Hodges, slowly. "Are you asking, or is that dipshit cousin of yours asking?"

Pretty laughed. "He is a dipshit. He wants to fight Chilly. Show him who's boss, or something. Ten o'clock tonight."

"Well, Chilly comes around at ten most nights." Hodges paused. "You involved with all this?"

"You know what? I hope Jackie gets his ass kicked." As soon as Pretty said it, he realized it was wholly true. That maybe if Jackie finally got hurt, he would stop all this nonsense and they could just hang out like normal people.

Hodges smiled. "I don't know, Pretty. Guess you haven't really seen what Chilly can do."

Jackie came back from the bathroom and put an arm around Pretty's neck. "Excuse us," he said to Hodges. "We need to talk, man to man," and he steered Pretty toward a booth in the back of the restaurant.

"We're going tonight at ten," Pretty said. "I talked to Hodges. He said that's when Chilly's around."

"Good, good, and you'll bring the gun?"

"Of course," Pretty said. "I have it. It's ready."

"You didn't tell him what we're up to, now?"

"Who do you take me for?" Pretty asked.

"That's a boy," said Jackie.

He paused and looked over Pretty's shoulder. "I don't know," he said, and then, "I don't know what will happen tonight, but it's going to be good."

"Once this is over and done with, let's stick to movies and stuff. I wouldn't mind taking someone to see a movie soon." Pretty pictured sitting in the back row, pinky grazing against Hodges's.

"Yeah, well after this you'll be a man and can pull any lady you want." He looked under the table at Pretty's feet. "So what are you doing wearing them cornholer shoes?"

That night at home, waiting for Jackie to pick him up, Pretty paced his room, nervous, just wanting the night to be over. Probably nothing would happen, he kept reminding himself, Jackie was mostly talk. He'd probably just give Chilly some dirty looks and make up an excuse for why they had to leave. Or not. Pretty went downstairs to check on his mother.

"You're home," Roger said to him, reading the paper at the kitchen table. Haldis was nowhere.

"Sir," Pretty said. His father seemed calm, probably in a good place, having recently emptied his anger.

"You don't look well, son."

"What do you know about Chilly Willie?" Pretty asked before he could stop himself.

"Bigger they are, harder they fall."

"Jackie's raising a fuss about him." Pretty sat down. His father was holding steady in his niceness. Pretty remembered the reasons why he did like the man.

"That Jackie," Roger said, sighing. "That Jackie ain't right. How many times I tell you to steer clear."

"He's family," Pretty said. "You always said he's family."

"The Herds is family by blood to us, yes," Roger said. "But don't get mixed up with it. He'll end up in jail like the rest of them. You want to be in jail?"

"You ever been to jail?"

Roger looked far away. "I served my time in the war, in case you forgot. Young men these days are worthless, you know it?" Roger stood and refilled his water. He was sober and slow moving. "I did things so you never have to. And look how your idiot generation repays it all."

Sometimes Pretty wondered if his father hated him. It was possible. Roger got up and moved into the living room, clicked on the TV. Sports.

Pretty walked slowly into the kitchen and called Jackie. "Come on and pick me up."

"You ready," Jackie Herd said, but it wasn't a question.

"I'll be up the road a bit, so Roger don't see you."

Roger did not say anything as Pretty passed by him on the way out. Pretty's shoulders were tense with waiting but Roger sat still. There was a beer on the coffee table now, and Pretty thought, good, maybe tonight was a bar night. Pretty walked up the road and realized he was wearing his cornholer shoes but it was too late to turn back and switch now. He thought of the word *cornholer*. Was it really a bad thing? He let his mind imagine Hodges walking next to him. What if they kissed? What would happen then, would the world split down the middle? Would something explode? Would his father actually kill him? He thought of the gun going off in the bathroom. He had almost killed him, Pretty considered. And yet. Not a word about it afterward, and still not a word about his siblings who had died. He wondered if he would be able to tell Hodges about all of this, and this thought felt just as exhilarating as the idea of kissing, maybe more.

Jackie's truck rounded the bend and Pretty jumped in. Jackie didn't even stop all the way for him, just slowed down to a creep. Pretty did not have Roger's gun, just a baseball bat in a bag, but in the fuzz of excitement, Jackie didn't notice.

Roger had only ever told Pretty one story from the war. He had been drinking, but he was still firm in speech. Pretty was ten, a child, and Roger was still youthful, still receiving comments from Haldis's friends about his classic good looks. It was a different time. Things were not altogether bad then, and Roger seemed to love Pretty and Haldis in a standard, expected way, for no other reason than they were his.

"His name was Sykes," Roger had started in. "He was my best friend. He knew my mother more than I did. I'd go out for lunch in high school, usually with some girl, but Sykes would go to my mama and eat the food she had out for me. They would talk about everything. What I'd give to be at that table with them."

Roger squeezed Pretty's knee and Pretty's breath caught in his throat.

"He signed up for the war," Roger said. "Guess why he did it?"

Pretty shrugged.

"Because I did!" Roger said. "Goddamn follower. Sykes was soft. He wasn't no fighter. But he says, he says, Roger, I'm in it with you, man, in it with you."

Pretty tapped his toes on the wood floor and Roger pressed down on his knee to steady him.

"But you know what, Pretty?" Roger looked at the ceiling. "You know, young boys like you have no idea what it means to be a man."

"No, sir."

"Sykes said to me, Roger, I'll go up ahead and see." Roger stood up and paced the room. "Said, I'll go see what's ahead."

"Yes, sir."

"Well, son," he said. "Goddamn Sykes got his fuckin' head blown off, didn't he?"

"Sir."

"I picked up his head and his eyelids blinked at me. I didn't tell his mama that."

"Sorry, sir."

"And you, a little wimpy shit like you," Roger said, looking into Pretty's eyes, "is all I have left." He grabbed Pretty's shoulders and shook and shook. Pretty felt his neck grow weak and loose. Haldis ran in and tried to pull Pretty away and Roger struck her hard across the face. Her lip bled. Pretty dared not speak of Sykes again, but would often think of a bodiless head in his father's arms. It seemed hard to fault the man for anything he did after that. Pretty and Jackie Herd peeked their heads in the doorway of the center. The music hadn't started yet. Chilly sat playing cards with three other men at a folding table, his large body perched on a little wooden stool with his back to the door. He let out a rumbling laugh that threw Pretty off. He assumed this was a man who did not laugh but here he was doing just that. Jackie grabbed Pretty's arm and pulled him round the side of the building.

"Think you better just get the gun now," Jackie said. "Let's do this quick and easy. From here. I'm a good shot. Right in the back of his head."

Pretty said nothing at first, shocked. "We're just here to make a razz. Scare him a little. Now you're talking about shooting him in the head? What are you, crazy?"

"Man, do your job."

Pretty looked at his blue suede shoes and resisted the urge to bend down and wipe a dirt smudge from the soft material.

"What is with you, man?" Jackie swiped at his greasy hair manically.

Pretty looked around. "Well, now, Roger found out—"

"Oh, shit, you little shit, you didn't bring it."

"Don't you want to talk to him before you shoot him?" Pretty asked.

"He disrespected me."

"Did he? Maybe you misunderstood?"

"His girl wants to be with me. I could see it in her eyes, but she ain't gonna step out on a guy like that! Look at him. He needs to move along."

"What if he ain't even that bad?" Pretty offered. "Who knows?" There was an urgency in Jackie, but where was it coming from? Pretty knew then they were seeing the world very differently.

Jackie shuffled his feet. He shuffled and shuffled and then walked into the building and headed straight for Chilly. Pretty looked back at the truck, thought maybe it was high time to start the engine like a good getaway man, but his eyes locked on the shiny orange Road Runner parked next to it. The door opened and Roger got out, swinging his long shotgun back and forth like a toy, half his lip curled up. Pretty backed into the wall. He looked into the building and saw that Jackie was into it with Chilly, shoving his chest with sharp hands, and the squat man was on his feet with his chin tilted up and eyes squinted and hot.

Roger smiled at Pretty and for a moment Pretty thought perhaps it was all a joke. It was over now, and Roger would laugh and take him home, and they might eat those ice cream sundaes and decide to forget about that dummy Jackie Herd altogether. They might turn the record player on and watch Haldis dance. Pretty would teach them the moves he learned at the flats and they would move their bodies around the living room. He could see Hodges another time, sure, any other old time. Just to make this all stop.

But Roger closed a hand around Pretty's arm and Pretty's feet came out from under him and Roger dragged his weight across the center floor.

Roger dropped Pretty onto the ground and it knocked the

breath from him. The men stopped and Chilly looked curiously at Roger. Roger gave him a nod and then turned to Jackie. He raised the gun and shot him in the foot. There was silence in the building and Chilly raised his arms above head, said, "Hey now, hey now."

"Sorry to interrupt the fine night you gentlemen are having. Please don't mind these boys, clear out of their minds."

Jackie howled like a wild dog. Roger turned to Pretty and said, "Help me get him to the car."

Chilly and the other men watched the spectacle as Roger and Pretty dragged the wailing Jackie Herd. Pretty half wanted to ask Chilly to help, to save him and Jackie from Roger. He wanted to say, "Tell Hodges I was here. That I meant to say hi." But he didn't.

Then from the other side of the barn Hodges emerged with a few other boys to see what the commotion was. He made eye contact with Pretty and then looked to Jackie's bloody foot. The boys ran but Hodges stayed planted for a moment. He glanced at Chilly then back to Pretty and started walking backward slowly, then broke into a run. Pretty thought he might run with him, but his body wouldn't move.

"These boys won't be back," Roger said to Chilly, kind as could be, as they got to the doorway. "My apologies again."

Jackie held his knee to his chest, and where his boot had been was now just a mass of wet and dark. They carried Jackie by the arms as he sobbed and Roger shoved him into the backseat. Blood smeared in a thick swipe on the white of the leather.

Roger beat the steering wheel with his palms and then said low, "Goddammit, Jackie, see what you made me do? Do you see what you boys made me do?"

Jackie made a moaning noise Pretty had never heard, deep and guttural. Pretty realized he was standing in front of the open passenger door. Roger was in a trance yelling at Jackie, sweat pouring down the side of his face.

"Should we take him to the hospital?" Pretty said.

"Try and try to protect this country, make sure there's freedom for everyone, and then two boys of my very own are too stupid to keep in line, take advantage of the education they so freely get, out making life hard when it don't have to be."

Roger was somewhere else now, his eyes welling with tears. Pretty thought he looked like a boy behind the wheel, sad and scared.

Jackie groaned and vomited on the floorboard.

Pretty should get in the car, should tell his father to drive Jackie Herd to the nearest hospital. But Pretty took a step backward. Then he took another step and Roger didn't flinch. Another and another, but Roger just got out and wrapped his shirt around Jackie's foot, not looking at Pretty at all. Jackie's eyes were closed. It was dark out but not densely so, and Pretty could see tiny lights far in the distance. Maybe it was a row of houses. Country people. Step step step away, and then he turned and ran back toward the community center where the music was now full blast. People everywhere. As if what had just happened never happened at all. He scanned the room for

Hodges and there he was, back turned. Jackie grasped his hand. "Can we talk?" he said. But it wasn't Hodges at all. In fact this person looked nothing like Hodges. The room felt like it was growing smaller and smaller.

He ran outside past the parking lot into waist-high blanched grasses. His blue shoes, he knew, were unrecognizable. He didn't have time to look down, but of course they were brown and caked with mud. Pretty tripped on a rock and fell. He hit his chin hard on the ground and stopped. He lay there. He heard his father calling for him. Saying he wouldn't leave without him. This seemed like a small tenderness that he could almost enjoy, if not for the fact that his father had transported. He was in the war again, looking for Sykes. Meanwhile Jackie bled on.

He fantasized that Hodges might find him like this, might hold him just like this. The need felt so strong. He wanted to tell someone desperately about this need, his mother perhaps, but he knew not even she would understand. He knew even she would look at him ashamed and she would say, don't tell no one about this, boy. You keep it to yourself. And that was the worst part of everything: he knew then, he knew so clearly, that it would always be like this and he would have to eventually be a real man, and he'd have to ask a Sarah or a Charlotte to the prom and an anger settled into him that would never leave him, not once, for his entire life.

Raisin Man

When Bonnie gave birth to Sims she was something like fifteen. The town said her daddy put it in her and ran off, and I let the rumor spread, maybe I even helped it along, but these things are easier to see in hindsight. At the time I was worried for my future, and what people would think if they knew that I had been with Bonnie, an odd, quiet type preoccupied with the history of religion versus religion itself, with books that had nothing to do with cooking. But when she opened her legs for me I felt something new and bright spring forth. Something to do with her thin summer frocks and the way she forgot to wear unders like a lady should. I think she reckoned we was going to run off together, but it wasn't to be. I was courting Clara and knew it was her flax-gold hair I wanted to inhale each night. Bonnie didn't understand my attraction to Clara. She said, How bored do you want to be in this life? And kept charging at me with an unusual desire not commonly found in women. It threw me into a stumbling trance for a time, but I straightened up. It wasn't until I explained my mother's Godly prophecy to her, how in the vision it was Clara by my side forevermore, that

Bonnie backed off, said at last she saw what kind of man I was. I assume then she thought she was done with me.

I married Clara, and she grew swole and happy with my seed. It was an immediate thing. I stripped her down on our wedding night and bloom she did with me. Each time I looked at her, I reminded myself she was the better choice, far more set and primed to bring me the family I had always pictured, been taught to picture, than Bonnie would have been. And blessedly I stopped seeing Bonnie around town. I thanked God for removing the temptation. I thought of her constantly, though, wondering what she was doing and who she was with, but I didn't dare ask after her. I didn't dare question the spell of God's grace.

But then there she was at the market one day with a cherub-looking baby wrapped in a tight linen against her chest, just a month before Clara was due to deliver our child. She glanced at me, then kept putting apples into her basket. She was very alone. A baby boy, she said. My heart lurched. I tried to get a look at his face but she turned. Mouthed, *yours*. The rest of the afternoon I tortured myself wondering if I had invented the entire interaction. I could not fathom that there were two dollies of mine grown separate at the same time, miraculous and frightful, but oh, what a shame. Only room for one before the Lord.

That was all about thirteen years ago. We didn't know then that inside Clara was a meek sliver of a girl who would look nothing like us, and would never return love in a way we could understand. Poor Clara was struck with depression when she first saw our baby, still slick with the brine of birth and looking listlessly into the overhead lights, so it was me who told the nurse to write down *Pearl*, a name we had decided on beforehand. What's wrong? I asked Clara over and over after the doctor had left the room and taken the baby to the nursery. She had looked at me.

That's not my baby, she said. Is what's wrong.

After a few days of this, I asked my mother if Clara's response was normal. My mother, by then, had seen the baby for herself, and had said simply, Well I can understand Clara's surprise. But I held fast to the idea that it was just a stage we would pass through, and one day the baby would cry, would suddenly wake up to us, and hold our fingers in her fist. I held fast that my love would be enough to pull Pearl into personhood, so it was me who bathed and swaddled her, me who warmed bottles and watched her. But over time, I am sorry to say that love, as I imagined it might, did not form. For Clara was right in her way. Nothing about the child felt like ours, and in the eerie silence of the house that should have been raucous with a new baby's coos and screams, I heard God: *Boots, did you think you had gotten away with it?*

My mind would drift to my other baby, pink and lively, poking his big eyes over the linen sling Bonnie wore him in around town, and I would hear my own response to God: O, *what have I done?*

I think back to that time, though, before Pearl came. It was sweet like cane. Clara was still alright, still waking with an appetite, sneaking finger dips of creamed peanuts, a fat pheasant. She said she felt wrong about something, but didn't know what. I said, hand to her bump, Woman, you are batty. But I knew something of what she meant. Gazing out from our porch, it seemed the sky was off. Gone the sun, the flat green fields bending with another kind of wind. That smog shade of gray swept over us, those smeared and heavy clouds. Nothing at all like light.

And then I had to watch Bonnie's boy grow up. She seemed to do everything differently. Named him Sims when I would have named him Samuel. Let him nurse whenever he wanted when I would have given him a regimen of formula in clean bottles. She wouldn't let him exercise his lungs, picking him up and wrapping him tight whenever he uttered even a whimper. I saw all this when I would go around to Bonnie's place about once a week to bring her any cash I could spare, to steal a glance at my boy. He grew and grew into a delight.

Then one day she said, This is enough of you coming around. I don't want your money no more. You taking care of your guilt just makes things harder. Makes more burden for me.

I looked at Sims, who was about big enough to work the vineyards, a kid still, but could be of some help.

Send the boy to work with me, then. Have him earn it.

Bonnie had looked at me long and hard. And why should I do that for you? He don't know you're his daddy. You'll make a right mess of things.

Please, I had said to her. Maybe I begged her. Maybe I got down on my knees.

Sims got taller, and Pearl got more difficult. He began to take on my likeness and Pearl was like someone I ran into again and again and could never remember their face. She sat at her desk most days, quietly drawing beautiful and haunted-looking birds. But she would never run to me, say, Daddy, this is for you! Instead she would let each sketch drift from her desk to the floor where I would pick it up later to put on the fridge. Doctors didn't really know what to tell us, couldn't say why she wouldn't talk or express anything. We had no answers. Some days it seemed manageable to go on like this, laying out her clothes for the day, brushing her long black hair into a ponytail and tying the ribbon. I had gotten good at that. Sometimes I would hug her stiff body. But then some days she was inconsolable, would not rise from bed but instead thrashed all the day as if fighting some invisible demon. On those days she would not get dressed, she would not even rise to use the bathroom but would instead soil herself in a great stubborn frustration.

Meanwhile Clara would be in the kitchen eating. Canned beans of all kinds, entire loaves of bread while standing up. I would tell her it was time for me to work, and ask if she was fine alone with Pearl, and she would say nothing. Sometimes, a simple no. For a time I thought if we could have another baby it would make things right, but Clara refused me. Looked at me sharply and said, Sims is a real nice looking kid, ain't he?

And he is. Now he's nearly fourteen. Now he's old enough to want something more from life, from me. Suppose that's why he's now gone missing.

And he isn't missing just because the crops ain't fit for nothing, damned March frost. At first I could blame it on that. Worst frost the town has ever seen. I kick at scrag vines with another farmer, Fenton, pacing rows. No need for Sun-Maid to come, nothing at all to collect. I could cry over it, all this crackle and dead, and maybe it's the chilled breeze anyway, but a tear comes down my face. When Fenton sees he says, Ain't no use, Boots, weather is weather.

But we both know weather is a message. This valley is frozen, dirt packed hard and cold underfoot. See, while the town's been so busy looking upward for answers, no one's bothering to notice. While they furrow away at how the Lord done us such a dark justice, taking from us our fruitful bearings, I don't wonder. It's what I done those years ago come back. My debt to pay. As far as I know, Sims has been gone four days, maybe more. Bonnie stepping deliberately through town as always, chin up. But I see her worry. I see her peer at me from under the brim of her straw hat. She don't know where he is, either. It's unbearable, this stillness spread over us all, clinging like chalk in the throat.

Where do you think he's gone? I ask Clara in our small kitchen as she peels potatoes for dinner pie. Pearl sits in the rocking chair on the porch with her birds.

Maybe Bonnie sent him to the city for school. They have all them new programs for boys. Them Future Farmers of America.

She can't afford nothing like that.

This isn't on my to-do, and it shouldn't be on yours neither. Clara pauses to listen for Pearl. Sometimes she appears close behind us, usually around mealtime to silently cast her need, but the surprise always spooks us.

We oughta try to get her into town more, I say. Take her around other people. See if she'll like it now maybe. She could hang her pictures up on the community board or something. Give her some purpose.

I called Dr. Wells and he acted like all this was my fault. He said we could try to learn sign language. Sign language! Called the pastor and he said to find the lesson in it. What do you think the lesson is here, Boots?

Pearl walks into the room and sits herself at the dinner table.

How was your reading lesson today, Pearl? I ask her, knowing full well Clara didn't even try a lesson with her. Hadn't tried a single one since the school told us there was no place for her anymore last fall.

Clara snorts. Lesson, she says. She drew another bird. Frame it for all I care.

I get close to Clara and whisper in her ear. She can understand us. Be nice.

Can she? I ain't so sure. Can she understand I'm about two days away from laying my body over the railroad tracks and—

Enough.

I can't do this no more. I'm in hell.

I put Pearl's meal before her and she eats it, looking at nothing, or looking at everything. I have begun to honestly wonder if she sees things we do not, if she knows things we can never know.

My mother always said to treat everyone like they were Jesus in disguise, I say.

I'm not understanding who Jesus is in this experiment, Clara says. Am I Jesus? Is she?

There's places we can take her. I reach for Clara's hand. I feel a rush of warmth for her. Guilt.

Places?

There's a nice home up the way a few hours.

I don't mention it was Bonnie who told me about it. That Bonnie sometimes listened to my woes and worries.

Clara looks at me and a little light comes into her eyes. You mean it this time, she says. You said stuff like this before and then the day comes and nope.

The bad days are getting worse. More of them lately.

You could say that.

Pearl finishes her meal and walks back to the porch where she will watch the sun go down. Then she will retreat to her bedroom and I will help her into her night dress and I will tuck her in, sing her one song, and turn out the light.

In the morning I press on. Clara is fixing waffles, in better spirits even while Pearl is in her room, doing her thrashes, another bad day.

So you think Sims is fine? I ask.

When you're asking after Sims, you're asking after Bonnie. You mean to say, Is Bonnie fine? Is Bonnie provided for? Why don't you just go on then? You'll do it anyways, why not go now?

Just don't think it's right, is all, a woman alone.

You must have thought it was right at some point.

I've done everything for you. I've stayed true.

I wouldn't have married you if I had known, you know that, right? I could have had my pick. You ruined my life. But my life ain't over. You said it yourself, Pearl can go somewhere. She can and no one would shame me over it. No one.

The other day I thought she said something, I say. It sounded like *thank you.*

You idiot, Clara says. If she said anything at all it was probably *I hate you.*

✦

There was a time years ago when Sims asked me about the raisins and working the harvest and how he could go on and do it the rest of his life, just like me, and that made me prouder than I've ever felt. He already knew so much, almost all of what I knew about the grape trays, and how to pray like the dickens for no spring frost; to let the fruit become sweet and sharp before plucking bunches, laying them careful to wrinkle in the natural fire of our sky.

The sun shines here in a special way, I told him. Beats harder and stronger than anywhere else in the world.

But why? Sims said, popping a grape into his mouth. He had to have been about ten years old then, wearing too-big suspenders hitching up pilled tweed shorts. Clothes I knew my money had helped buy. Still, I felt bad for not slipping more into his pay envelope each month.

My mama used to say that God came down and ran His mighty hand on the land, blessed this place, I said. Sims drew close, his head up under my chin.

My ma says it's the deepest hole in hell, Sims said. She says it's so hot our house is going to boil out.

I shook my head. Your ma ain't able to see the riches here. Without the heat, how would we survive? How would raisins come to be?

She don't understand, Sims said, and turned from me. The way that we do.

Sims's shoes were too big, too, and he stood straight like a line of fishing wire was stringing him up from the clouds.

Been thinking I could be a better farmer if I lived with you and Clara, he said. I could help tend Pearl even.

Yes, he was mine through and through.

That way I could wake up early with you and work. Sims tugged a vine. I would devote myself to the harvest. You won't have to do nothing. I can take care of myself.

Who'll take care of your mama? I asked. She needs a man in the house. And you need to finish your schooling.

I don't care for lessons, Sims said. I just want to do what you do.

Do you care for raisins, Sims?

Sir, I do, he said.

But do you really?

He began to cry and he crumpled himself down on the dirt. He was sentimental in a way I'd never known, and at times being around him muddled me up, and I would find myself saying things. I walked over and sat with him.

You'll work with me and take care of your ma, I said. You can do both things, how about it?

She wishes for you, he said.

Does she now?

She does. She wishes you hadn't never left us. And I wish it too.

It was a mistake me being with your mother. It was me being young and selfish. Sinful.

So I'm a mistake.

I stood up and yanked the boy's arm. He wiped his eyes.

Looked up at me and it was like looking at my own father, those thick eyebrows, that sparkle green. I thought for just a second what it would be like to bring him home, let him stay. I supposed Clara would have left me. Which seemed unthinkable at the time, but now seems neutral like a leaf falling from a tree, going back to earth.

Never, I said. Never for one second were you a mistake.

But I knew the damage had been done. He had probably been thinking he was a mistake roaming the earth for a very long time.

He turned from me and began his walk home, down the dirt paths between rows. I followed him, my feet moving before my mind. He must have heard me behind him, but he never looked. I pictured my own girl unable to even look me in the eye. I watched Sims's little muscle-bound legs step like an acrobat over branches and rocks. Throbbing with adventure, going everywhere fast. When I reached the end and the field was clear, I stopped. I watched him walk to the main road and he got smaller and smaller, just as the sun finally lowered behind land. I should have gone with him then.

Our home is the Gifts of the Spirit Church. It's where me and Clara was married and it's where my mother laid my father to rest. It's where I met Clara when she moved to town and was hot for a husband. It's where Bonnie won't step foot even though I've tried to save her more than once. When we go to church these days we leave Pearl at home. I tend to think the Lord would want her there, especially her, but Clara thinks otherwise.

Fenton's a regular here, too. He hired me up as a boy and taught me everything to know about being a raisin man. You might think being around the vines so often would wear off that pine for the taste of grape, but still, each morning when I rise, my mouth opens and closes for them tiny dried-up heavens. We put them in our barley meal, we put them in our pockets, I suck them till they go fat in my mouth and I swallow them whole. I take home more than my piece, slipping Sims bags of ripe and bags of dried before he goes home each eve. Now there's no one to smuggle with, no boy to clap on the back, squeeze his shoulders at the end of a long day's work.

Shortly after I married Clara, Fenton came out to find me deep in the rows and asked if I was a prayer-minded man. I said, Yes of course I am, you know I am filled by the Holy Spirit. He pressed me down and we knelt together there in the dirt. His white hair swept back in the small hot wind, and Fenton prayed.

Father, he said. Please do not condemn Boots for his missteps. Please give us strength, and please stave off the retribution of Boots's immorality so he can be of good use to the harvest and to our town, Amen.

Who all knows? I asked.

God knows and God's enough, he said. But in town, well there's no saying. I, myself, can see a man in sin, wearing it around like cuff and chain. Sulking around my orchards bringing to us the dark.

I'm going to make it right, I said, thinking then that a right-ness was possible.

The Lord makes everything right, Fenton said. He hung his head. But it won't be easy. No, it's never that.

Those words seemed harsh talk to me then, struck me as superstitious, but of course now I see.

After the service I usually like to take a slow trip to the pisser to avoid small talk, but this Sunday I go up to Fenton and start in about Sims. I know he will be with me in my worry. Sitting in the pew, he shakes his head slow and rubs a thumb over the golden words on his Bible.

I ran away when I was about his age, Fenton says.

What would make a boy do something like that?

Came here. Stayed here.

Do you feel it? I ask him. There's something in this air. Where's the sun?

It should be back, he says. The Lord is offering the freeze, now. All offerings have merit.

How can you say that? I ask. Frost killed every damned grape.

We sit together a while longer, then he turns to me. I begin to sweat and it gathers about my brows. He puts a hand on my shoulder.

It would be all right for you to go looking, he says. He clears his throat and pats my back hard. No one came looking for me. Always resented that.

We're fixing to take Pearl somewhere. Someplace nice they can care for her real good.

I wonder, Fenton says carefully, if that will offer you any peace.

Clara came to rush me away. She don't understand it. Don't have time for my concerns. Wants to get home to eat a rack of ribs, a can of kidneys, anything, everything from the cupboards. Sundays she pretends Pearl don't exist at all and eats herself sick.

It's like I got a tapeworm in me, Boots, she says. It's eating me out of all my marbles. Let's go.

It's her showering day, I say to Clara.

Clara waves to no one and says, You take her out to the driveway then, and spray her down. You do it. I ain't doing it anymore. She's practically grown.

I think I better go looking for Sims.

Why don't you call the goddamn police? Tell them they better find that kid before you die of worry.

It's just that I miss the boy around, I say.

Oh, God, Clara says. You would. Love that damn kid, don't you? Well, we all know why.

I think to myself as I start the pickup, but don't say it aloud, of course, that it was just Sims wanting desperate to be like me that had me in a tizzy, just wanting me to be his dad. So simple. Just wanting to be a raisin man.

When we get home Pearl is standing on the porch, her white dress red with blood.

Oh my god, I yell. Sweetheart, did you hurt yourself? I look around for a knife, signs she might have slipped and fell, but see nothing. Clara stands with her arms crossed.

I hoped it would never come.

I realize suddenly it's her time of the month.

Well now we really can't manage this, Clara says, as if this had settled it. But I know something of what she means. It really is too much for us.

I kneel next to Pearl's chair and say, Honey, Sugarbee? We're gonna take you someplace nice real soon. Would you like that? They have a garden you can sit in. It's cooler weather too, won't be so hot there.

Pearl's hand twitches like she's going to take my own hand, like she's going to stroke my cheek, her father. But no. I want to believe she knows we love her, but it is hard to say, in this case, what love is.

That night I fire my gun into the dark field behind the house. I been out here most the evening, unwilling to watch Clara do her Sunday feasting while the girl thrashes in her bed, sweating and miserable. There's a rustle in the brush and I figure if I hit something, then let it be. But then I picture Sims out there, and what if I shot him? For a moment it calms me, but in the next second I beg the Lord's forgiveness. Oh, where is he? I ask? Where is my boy?

I lie on the ground. On my back looking up, I trace the tip

of the gun around my lips and it is warm, even in the cool of the night, and I think about Pearl in her room alone in the dark. I get up. Inside, I drink a glass of milk. I pour some whiskey into it, then drink the whole bottle. I think of how just a few weeks ago, while we was out pruning the vines, Sims said to me, Boots, this place used to be named Collis.

Who told you that?

My ma, he said. She read all about it. Don't it sound like some disease?

The boy laughed with a high-pitched squeal and ran at me. He jumped into my arms and I caught him and he kissed my mouth and buried his face in my neck. It was such a dear sweet moment that I nearly forgot that men don't behave that way. But there was no one to witness, dusk in the fields, Fenton gone home. I enjoyed those after hours, I did, and I even lied to Clara more times than I can count about working late. Just to sit there in the dirt like a kid and talk about anything.

Can I do this? he asked. I was still holding him, his long legs dangling, toes brushing ground.

I don't know, I said. I set him back down and gave him a light shove. Well, hell, you ain't a little kid. You're a man, ain't you?

He looked over my shoulder.

You're a man, ain't you? I shoved him harder.

I got to go now, he said.

Better get home to that ma of yours, I said as he walked off. She don't like it when you're late.

How do you know what she likes? he asked, turning around.

No mother wants to serve a cold supper, I said.

She don't understand why you chose them over us.

Excuse me, boy?

That girl of yours, he said, pounding his chest with his fists. She ain't out here tending fields. I am. I'm here.

The red that had brightened his thin face was gone, and he looked sallow, all of a sudden, or maybe it was the last wisps of overcast light. Who could know?

Now into April, Sims gone a few weeks, I can't take it no more. The grapes are dead in the fields and I have some extra time. I go to Bonnie's. She lets me in and gives me a piece of plum pie and I nearly finish it before we speak a word.

You gonna tell me where the boy is, or do I have to sit here all day? I ask.

Gone for a visit with some relatives, she says.

He ain't got no relatives.

It don't concern you, Boots. She sits down in a chair, eyes sunken back looking older than Clara, somehow, though I know her to be several years younger.

You don't believe that now, do you? After all this time, you can't act like I ain't been some kind of father to him.

You've been an almost father, which is almost worse than no father at all. He keeps thinking he'll win you over, but he can't.

Find him.

He just wants a pa, she says. Knows you're it.

I shake my head. Could have told him otherwise. Could have helped make this all work.

Yeah, but nothing could have kept you away from that boy. He knows he's yours. His heart can tell.

Bonnie. I get up and hold her shoulders. He could be dead. He's a boy.

He's your boy, she screams.

Where would he have gone? I ask.

You deal with it. I've given over my life to all this. Now you deal with it.

Fresno, I think. Must have hitched there, probably working for some farmer. Hopefully not far, I say. I ain't running to Hades and back looking.

But I feel the truth run thick in my marrow. And it is only this:

I would go anywhere in the world.

Clara makes another batch of potato pie that night. I have found three hairs in my portion, and I suspect she's doing it on purpose.

There is a steady knocking coming from the girl's room.

What's she doing in there? I ask.

I've given up trying to know.

Just a few more days with her in the house, think you could try harder.

Try harder? Try harder? The nerve. You aren't here all day

long with her. Year after year. Does something to a woman's mind, you know.

Once she's gone, she's gone, I say. Then what? You're gonna be fixed?

There's life after this. I'm only thirty-one years old.

We could try again, for a baby, I say.

She tips her head back and cackles.

I remember Clara's girth expanding by the day, her skin so pulled it was liable to split, the immense energy it took her to make Pearl. The tiger stripes flanking her sides, red rips she looked at with admiration, dreaming of a little sweet babe to rock back and forth. Can you believe I'm gonna be a mama? she would ask me, swaying from puffed foot to puffed foot. I'd touch that hot skin and feel a vibration. It always unnerved me.

If I had done right by Sims, he wouldn't have run away, I say to her now.

Had you done right by me, we wouldn't have had Pearl. We would have had the daughter we was meant to have. We'd probably have a whole flock of kids jumping up and down. And I. I would be happy.

Will you ever forgive me?

Like I said, once we take her in, no more of this life ever again. New and new from there on out.

I lean to kiss her forehead, try to find my love for her.

◆

I have predictions of where Sims might be. One idea is that he is sleeping in a barn tending someone's cows or horses, doing fieldwork like I taught him. Maybe he's taken up with some girl living in isolation somewhere, or with her family who don't care they're really still children, because that sort of thing happens a lot with the folks living in long stretches of nothing. Or I figure he up and went further than I'd be able to find and was starting new somewhere none of us had ever been. I drive forty miles down the road, stop at the fuel station.

Seen a boy through here, sir? I ask.

Got to be more specific, the man working the register says. BRUTUS, his nametag reads. A stringy look to him, old. I seen a lot of boys.

This boy's a real nice kid, I say. Tall as myself nearly, blond, covered in freckles.

I'll assume you mean the kid asking for work, asking after any kind of work.

May have been, I say. Point me straight?

He come around here, slept three nights in my shed out back, and took some job with the Sander family up the road, Brutus says. And this is all I know of it. I'm a generous man, liable to help a kid in need.

Sander family, I repeat.

Brutus stoops and leans over his large hands rolling a cigarette. Kid said he ain't got no daddy, no mama, no God, and no love. You ever met a person like that?

Only an empty soul would say that, I say. Not this boy.

Maybe a boy would say that if he had too much anger inside.
I suppose.

Boy some relation to you?

I almost say no. No, he's not. But then, I enjoy myself.

Sure is, I say. That's my son.

Oh no no no. The man steps back. He doesn't have no father. He was very specific about that. No father at all that wanted him. Now here, all this time I've been handing out free food to a runaway, he's got a perfectly fine father out looking for him? I ought to call that family up right now, tell them he's a liar.

No need for that.

Well, you're gonna go get him, ain't you? I'll just call and tell them you're on your way.

He picks up the phone and begins to dial. I picture Sims taking up with another family just miles down the road from his rightful origin. All the shame there is to feel, I feel it then.

I'm not actually his father, I say. More of a father figure. He works for me. In fact, he's my employee and he's been skipping out.

What now? He holds the phone away from him. What ya say?

I'm not his father.

He hangs up, confused. What are you on about, now? Talking like a looney tune. Maybe you should be on your way.

My daughter. We're taking her in. To one of them homes. It's real nice. Need to deal with that, and then maybe. Maybe the boy can be with me.

You gonna make it? Brutus asks. Look a sad sack mess.

It's too much, I say. You know I was young when all this happened. I didn't mean for it.

Gone off some end, you have, he says.

I move out quick and make sick around the back. I can't form sense of nothing. I sit in my truck and I try to imagine what happens if I find Sims and take him back with me. Imagine us just driving and driving, never seeing Clara or Bonnie or Pearl again. Just two men, driving and driving.

I go up the road to a grand red house. SANDER, it says, in rusted letters across the mailbox. I stop the truck and look out at the yard. I see three boys in the front throwing a baseball. I see his strong legs running, arms catching. And I know it's him and he looks like a boy among brothers. His outline pressed against the end of day glow. The boys don't care about a truck at the bottom of the drive, just a man passing through, pulled over for a piss, a drink of water, a chance to clear the mind. It's easy to imagine what some folks would do in this moment, the right thing in front of them, a boy without a father. A father sitting still and broken within the range of scent.

I think of Pearl and Sims side by side. Both the fruit of my loins, but both such sorry tries. Like untended crops growing dry and gone in a lost field somewhere. When they were both babies, if you can believe it, I felt I had accomplished something of worth. I thought, I can have both things, why not? But any God-fearing man can tell you, there is never such thing as both.

I take a look at Sims as he bends forward to scoop a grounder. The sun moves behind the house and I see him clear. His cheeks red and alive, his eyes on the ball. I see him squint. He is still for a moment and I imagine his legs breaking into a run toward me, everything fixed. But he doesn't run. He lifts a hand and waves, the saddest wave in the world, and I crash into tears. He goes back to playing ball. I wonder, and I hope that maybe he is young enough to survive this. Me, there is no hope for me.

I drive home. By now I suppose Sims told the Sander family everything and finally heard the truth in his own voice. Finally found someone to listen.

Clara fixes a nice dinner, knowing it to be our last with our girl. We try to tell her what the place will be like, how she will get to have her choice of breakfasts, all the drawing supplies she could need. I keep thinking it's possible under God's grace that Pearl will speak to us, look at and not through us.

You'll love that, won't you Pearl? Clara says.

Sure she will, I say. And I read they bring in a musical group once a month. She loves music.

I look into Clara's eyes. We both know she's never once tapped a toe to any kind of music, but who are we to say what she loves. I know there are infinite rooms in her mind.

They should be taking us away, Clara says. For not knowing how to care for her. For just giving up.

Now. That's not fair. We tried. Remember all the drives we used to take her on? How about all the books you read to her? She knows we tried.

Remember that class in the city that was supposed to help? We never went.

Can't leave a farm unattended, I say.

I knew then we were in way over our heads. But you just wanted me to fix it. You wanted magic to happen.

We had to try.

I seem to remember it was you who had to try, Clara says. I knew my own limitations.

Well, maybe I did want magic then. Maybe I wanted you to snap out of it and be a mother.

Maybe I wanted her to be a daughter.

Well. No one got what they wanted, did they?

We bathe Pearl before taking her in. I feel giddy, like we are getting ready for something special, a first day of school. As if she senses something new, Pearl is calm and compliant. Clara braids the girl's hair. All is easy and all is well until we tell her it's time to get into the truck. No, she doesn't like that. It takes all our might to get her outside and by the time we make it to the door of the truck, it's clear she will need the swaddle. Clara reaches out and slaps Pearl.

Now? I say. Right now, you got to hit her?

I don't know what came over me. I ain't never hit her before. Just back up.

I wrap her tight in linens and lay her in the bed of the truck. She likes watching the clouds as we drive. It will calm her, I say to Clara.

Whatever, just go, just drive.

When we get the truck a little ways down the road Clara starts sobbing and I join in loud and fierce and we cry off and on nearly the whole drive, sounds I've never made in my life come out of me and it feels like something is releasing in me and it feels terrible and terribly good.

A few hours later a city materializes as if from a dream. Nothing like the valley. A brick building is before us, tall and assured. Before we turn her over, Clara puts a swipe of her rose lipstick across Pearl's mouth. I've never seen her do such a thing, and I can't help but stare. She looks up at me and says, I always wanted to do that. Just never got around to it. We hand her off to some nurses and they put her in a kind of padded chair. She's exhausted from the journey, and we know just what a rough night it will likely be.

When can we visit? Clara asks them quietly.

But no one hears us. I expect her to ask again. When she doesn't, I open my mouth, try, but nothing comes out. I know we'll never see her again. She never spoke a word to us in all her time. Or did she? *Thank you/I hate you.*

✦

When we return home we make a small pile of her things in the back. Clara instructs me to place my photo of Sims on top.

He is in this, too, she says. It's all got to go.

It's the only picture I got, I say.

She lurches forward and grabs it from me. She rips it in two and throws it and it lands on one of Pearl's sleeping dresses. It don't matter, Boots. It's just you and me now.

She lights the whole lot on fire and we stand in the heat. I hoped it would feel like goodness, and bring us closer, but she stands far from me.

We move away from the valley and east to Albuquerque where we wake every morning in a room that don't feel like our own. We had to get out. Everything looked like Sims there. I'm a coward of a man, this I know. You might be picturing me now, skinny and crooked, a waste load of shame. But I'll say that I am muscle-bound, robust. I look as if I could pick up a steed and throw him yards off and the ladies through town are sure to give me a glance. But in the everyday, we all don't go to heaven, oh, no. Not every person can be redeemed. There is a calm in that acceptance, and I feel it now weigh solid on my chest as I clean my guns. Not every man comes out in the favor of grace.

I have not heard from Bonnie and I don't go by Boots. I've taken up being called Mansar by neighbors and folks about town, and my wife calls herself Reagan. Most eves we sit on the porch and drink and she rocks back and forth speaking of her baby girl like we promised we never would.

Pearl was a beautiful name for a little one, she says.

The most beautiful, I reply.

Do you think she misses us?

I don't think she misses anything, I say. Every day the same to her.

But deep down, she do.

What's done is done, I say to her, and reach for her hand. She pulls back from me. We are not old, though I feel older than dirt.

The sky never looked like this in the valley, she says. Here it's bigger.

I look up. It is July and it is hot, though a different heat than what we knew. Here the puffs of white clouds ripple endlessly against deep cool blue, higher than heaven. Everything is turquoise. I think to that March frost whenever my mind goes quiet, the moment we knew the crops were dead and gone, and realize I know not one raisin man here. I feel the devil sinking into me and I converse with Sims in my head. He asks me how I like Albuquerque. I tell him it ain't as fine as Collis, the place that sounds like a disease.

Heartbroke

Dear Pretty,

You've been asking about Johnny and Jane like I hoped you would never, and it's got my mind in a twist, remembering myself reaching out for those little babies in all that smoke. Johnny was only two years old and Jane was nine months. "Not much life to remember," Roger said when I wanted a proper service. "Babies that small are too young to break a heart," he said when one night all I could say was that my heart was broke and Roger told me to be done with it, to forget it. But let me tell you something. A mother doesn't forget her babies, no she don't.

I was pregnant with you when the oil stove blew up, when the house caught fire, when I ran in to the nursery and carried out those babies. One minute I was hanging laundry to a line and the next the house was in flames. I wrapped them in the sheets on our front grass, Jackie Herd's mama helped me, and we thought of course they would be fine. We were of a time when these things happened and people walked out of the rubble of war on two feet. I didn't know I was pregnant then. I was feeling tired. I'd just been complaining to Jackie's mama about how tired those babies were making me. I said some other things I can't bear to think of.

When you came out nine months later I didn't want to hold you none. I didn't want to look at you neither but you know it was Jackie Herd's mother who slapped me and told me this was my reward from God, my angel come down to fix all the mess of loss. To my understanding then and now, it don't work that way. I'm writing you because I feel I done you a disservice in this life. Seeing how things have gone for you, I worry I poisoned the air of your first breath. I worry it's all my fault.

I'm tired now. Let me try again later.

Dear Pretty,

The day of the fire was sunny and hot, my white house-dress soaked through. Jackie Herd's mama was going on and on about Willie, her husband, and his late hours at the bar and for shame, for shame, and I shook my head and let her go on, so boring she was, telling me the oldest story in the book. All the while I was thinking about what I called then *the other life*, my life if I had not met Roger that day at the hot dog stand, if I had just been strong and not fallen for blue eyes. What do blue eyes really get a person? I'll tell you. Nothing.

I didn't know about oil stoves exploding, about fires sweeping a house in minutes. I didn't know.

Now I'm an old woman alone. You visit for Christmas still, you call me once a week. "Hey Ma," you say. You don't talk about feelings. But here I've been sensing I don't have too terribly long left and there's things I need to say. I remember that night when you were just a teenager, and Roger shot off the gun in the bathroom and I thought we were both going to die, and all I saw was the ways I'd failed to protect you from him.

It is true that when you were about five and off to school the Lord granted me an expansion of heart, some relief from my grief over Johnny and Jane, and it was as if I was seeing you for the first time, my bright-faced boy, my sweetheart. I started making you sandwiches with glee, sewing your clothes just right. I cared so much suddenly and all at once. But it wasn't soon enough. I had already put my sadness into you.

Dear Pretty,

I don't know why a woman like me bothers with pen to paper at all. Once when you were off in Vietnam, Roger saw me writing and he said who do you think you are, a damn scholar? I told him it was Bible study and I prayed he wouldn't come close enough to see I'd been thinking on those babies again. A woman at church I had confided in said, "Well, Haldis, why don't you write those babies a letter?" Like it would cure me of what had happened. I tried. I didn't get far. Just *Dear babies. Oh I'm so sorry. Will I get to see you in heaven? Don't forget me . . .* That's all I could get out before it was too much.

Pretty,

I was tired the day them babies died. My arms were heavy and my head hurt. I was wishing I was free from the nausea I felt, and the day in day out sameness of changing cloth diapers then washing those diapers, and then changing them again, and I really wasn't right in the head. Having babies switched something in my brain. I was just starting to sort that out and then they were taken. I was feeling like being their mother was hard when other women made it look easy, as natural as anything. So while I was hanging sheets on the line that day I fantasized that I was alone on a beach. Just alone listening to the waves. That's the only reason I can imagine the Lord smote me like He did. I always figured that it was my thoughts of the other life that made me deserve this. I've been paying ever since. At the hospital they gave me something that made me feel cloud high but they didn't send me home with anything and I think that was a smart choice but not the right one.

The news printed three small clippings no wider than two pressed fingers. The first said that Johnny was dead. It said his sister was in the hospital and that she wasn't dead yet. It said by the time I got to the crib it was already on fire. It said I suffered burns on my hands and arms carrying them out to the grass. Smoke inhalation. I remember feeling surprised that no one reacted correctly, that no one took me behind the house and shot me.

But then, see, there wouldn't have been you. And that's what I want you to know. That now, my time on this earth almost over, I do understand you were my gift.

I feel I'm still not getting something right here. I'll try again tomorrow.

Dear Pretty,

I always worried you'd turn out like Roger and imagine my terror when you started in his footsteps. The war ruined him. I wrote letter after letter to the military when he came home, injured badly and not right in the mind. Angry and drunk. I said, "Something happened to him there, fighting for this country and now you need to help me." There was no help to be had. And then you signed up for the Vietnam War against my wishes. I came into your room and told you not to do it. Told you to go to college, to work at the Billy's Gas 'n Stuff. For God's sake go be a miner in the hills and get the black lung but don't go fight in no war. I knew who you were, Pretty. You weren't no boy for the war, and if you came back at all you'd be ruined. I told you, believe me. You'll never sleep again. You'll be up all the night howling at the moon. You'll be haunted. Look how right I was.

Pretty,

Each day I think this is the letter I will write that will finally explain everything and you will read it and it will change you for the good. I think, if I can just describe to him what it really was like to lose those babies that day something will be fixed. For me. For you. Maybe even those babies up in heaven will forgive me. I never told a living soul but I went to see a medium some years back to try to talk to them. I explained the situation and she said something about them already being incarnated into other lives. She said you were Johnny. That Johnny's soul went into your body while you were still in my belly. That I should feel lucky. I don't claim to know much about that stuff but I don't think that's how it works. I said to her, "Didn't that baby in my belly already have his own soul?" and she was so sure to tell me that no, no you didn't. But you aren't Johnny and he wasn't you. A mother knows the difference. She didn't even try to explain Jane and I went home more angry than ever.

My heart is broke broke broke and the repairing of it would be worse than death. Roger never outrightly knew I lived in such desperation. And when he died there was some relief because I could finally relax and spend long hours of the day just replaying the fire over and over. I put their photos on the walls and I began talking to them as if they were there. Now I look back and think that I probably hated being a mama to you when you were young because there wasn't nowhere for me to put this pain. I had to hold it inside and who was there to absorb my anger but you.

But you just wanted to be loved. You liked your mama to iron your underwear, and you liked your mama's fried canned oysters and you liked the pork chops I made with tomatoes and rice in the glass dish.

Dear Prettiest Boy,

The next news article they printed, no bigger than my thumb, said that the nine-month-old girl died too. That was the day I decided I'd only ever listen to the sad cowboy songs my father had listened to for the rest of my days, the slow and crooning dawdling songs that used to depress me in my youth, as if I had anything to be depressed about. But then I understood those songs and what they were for. I knew the day I lost them babies, my ears didn't deserve to hear no happy music never again.

P.S. The last article mentioned a service being held for them. But I don't remember that day. Did it happen? Roger had said no, what's the point, but maybe I fought for it. Maybe for once, I won. But don't ask the mother of gone babies about anything logistic. Don't ask me about the facts of my days. They are gone before they even arrive.

Dear Pretty,

One time I watched you outside the Tastee-Freez but you didn't know I was there. I was gonna get me a vanilla cone and eat it in my hot car the way I liked to do sometimes, trying to focus on only the bright cold flavor in the back of my throat, throwing the wrapper from the cone out the window on my way home. But there you were round the side of the building with that boy who worked there and the two of you was thinking no one could see. And I saw the way you were looking at him and you had your arm up against the wall and your hip cocked to the side and it made me blush when you combed your hair in front of him because of course you looked like Roger when you did that. I knew for certain then what I'd always wondered. I knew then it was true.

I cried in the car watching you because I realized my heart wanted something unthinkable, a world where you could just be yourself, and I wasn't sure where that idea was coming from as I had never known such a world.

Dear P,

These letters feel more useless by the day. I'm writing to ghosts, waiting for the perfect words to come fix it all. I want you to know that I prayed all the time for a day when I didn't think of those babies. That I could have a day where I looked at you and only saw you. Where you could feel my joy and know it was safe to be joyful. But I don't think I ever accomplished it. It's always in me and always in you. I'll see fire every night when I close my eyes. I'll let your daughter eat mint chip ice cream for breakfast when she visits. I make believe she looks like Jane, what Jane would have looked like. What do you think this life is for?

Dear son,

I wish life had been easier on you. I am sorry for that. Maybe I should have left Roger, taken us both into the other life. I never did. Will you forgive me? I hope you know that I loved you even when I didn't know it. I can look back and see easily that as long as I was alive, I loved you.

I see those babies when I hear my sad cowboy songs, but I also see you. You'd think I'd stop listening to those old heartbroke melodies since they hurt me so. But this life don't make sense and I don't just listen to sad cowboy songs, no. I go looking for them.

The Bare of Our Chests

My daughters jump and skip across our lawn, their golden hair matted against sweaty foreheads. My wife and I sit on lawn chairs wearing visors, drinking sweet tea with lemon wedges floating amid the ice chunks. On the other side of my fence lives a family like ours, and beyond them, another family, similar in many ways. I think of how many backyards I would have to travel, all the fences I would have to hop, until I would find the lawn my mother and I used to spread our bodies across. Summer nights, just her and me, when she would whisper stories and run shivers down my spine, defying the heavy heat. How many miles until I could step across that grass, the little blades of dry green we crushed under our backs? In the summer I think of her the most. There are times when my daughters will say or do something a certain way, and I see her face in them, and I hear her voice, and I think of her watching me still, each summer, our secrets fading as all things will, with time and careful silence.

✦

Aunt Lowette was mostly a shut-in by the time I came to stay, but she went out for necessities. Married once but Richard ran away and died. There was proof of them in her bedroom, though, a wedding day photo, small and sad, with my mother standing beside Lowette, flowers crowning her golden locks, the beauty of the two. Aunt Lowette's mouth set in a thin half smile, her arm looped in Richard's, a stoic man in a suit with pants too short.

I was sent to live with Aunt Lowette after my mother vanished, after she poisoned old man George. Aunt Lowette said she could only take in one of us, and Elaine was too young, would be too much work. I tried to convince her I would take care of her, as I always had, seeing as my mother left me in charge of five-year-old Elaine all the time. But the police and the courts didn't care about my mother's wishes. Didn't care about us much at all.

Right from the day I arrived, Aunt Lowette lectured me on the evils of the world as if I didn't already know. Laid it on thick after I did something that wound her up, like wave to neighbors or suggest we answer the doorbell when it was clearly a UPS man holding a package and clipboard. I started to undo the locks, but Aunt Lowette rushed over and grabbed my wrists.

"What if it's the books I ordered?" I asked.

"Opening the door to your home is a fool's game, Maynard. You open it even a crack, you're inviting anyone and the dickens in. Don't be stupid, boy."

We were crowded against the door taking turns with the

peephole, and she could see my disappointment. "If he's the real deal, he'll leave a note and we'll pick it up later," she whispered.

"It's a package, ma'am," the man said through the door. Aunt Lowette and I jumped and my cheeks grew red even though the man couldn't see me. "I would just leave it but it requires a signature." Aunt Lowette put her finger to her lips and shook her head. When I looked through the hole again, he was gone.

We sat down together at her small kitchen table while she ate a bowl of chalky oats and yellow mustard with brown sugar. I thought she was going to go on and on about the delivery man but instead she shifted.

"You know, your Uncle Richard used to break my dishes after every meal, china flying everywhere like goddamn shrapnel."

"How did Richard die again?" I asked.

"Oh, your mother's told you, don't play me. That woman couldn't keep nothing quiet."

"Is it true he hanged himself?"

"My sense is that orange-haired woman he was surrounding himself with toward the end made him do it."

My mother had called Aunt Lowette a *withholder* and said she wouldn't submit to Richard's needs. The lack of affection drove him mad and turned him into a regular Mr. Hyde when he drank.

Aunt Lowette shook her head. "The last thing Richard ever said to me was in a letter, and in it he said he had gone off with the wrong woman and could I please take him back. And I was considering it, Maynard. But then came news that woman found him stiff and stupid hanging in the closet the two of them shared."

"I'm sorry," I said.

"Don't ever apologize," she said, wiping mustard from the corners of her mouth. "Opens the door for people to step all over you." She glanced at her reflection in the sliding glass door. "When we go out, remind me to get you some cereal, and Clairol if they have it. Golden Sunrise."

I looked at her stringy brown hair striped gray.

"Now that you're here, I had better keep up appearances," she said, and left the room to get dressed for our errands.

Aunt Lowette's kitchen was cluttered but barren at the same time. Empty boxes of easy rice, questionable lunchmeat, off-smelling juice, little mountains of cardboard wrappers, and Tupperware pitchers full of too-sweet tea. Oats were the only safe thing to eat, but I really couldn't stomach them. The fridge was covered with pictures that at a glance could be mistaken for a collection of family photos, but on closer look, they were clipped images from J. C. Penney catalogues, happy-looking children posing in new school clothes and backpacks, staged families caught in the middle of exclusive laughs. Each one was held up by its own magnet with care. There wasn't a single one of me or Elaine, or my mother, or anyone I knew. My mother had told me of Aunt Lowette's downward spiral after Richard died, her retreat into becoming odd and unkempt. I didn't think much of it until I arrived in her home. She had been little more than a made-up character to me and my mother had always spoken of her like she was dead, a person of past regard.

Aunt Lowette and Richard moved to Fresno when they married and took my mother with them, just fifteen at the time. They settled on the good side of Shaw Avenue, the dividing line that separated people by finance and race, in a duplex with two wicker chairs on the porch and a straw welcome mat at the door. It was a dream come true, California at last. Fresno, an agricultural paradise, was perfect because Richard had plans to become a raisin man. My mother got a job right away hosting at a restaurant. She found herself pregnant by mistake with me soon after. Because she was still a child herself, Aunt Lowette and Richard let her stay even though I was a colicky baby. But when she started bringing Wayne around, a twenty-something-year-old man she met at the supermarket with me on her hip, it seemed to be too many people in one space. Wayne didn't mind my mother's complicated situation, or her age, so on Wayne's dime we moved ten miles away to the Lakes apartment complex. Wayne and my mother stayed together longer than anyone predicted, and when I was ten they made Elaine, my baby half-sister who seemed world-weary even as a newborn, her features heavily drawn and shadowy. More than anything she preferred watching television all day. I'd make her pancakes shaped like Mickey and she'd smile and say "good."

We lived like a family above old man George, the longest tenant the Lakes had ever had.

I am older now, with children and a wife of my own, and I think we will always be here, in this valley, though it remains a place of private confusion for me. Years here blend into stages of weather and people recall things by season. I think of Aunt Lowette when the fog settles over the expansive gridded neighborhoods and blankets the rows of Sun-Maid vines and the fig trees harden with frost. In the summer I think of my mother, when the dry heat stretches the days and our bodies cannot remember anything but sweating deeply from the inside.

And September belongs to Elaine and the raisin harvest, and marks the season I tried to keep her safe and manage things after our mother left. My mother had said to stay inside with the door locked and lights off until she came back for us, but until then I had to make it look like we had all up and left. When police knocked on our door I panicked and hid Elaine under the kitchen sink and curled myself in the corner of my mother's closet. They beat the door in and found Elaine immediately. We had lasted only three days, and even still I wonder if I did something wrong, fumbled my mother's last instructions. Elaine was taken away and sent to live with Wayne's parents in Portola up by the mountains. It's funny how fast children can be reassigned—blood relatives come first, as if sharing DNA equals capability. Foster care is a swift second, and where I assumed I was headed, having not seen Aunt Lowette, my only next of kin, since I was a small boy. Elaine was carried off in a stiff little ball. She didn't cry when they took her from my arms, or even look back at me, knowing already, perhaps, that it was best to move on.

"She slow, son?" a detective asked me, scribbling in his notebook. His name was Geary and he had made me a cup of cocoa. He was an older man with wiry eyebrows and flushed cheeks with a wide space between his two front teeth. A long off-white braid hung halfway down his back and he wore a felt cowboy hat with a turquoise tassel. His voice was deep. I hated him on sight.

"Elaine was going to start kindergarten next year," I said. "I taught her to write her name already and she'd memorized half her story books. So, no. Not slow."

"She don't seem right to me." The notebook was tilted just so I couldn't read it.

"My mom said Elaine is in her own world and smarter than us all," I said.

"Is Elaine smart enough to tell me what happened to the old man? Or can you do me that kindness?"

I knew this was coming. I thought of what my mother might say.

"You hear the question? We're just having a little man-to-man chat, now. Put the cocoa down, son."

"I'm not your son," I said.

"Wipe your face." He handed me a napkin. He wrote something else. I wondered if they had already caught my mother and this was a trick so see if we shared the same story.

"You were upstairs with the little one the whole time then? You hear anything unusual going on down there?" he asked.

"No, I was reading to Elaine."

"What book were you all reading?" He closed his notepad and waited.

Aunt Lowette appeared in the doorway. "Think that's enough now. You be on."

"Summer nights here are hard to beat," my mother used to say, ceiling fan on high, sucking a frozen pineapple pop. She stood in front of the window, thin tank top clinging. "Feel that breeze? Come on, let's lay on the grass. Bring the spray bottle." After Wayne died, this was our ritual. Little Elaine would fall asleep and we would sneak out to be alone. One of us would shoot water straight up over our heads, and lean back, letting the fine mist settle on the bare of our chests, and my mother would tell me about her life before everything. She had been barely sixteen when she had me. I have never admitted to another soul, but I liked to pretend she was my girlfriend sitting alone out there on the grass, the glow of streetlamps softening her to look younger than a mother should.

She said she always felt cosmically connected to me, like our souls were meeting again and again in different forms and lifetimes. That I was a different breed than Elaine, from a different father, a man who took my mother on the gravel behind Ned's Family Valley Dining after her night shift as a hostess. I don't think my mother ever loved Wayne either, but he was safe and made sense, which to her must have looked a great deal like love. He died simply, in a car accident not long after Elaine was born, and after his funeral he was easy to forget. The sadness passed over us quickly, as if he had never been there at all. Of my father, though, my mother said from what she could see by streetlight, he was a handsome man with nice eyes and was gentle with her, all things considered. She used to tell me that God wanted me in the world so bad he made it happen against all will and all sense. I was coming no matter what.

Aunt Lowette came out of her room finally, dressed and ready to take me to pick up the package that was now being held at the UPS store. It would come last on our list of chores, so first she drove us in her powder-blue Chrysler New Yorker to the Dollar Tree. Inside there was a girl who looked about my age working as a greeter, wearing headphones and a green vest over a tight white T-shirt.

"Welcome to the Dollar Tree, please enjoy your visit," she said at us, raising her eyebrows. When I got closer I read the name on her tag: LOLLI. "Please let me know if there's anything I can direct you to. Ma'am, need a cart?"

"Give me one that ain't sticky." Aunt Lowette looked suspiciously at the lineup of carts. "Have any of them wipes? Anti-bac-ter-ial?"

"No ma'am, this isn't Wal-Mart," Lolli said and pulled a cart loose from the bunch. "Ain't seen nobody cough on this one."

"Thanks," I said, and our eyes met. She had thick-cut bangs across her forehead and nice green eyes.

I chose a box of off-brand Lucky Charms and a box of Waffle Crisp, then found some imitation Clairol. Aunt Lowette piled the cart with French toast–scented candles, and we checked out. Before we left, I turned and walked over to Lolli and slipped a piece of paper with my number down the breast pocket of her vest. By the time it startled her, it was already done, and I looked back and smiled. She stared, confused. I didn't know what had come over me. I had never talked to a girl before. The action of it was my mother, something she might have done to a man she half liked at a gas station.

The package was books after all, but not what I had been expecting. I had ordered a few mysteries, a novel about a cult with a gold cover, and a book on bird-watching with some unused birthday money, but the package we picked up came from an address in Miami, Florida, not from any bookstore, and I waited until I was alone in my room to open it. There was a journal with cherubs floating across the cover, and I recognized it immediately as the one that used to lie next to my mother's bedside table where she copied down inspirational quotes and notes about her days and wrote little fairy tales about goblins and pretty witches. I had never dared read it and holding it in my hands felt wrong. I opened the front cover, and there was a line of writing darker and fresher than the scribbled drawings around it. *Hello Maynard. Just a note to say I'm doing all right. I read this on the wall of a pisser yesterday:*

"Even if you are on the right track, you will get run over if you just sit there." Some guy named Will Rogers said that. Pretty smart. Love you, kid.

I slumped on the ground and held the journal to my nose. It smelled like her, like her breath on my neck, lightly scented by Marlboro Lights and spearmint, like her shampoo—no, like her hair a day after she had shampooed, lightly used, a bit salty but spiced, cardamom in a sugar cookie. It was my first heartbreak. If my wife left me tomorrow, the pain of my mother's absence would resound over it as my greatest love lost.

The other book was a small paperback of Oswald Chambers's daily devotions, something she carried around in her purse. I flipped through pages hoping to find some clue, a secret code maybe, directions to where she was. There was nothing, just some sketched drawings of animals, little wolf faces and mountain lions, ticket stubs, and some photographs of herself that were very complimentary, one that I had taken. I expected inner musings about George, her anger over what he did to little Elaine, the next step of our plan. But the package more or less confirmed my worst fear. She had never meant to come back for us. There was no next step.

My thoughts drifted to Lolli then, and I wondered what I would say if she called. I had never been on a date. And I thought that if Lolli called I might take her to the movies, I might kiss her in the back row and I would reach up her shirt and feel what was there. But it would mean nothing to me and I knew no matter what I found, it would never compare to my mother's hand on my knee in the car with the radio turned up, her chin tilted back laughing and screaming along to Bruce Springsteen.

I arranged myself in bed to reread her journal. A few minutes later, Aunt Lowette walked in and sat by my feet and tried, I think, to comfort me.

"Maynard, it's time we quit pussyfootin' around, and talk about this thing. I got to know. You only have to tell me one time."

I nodded.

"Why'd your mother go and off the man? Some money thing?"

"No. It was something else."

"Tell me then," she said to the wall.

"She didn't run because she was innocent."

"She probably got the whole idea from me. Such a copycat."

"How do you mean?" I asked.

"When Richard and I were first wed, he did terrible things and it came as a shock. Never hit me till we were hitched. Case of bum luck, but your mother saw it all and she hated watching mean old Richard get higher than a Georgia pine and knock me silly. After he would pass out in his chair we would sit on the patio real late. Chitchat about ways to kill the son of a bitch."

"Like what?"

"Oh, well, you know us after our wine bottles were low and the crickets got loud, I suppose we pretended to be real brave. One time we did put some Benadryl in his mashers for some peace and quiet, but nothing to squirm over. Put him out over thirty-six hours, scared him so bad he marched his ass to an AA meeting when he woke up, and we laughed, oh we laughed, your mother and I. The man thought he'd died, gone to hell, and come back. We wasn't going to do serious damage, but it felt good to talk about, I suppose."

"Maybe some people have it coming."

"I always said the easiest way would be antifreeze. I got it off *Matlock* or some hootenanny." Aunt Lowette laced her dry fingers together. "When I heard she put that in the old man's soup I had to chuckle." Aunt Lowette smiled. "Chuckled even harder when I read it was really asphyxiation that finished him off. Girl never had any patience."

"He wasn't a good man," I said. George had loved my mother. She was easy to love and attracted caregiving men all the time. She had a quality that made you want to hug her and then put her in a cage and feed her with a small spoon.

"Always a greedy little thing. That's why her and I fell out. I'm sure she always told you I didn't care about you all, but that wasn't it. She was stealing my money."

"George gave her money when she needed it. She would just walk downstairs and spend time, do the crosswords with him, and then we'd be set."

"Maynard, don't believe your mother's trash. She was doing more than the crosswords."

"She did what she had to do," I said. I felt sick as I thought of the way his eyes followed my mother, his velour tracksuits, his greasy upper lip, the multitude of conditional offerings. Bizarre requests that my mother carried off with a smile: a bottle of wine if she sat on his lap, a hundred-dollar bill if she cleaned his apartment in a bikini. "When she lost her job as manager at Arby's, we were broke."

"So he helped you all out, and then she turned on him?" Aunt Lowette asked.

"It wasn't that simple," I said.

George had marveled at how much little Elaine looked like our mother, even though I couldn't see it. Mommy this, mommy that. He would have her climb onto his lap and he would pet her head like she was an obedient puppy.

"Elaine, you are the spitting image of your mommy, aren't you?" George said one afternoon while our mother organized his cassette tapes in a sheer bra and panty set. "Your mommy is so pretty. Look at your mommy. When you grow up you're going to be even prettier, aren't you, Elaine? Show me a smile." Elaine faced him and parted her lips to reveal two rows of sharp baby teeth.

"I don't know, George," my mother said. "Wayne wasn't much of a looker. That little girl could go either way. All kids are cute to start."

"I think Elaine should put on the new dress Daddy George bought her." George set her on the ground. "Let's get her into the new dress. Elaine, what do you say? You want to come back here and let Daddy George help you with your new dress?"

"She doesn't want to wear a dress right now," I said. "It's too hot. It will itch her."

"You stay out of it, kid," George said to me. "I bought it special and she's going to wear it. It's made for a little princess."

Elaine had walked to the bedroom and George followed.

My mother loved when George wasn't around because then she could stop cleaning and have some peace. She got up and flicked on the TV to Sally Jessy Raphael, her favorite, and power-walked on George's treadmill eating Lemonheads.

"Oh, Jesus H., Maynard, that poor little thing. Makes me sick. Old pervert." Aunt Lowette wrapped her arms around herself and shuddered.

"I just thought he liked my mom. If she had known he was messing with Elaine she would have made him pay a lot sooner."

"Now tell me, did you help her do it?"

"Elaine is my sister. I would do anything for her."

"You would do anything for your mother," Aunt Lowette said.

"She hasn't forgotten me. She's just waiting until things cool off."

"I hate to say this to you, but you're nearly a man. Your mother ain't coming back, and my guess is ain't nobody gonna find her."

"What do you think she wants me to do now?"

"I'd get your story real straight. Wouldn't put it past the little chicken to blame it on her boy."

"She would never do that," I said. "I already told the police I have no idea what happened."

"I been lied to a good amount in my day, son. And I've lied to my own self, too. So I know how it is." She patted the bedding over my legs. "When you got more to say, you let me know. And shit, I like you, kid. Always wanted myself a boy."

"What about Elaine?"

"That Elaine's half-related. She got herself covered up there, growing up near the snow with some real nice folks. Let it be."

My mother and Aunt Lowette grew up in Boonville, Missouri, in a small run-down two-bedroom house. Their Daddy Leon was a good-for-nothing, a criminal at best, involved with drug mobs and the deaths of men who had done him wrong. My mother told stories about her childhood that writhed with amazing twists and turns, villains and beautiful powdered women.

"Your Aunt Lowette and me, well we would hide under the kitchen table while Leon and Mama Belle would have it out. Screaming the most horrible obscenities." We lay on early summer grass, just her and me. "Daddy Leon would work hisself into a rage and his target would center right on Mama, the boney thing. But she fought back. Her sister Wanita gave her a small pistol on her wedding day, and I only saw her draw it once, the day Daddy Leon tried a go at Lowette."

"He hit her?" I asked.

"He was gonna put the devil in her something fierce," she said. "But Mama got between them and pulled that gun. Never heard the house so quiet. Daddy never went after Lowette again—a first and last time situation."

"Tell me what happened next." I loved her stories. Her voice would fall in tone to match the characters with spot-on accents and expressions.

"Ain't I told you a million times? You love the blood and guts, don't ya?" She poked my ribs and we lay on our backs, eyes to the sky. "One day Daddy Leon and Mama Belle met up with Wanita and her husband at the Other Bar in the middle of downtown, and Mama had her pistol, of course, prepared for anything. From there they went out back where they was meeting some of Daddy's business associates, and 'fore they knew what was what, they was gunned down in a drive-by situation."

"I don't understand why someone would have killed Mama Belle." In pictures, the few that I'd seen, Belle looked like an old-fashioned version of my mother with her sharp nose and round eyes. A deer.

"Don't ever be fooled, Maynard." She rolled to her side and put her hand on my chest. "Mama Belle took her share of beatings, but it don't mean she was good."

"Did you love her?"

"You come into the world loving the one who made you."

"You said God made us."

"And that's the truth, Maynard, but when you're born you got the devil breathing down your neck and you're told to love your mother."

"You're so brave, Mom."

"Honey, you ain't got no choice growing up the way I did."

"Did Mama Belle love you more than Lowette?"

"I think she could see who was the most loyal," she said. "No matter what hell that woman put me through, I kept my mouth shut and stood by her."

"I love you, Mom." I hugged her. "I'll never let you down."

"I know you won't," she said. "You're a special boy. You just do what your mama says and everything'll turn out."

Fingers entwined, we walked back into the apartment together. Little Elaine was asleep on the couch, her Disney movie just a blue screen, a half-empty bowl of popcorn on the floor next to her. We stood and looked at her chest rising up and down with breath, her nose small and upturned, eyebrows crinkling with dreams, and I remember feeling something roll through, a bad thing. My mother let go of my hand and narrowed her eyes at Elaine.

"She been acting funny to you, Maynard?"

"I don't know. Quiet I guess."

"More than usual, though?"

"Maybe we shouldn't take her to George's anymore," I said.

"What makes you say that?"

"I don't think she likes him much."

She spread a blanket over Elaine. "He sure likes her. He does a lot for us, too."

"Can I sleep with you tonight, Mom?" I asked.

"Maynard, you're becoming a man," she said.

But I knew it didn't mean no. We got into her bed and just before I fell asleep my mother sat up in the dark. Shook me awake. "I think he did something," she said. I knew just what she meant, and we both felt something press into us, too heavy to ignore, for we knew little Elaine was a particular girl and never slept on the couch, loved her bed and stuffed toys, and this change confirmed a truth to us that seemed to arrive fully formed, where before in its place there had been only our endless and ordinary days.

The day after our talk, Aunt Lowette and I kept our distance from each other until evening when we played cards while her Clairol set. I helped her rinse it out in the kitchen sink, running my fingers through her thin, soft strands. She dried it in the bathroom, and when she emerged I was shocked. The blonde had taken pretty well to her pale brown, and she had pinned it up in little billows around her face. Dark lipstick was smeared on her mouth and if I squinted I could see her relation to my mother.

"What do you think?" Aunt Lowette laughed.

"You look great."

She fumbled a bit with her record player. John Prine filled the room, and we danced and sang, my hand on her waist. After a few songs, Aunt Lowette poured us each a small glass of brandy, and we sat down on the couch.

"I used to be a fun girl," she said. "Your mother, after she came along, made me feel old."

"You're still a fun girl, Aunt Lowette."

"I'm sorry if I upset you last night," she said seriously. "You know your mother done some terrible things, but it don't make you bad, too. I want us to get along here. We're the only family we got."

I wanted to remind her this was not a sure thing, that my mother was still alive, somewhere out there, and would pick me up any day, any minute really. But I was quiet.

I helped Lowette to bed, a little drunk and sentimental. "Don't ever apologize," I said. "Remember?"

The phone rang and I dashed from the room to pick it up, thinking it was my mother, but it was only Lolli. I had nearly forgotten about her, the whim of Dollar Tree no longer on my mind. But a wire was running through me. I'd be up for hours and hours. I asked her to come over even though it was late, assuming she wouldn't be allowed, but she came within a half hour. We tiptoed straight to my room and closed the door.

"Was that your mom in the store with you?" Lolli asked, flopping herself on my bed. Her hair was up in a tight ponytail, bangs pulled back. A little roll of flesh popped over her tight blue jeans, and her belly button piercing shone, two sparkling rhinestones protruding.

"Yeah, it was my mom." I sat down next to her.

"You two don't look much alike," she said.

"No, well, I take after my father. He died years ago."

"How did he pass?" she asked.

"It was a plane crash. Well, he actually survived the crash, but then died in the ambulance on the way to the hospital." I felt a rush. It was so easy to just make up a different story.

"I'm real sorry. Is that why your mom looks so sad?" She scooted herself closer to me. "Some women really wear their sadness in their facial lines. My mom works at a beauty parlor and tells me all about it."

I put my arm around her. "We were never the same after he died, it's true."

"Hey, I've heard of this," Lolli said, reaching for the newspaper clipping on my bedside table with my mother's picture and a headline that read KILLER STILL AT LARGE. "Can you believe someone would murder a poor old man like that?"

I grabbed the clipping from her. "I can, actually," I said.

"What, you think he deserved it?"

"The news people don't tell the public what's actually going on," I said. "Don't you know that?"

"Calm down, I didn't mean nothing by it," she said. "I could be a news person one day. But I wouldn't want to report any murders or nothing, more like writing about dating and movies."

"Yeah, I bet you'd be good at that," I said.

"I was surprised when you gave me your number. Never had a boy ask me out like that before," she said.

"You've never met a boy like me before." I was another person then, and the words I was saying had a life of their own, and this Lolli was taking it in, drinking it up like pure water, clean and real.

"Can you take your hair down, like you had it yesterday?" I asked her.

"Looks better that way, huh?" she said, shaking her head, bangs brushing her eyelashes. "Like me now?"

"Yeah, sure. That's better," I said.

"I'm on the pill, you know."

"That's good," I said. I didn't move and didn't have to because Lolli sort of lurched toward me, kissing me with a forceful tongue. I had never done any of this but it turned out it was just what bodies were designed to do, and it wasn't hard at all and for a moment I thought it could even be a solution of sorts, a way to forget. Until I closed my eyes and saw my mother.

The way she looked in the morning making cowboy coffee over the stove, the time she peed herself laughing in the aisle of Walgreens as we were shopping for toothpaste. I buried my face into Lolli's neck and grabbed a handful of hair to smell and bring me back into the room before I thought of George, the way he sat in his chair all day, his lips greased with sausage. Her hair smelled not like my mother, but something else, light and fruity, generic like her matching bra and panty set, bright pink and lacy and stiff with newness, the same set probably every girl her age had stolen from the mall and I stayed with that for a minute but then there it all was again like a movie I couldn't pause. My mother hurrying us out, the horse races still playing on George's television.

I thought I heard the door creak open and I felt terrified that Aunt Lowette could walk in at any moment and then the whole thing felt spoiled. Lolli all the while had no idea of my thoughts and afterward said, "Alright," like she expected some fanfare or something but I could barely breathe. I was frozen in fear that I would never live a normal day of my life. I saw it all before me. I let Lolli walk herself out and I lay awake and my body thrummed as if an emergency had taken place.

Lying in bed together the night before George died, my mother had said to me, "Whatever comes tomorrow, Maynard, never tell a soul what's happened to little Elaine. She ain't very old, let her have half a chance at forgetting." There was, even then, a small part of me that wondered if we were imagining things. That our worst fear had taken up a residence in our minds, yes, but perhaps wasn't real. It was true that neither of us had seen George actually do anything. We were going on feeling, something my mother always told me was more important than anything else.

"I won't tell anyone," I promised.

When Detective Geary would stop by in those first months at Aunt Lowette's, I tried to always be ready. I had hidden my mother's journal in a dishwasher soapbox and covered it with towels deep in a kitchen drawer. Even if he had found it, it would have led him no closer to catching my mother. She was smarter than to stay in one place.

"Anything odd you remember about your mother's relationship with George?" he asked, sitting across from me at Aunt Lowette's little table. She poured him a glass of sweet tea and pretended to straighten up the kitchen. "We just can't pinpoint why she wanted him dead."

"Sir, George enjoyed my mother's company and that's all I know of it. I can't say much more than that."

"You can't say because you don't know, or you can't say because you won't?"

"My mom was nice to everyone." I shrugged.

"Son, there is a part to this that just isn't adding up." Detective Geary took a long drink of tea. He was wearing dark jeans and a boxy white blazer. The same cowboy hat. "You don't have to protect her, son. She didn't protect you."

I looked at Aunt Lowette who was folding the same stack of cloth napkins over and over.

"Tell me one more time what were you doing while your mother was downstairs," Detective Geary asked.

"Goddammit," Aunt Lowette said, throwing a dishtowel to the floor. "You're like a broken record playing the track of stupidity. He already answered you. He was making Elaine some macaroni and cheese."

"Now, last time I asked, you said you were reading her a story." He looked at me.

"Don't you ever eat before you get your bedtime story, sir?" Aunt Lowette went on. "Sheesh. These questions. Go find your kicks someplace else."

"Which is it, son?"

"I think it's time you go, you're upsetting the boy, can't you see?" Aunt Lowette said. She came over and rubbed my back and I put my head down on the table. "He misses his mama, can't you have some compassion? Coming in here talking like he done something wrong. My sister's the one to blame, leave the kid out of it."

Detective Geary got up and smiled. "Ma'am, I'm real sorry, didn't mean to upset anyone. But we have to remember an innocent man lost his life, and Maynard here may know some things that could help. The smallest detail could turn the whole case around."

Aunt Lowette walked away.

"We'll let you know if we have any other questions," Detective Geary said. "Thank you for the tea, ma'am."

I will never know how much Elaine remembers from that time. I've read that our minds can do us favors and block out trauma. There is even a thing called childhood amnesia that is very common. If I had spread little Elaine's troubles to Geary, told him the truth behind it all, it would only complicate the thing, make their case files thicker with our business. I loved my sister, and I felt I was the only one looking out for her, that understood her. I believed it was my job to do this one act of kindness for her. And as much as it pains me to hear them contemplate my mother's sanity, label it a random act of evil, I keep my mouth shut and commit to their simple conclusion. Who needs a record of what only my mother and I can understand?

When I was thirty-six, Aunt Lowette passed away, a failure of the heart. We held a small service for her and I put it in the papers, hoping my mother would see it somehow and come out of hiding. I looked around the cemetery for a beautiful woman in disguise. But she wasn't there. No one but my wife and baby girls stood with me. I couldn't help but think that once the dirt was packed over Lowette's casket, it meant one less person who had half a mind at the truth of what happened that afternoon during George's lunchtime, and I felt unexpectedly lighter.

Because during our last conversation before I moved into the Fresno State dorms for college, Aunt Lowette and I got drunk on her porch and had story time. She told me of when she and my mother were locked in the trunk of Daddy Leon's Chrysler LeBaron for an entire night for no good reason, and I told her about that afternoon in detail, the thing that still keeps me up at night, even now, all these years later.

My mother had filled a plastic water bottle full of bright green antifreeze in our apartment and snuck it down in her purse. "Dogs love this stuff, can you believe it?" she said. We stood over a simmering pot at George's while he faded in and out of naps in his chair. "Can't have it around unless you want to kill off your dogs."

I stirred it into the soup and ladled some into a bowl and put two saltine crackers on the tray.

"Go on," my mother said. "I'm gonna clean up."

I carried it to George and roused him.

"Kid, can you find my races, can't work the damn thing." He

thrust the remote at me and tucked a napkin into the front of his shirt. I clicked to the right station.

He began to eat, blowing on small spoonfuls and slurping. "You know, Maynard, I think a young kid like yourself should go off to some boys' school, where they teach 'em how to be men. You're like a goddamn puppy trailing after your mommy."

I said nothing. I tried to visualize him as a baby wrapped in a bundle in a faceless woman's arms. But I couldn't see it. I could only see his sagging cheeks and hedged white bush of a mustache. He was a careful groomer and meticulous. He liked his routines, his lunch served on time.

"I wanted to be a jockey," he said and put the spoon down. My mother walked in and leaned over him, straightening the pillow behind his head. "My father said, 'Sorry Georgie, you're too big.'" He laughed. "You can't tell how little those men are on the television screen. Tiny things." He patted my mother's butt. "This isn't your best recipe, honey."

"Eat up, George," my mother said and walked down the hallway. George began to eat faster, his beady eyes glued to the television. His waxy scalp shone with new sweat and he leaned back in his chair. "Kid, get me a glass of water. I feel like I'm coming down with the summer flu."

I wasn't sure what to do. My mother had said to just let the antifreeze do the work. I was scared that water would ruin something. I pretended I didn't hear him.

"Get me some water, kid." He began to cough and knocked the tray to the floor. I was supposed to keep him in that chair and not let him go traipsing through the apartment. I stood before him and braced my hands on his shoulders.

"Just stay there, George," I said.

"Out of the way, I need to get to the bathroom," he sputtered. Vomit poured from his mouth, pale green and foamy down the front of his navy blue sweat suit. He put his head down. "Boy, get your mother," he said between heaves.

"Mom," I called. But it was quiet. "Mom!"

I ran to the bathroom where I found her sitting on the toilet, sort of looking into space. "He's barfing everywhere, what do I do?"

"He's a miserable man. Put him out of his misery."

I ran back to the living room where George's thin legs quivered, and I smelled shit. It was like his entire body was emptying itself.

My mother came up behind me and handed me a pillow.

No, couldn't have, she wouldn't have wanted that for me. She must have done it herself. Yes, that's it, she had the pillow. But when I close my eyes again it's me who is holding it, me who is pressing it over his face.

"Think of Elaine," she said.

"Is it done yet?" I asked. "Mom, is it done?"

I felt George relax under the pillow and my arms burned. I let go and his face looked shocked, confused, his jaw twisted at an odd angle.

"I think he passed out," I said.

My mother shook her head. "No, Maynard. That there's a

dead man." She didn't look at me. I stood staring at George, his legs splayed apart, the immaculate velour pants saturated in vomit. He wore a gold chain around his neck. His glassy blue eyes looked past us, down the hallway into nothing. My mother yanked the chain from his neck and pocketed it.

"I got the money from his safe, and it's more than I thought, Maynard. We lucked out." She stopped and looked at me. "There's no time to sit and think. Move, get yourself washed."

I went to the kitchen and ran my hands under scalding hot water.

"I'm just going to finish up here and you watch Elaine," she said. "I'll be up in a bit and then we'll go."

"We had to do that, right?" I asked. "George hurt Elaine. He was a sicko."

"Honey, like my Daddy Leon always said, 'If the world don't treat you right, go ahead and treat yourself to the world.'" And then she kissed my cheeks and wiped away tears I didn't realize were there. She kissed my mouth, our lips dry.

"I always thought she made you do it," Aunt Lowette slurred. "I did."

"You didn't."

"I did, Maynard. When you came here that first day and you wasn't scared or nothing, reminded me just of your mama the day Daddy Leon and Mama Belle were shot down in the street. The girl never cried a drop. They were our parents, after all, and you're born with a connection to your parents whether you like it or not. I felt a sadness the girl never felt. You and her have the same look in your eyes, always have. That's how I knew."

"How could she have left me after I did everything right?" I asked.

"Maynard, in life I really believe we get one free pass, maybe two. Yours is long gone and used up. Now forget her. She forgot you. Children do what they're told."

She reached over and laid her hand on my hand and we rocked the wicker chairs back and forth. We didn't talk for a few minutes.

"I think it's over now, Aunt Lowette," I said. "Geary never comes around anymore, nothing in the news."

"Can't say I haven't prayed for it," she said. "This is your mama's sin, boy. Don't forget it."

Last week I got a letter from Elaine, return address Portola, California, still.

> Hello, Maynard. I hope this finds you and your family well. I am in a bad way, and will be going to stay at The Meadows, which according to my map is not far from Fresno, just in the hills, maybe an hour drive. It's been a very long time. My therapist says that I need to ask you

the hard questions. She said that these things don't die on their own. Hope to hear from you,
Elaine

I look up the Meadows and it says that it is a drug and alcohol rehabilitation center for women. I tell my wife about it.

"I'm not sure we should expose the girls to that kind of thing," my wife says, washing dishes over a steaming sink. "It seems disruptive. Why now? She probably wants money."

"It might be nice to see her," I said. "She was my sister. Is."

"Your family was never really a family. We're your family."

"You're right."

"Put the past to rest, why don't you?" My wife turns and faces me, her shirt wet in splotches. "You barely know her."

I walk over to my wife and kiss her mouth. Cup her face in my hands. "Fine, if it's what you want, you know best." And we haven't talked about it since. My wife, she grew up in the church, and loved her parents in a measured way, and when an issue was resolved it was resolved, no reason to keep digging around, which is, in many ways, why our relationship works. I put Elaine's letter in my drawer and lock it. I copy down on a slip of paper something our preacher once said, *The old you is dead, and you are made completely new—why delight in morbid reflection and shame? God doesn't have time for it,* and mail it back to Elaine.

But I know I will go to her. I won't be able to stay away.

I play with my daughters in our yard and my wife reads her magazine and we all run through the sprinklers. I think of how perfect we look, our lively children, strong little girl bodies sprinting through water, enduring the same heat I've known so well for so long. I see Geary every now and then at the market or at Sunday service, and he tips that felt hat to me, and hobbles by with his cane, still stately in his pressed shirts and buffed boots. My mother remains a kind of Fresno legend, and because they have no mug shot, she is forever captured by a photograph I took of her that last summer on the grass, her head tilted to one side, the late afternoon sun illuminating her blonde hair like a halo. Her eyes aren't looking into the camera but beyond, past me, past the apartment complex, past the restaurants where she used to work, to the stretches of Missouri and outward, and I imagine her sprawled across unknown grass, somewhere, Florida maybe, but probably further, thinking, as I so often do, of our nights together those years ago, and what exactly measures love. And whatever it is, I believe I have succeeded. I have loved her no matter what.

Acknowledgments

First, a special thank-you to my sister. You and I understand the depths of this dark magic, and I am grateful to not go it alone. Thank you for your unwavering support. Keep on keepin' on, Lerline.

To Brenon, Harper, and Finn, you three are my everything. I know no greater joy than being yours.

Because this book is so near to me, and I have journeyed with it for so long, I must go back to the beginning and thank the teacher who helped me see what my short fiction could be: Charles D'Ambrosio, thank you for the education. I carry it always.

A huge thank-you to the luminous team at Catapult for all it takes to put a book into the world—it is an immense honor to get to work with all of you. Jonathan, Megan, Alicia, Katie, Wah-Ming, and everyone else, all my appreciation.

Thank you to my brilliant agent Samantha Shea, for reading all of these stories many times over and seeing the whole heart of them.

To booksellers everywhere, and everyone who read *Godshot*.

Your support has made me feel connected to a larger heartbeat. *Grateful* feels too small a word, but yet, I'm grateful.

A huge thank-you to my writing community who read these stories in various forms—especially: Gen Hudson, T Kira Madden, Kimberly King Parsons, Allie Rowbottom, Anna Weatherford, Molly Tolsky, and Annabel Graham; thank you for being there.

A special thank-you to Stephanie Danler and Lauren Groff for your beyond-brilliant work, and for reading mine. You light the way.

To dear friends and family, too many to count, thank you for your care, kindness, and support.

To Putz, thank you for everything.

To my mother, thank you for writing things down for me to find. Your essay about miners inspired the first story in this collection. I am captivated by your talent, your instinct for rhythm and language and story, and the way you bring your subjects to life, both on paper and on a simple phone call. No one tells a story like you.

Finally, and mostly, a choked-up thank-you to my father, Phil "Flip" Bieker, who died before this book could be held in his hands, and long before I was ready. Well, I would have never been ready. He read most of these stories. He'd say, "I don't know where you get this stuff." But then he'd grin. "I guess from me." Thank you, Dad, for the way you never failed to point out the absurd, delighted in the strange, and always got that triple scoop. These stories are like you: tough but brimming, achy-breaky. I hope you know I always saw you. You liked to say, "When the going gets tough, the tough get going," and now, though I can feel out so many meanings in that one line, I'll choose to hold the best version of it with me, the one that means *Keep going*. It's hard, but keep going.

© Jessica Keaveny

CHELSEA BIEKER is the author of the novel *Godshot*, which was a finalist for the Oregon Book Award, long-listed for the Center for Fiction First Novel Prize, and named an NPR Best Book of the Year and a Barnes & Noble Fiction Pick. Her writing has appeared in *The Paris Review, Granta, The Cut, McSweeney's, Literary Hub, Electric Literature*, and other publications. She is the recipient of a Rona Jaffe Foundation Writers' Award and a MacDowell Fellowship. Originally from California's Central Valley, she now lives in Portland, Oregon, with her husband and two children.